Meet Me at Blessed Creek

Mindy Killgrove

Meet Me at Blessed Creek

Mindy Killgrove

* * * * *

© 2024 by Mindy Killgrove

All rights reserved. No part of this book may be reproduced, stored in a retrieval system, or transmitted in any form or by any means without the prior written permission of the publishers, except by a reviewer who may quote brief passages in a review to be printed in a newspaper, magazine or journal.

The final approval for this literary material is granted by the author.

First digital version

All characters appearing in this work are fictitious. Any resemblance to real persons, living or dead, is purely coincidental.

Contents

Chapter One

Chapter Two

Chapter Three

Chapter Four

Chapter Five

Chapter Six

Chapter Seven

Chapter Eight

Chapter Nine

Chapter Ten

Chapter Eleven

Chapter Twelve

Chapter Thirteen

Chapter Fourteen

Chapter Fifteen

Chapter Sixteen

Chapter Seventeen

Chapter Eighteen

Chapter Nineteen

Chapter Twenty

Chapter Twenty-One

Chapter Twenty-Two

Chapter Twenty-Three

Chapter Twenty-Four

Chapter Twenty-Five

Chapter Twenty-Six

Chapter Twenty-Seven

Chapter Twenty-Eight

Chapter Twenty-Nine

Chapter Thirty

Chapter Thirty-One
Chapter Thirty-Two
Chapter Thirty-Three
Chapter Thirty-Four
Chapter Thirty-Five
Epilogue
Extended Epilogue
Prologue
Chapter One

Chapter One

Are You Still Here?
Missy

"Are you still here?" Nathan groaned.

"Yeah," I grunted, wriggling a little, trying to ease my way out from underneath his left arm,

which lay heavily across my stomach. "I live here, so…"

"This is your apartment?" He smacked his lips, then made a displeased noise, like he wasn't altogether satisfied with the smell of his own morning breath.

"Where did you think we went last night?"

"Honestly…" He exhaled weightily then rolled to the left, moving his arm off me so I could scoot away and establish a bit of space between us. "I'm not sure. I can't remember much after we started dancing and…"

Self-consciously, I pulled the sheets up a notch higher, covering myself. "Then you don't remember how we…" I allowed my words to trail away, not wanting to come right out of the gate, testing his memory, trying to determine just how much of the night we spent together had been lost in a fog of champagne and sweet kisses.

Nathan turned all the way over so that we were face-to-face. I hadn't been able to shimmy far enough away from him to create a wide chasm between us, so his elbows bumped mine and I could see the look of surprise clearly etched on his handsome features.

Oh, Nathan Hamilton…

Even slightly hungover, the man still looked amazing. His chestnut brown locks which were highlighted with gorgeous honey-colored hues were messy and tangled, probably because I'd been running my fingers through them just a few hours before. The soft morning sunlight that was peeking through the curtains in my bedroom touched his blue eyes, making them sparkle like the surface of a backyard pool. And the faint dusting of freckles on his nose and cheekbones was almost non-existent because his complexion was slightly red, possibly from embarrassment or perhaps because he'd been sleeping with his face pressed against the pillows.

I resisted the urge to lift my hand and stroke his cheeks. As tempting as it was to renew the intimacy that had always come so easily to us, I wanted to have this talk with Nate. We *needed* to discuss what had happened here last night. And if I made light of the situation or allowed the two of us to get carried away by our passions again, we'd be no better off than we were before he'd come to town for this quick visit.

"I...I'm almost afraid to ask this, Missy, 'cause I'm pretty sure I already know the answer..." He stopped and a small, impish smile quirked the corners of his lips. "But what did we do last night?" Slowly, he propped himself up on his elbows and surveyed my bedroom.

For the first time, I focused on something other than the man sitting in my bed. There were two glasses of water, both half full, resting on my nightstand. Our phones were right next to them, but neither of us had remembered to plug them in, evidently, because the charging cords dangled uselessly over the edge of the nightstand. While I had the top creamy white bed sheet pulled high up to my collarbone, my comforter had been kicked on the floor. It lay next to our clothes. Nate had worn a dark blue suit with a periwinkle tie and my aquamarine bridesmaid gown was heaped right on top of his shoes. I tipped my head to the side and gazed at the dress for a long moment.

Adair got married. She really, really did it.

I'd watched her walk down the aisle. I'd heard both she and her husband, Wes, utter their vows. And yet, I still couldn't believe that fact.

I'd been there the whole time, standing right by her side. I'd spent months helping her prepare for this occasion, but I still thought it was out of place in the grand scheme of things. I never imagined that Adair would be the first one in our group to get married, and now here it was, the day *after* her wedding ceremony.

I glanced at the clock on my nightstand, ignoring—or attempting to ignore—the rings left there by the water glasses and saw that it was already 10:30. I hadn't slept this late in years. On a regular day, even a weekend, I would've been up for hours, already burned through a workout and then headed on with the rest of my day.

When I want time to stand still, that's when it passes the quickest.

That thought brought my attention back to Nathan. He'd been saying something while I was off daydreaming, and now I felt a bit of guilt for not actually listening. I made a solid effort to start tuning in and give him my full attention.

"So, what exactly happened last night?" he asked with his eyebrow hooked high in the air.

Turning once more onto my side so we could be eye-to-eye, I answered in my most nonchalant way, "Adair got married."

"Yes, she did," he said and grinned widely. "That was some reception, huh?"

We both snickered at that suggestion. Jessica Adair and Wesley Jefferson, her groom, had spared no expense in throwing the bash of the century. While the ceremony itself was relatively intimate, the reception could be best described as expansive. Adair had invited most of her clients and she'd even insisted that Ian Whitley and Cora Collins, the newest additions to her record label, perform throughout the evening. I couldn't decide if she was celebrating her marriage or her new catalog of artists. Maybe it was a little of both.

Jessica Adair had built DieLou Records from the ground up and she had every right to be proud of her work. She'd spent obscene amounts of time and money making her business successful, and it felt right to pull the biggest day of her life and her greatest achievement together in one colossal event.

Plus, I'd never been to a wedding that was so spectacular.

I thought I'd mention that to Nathan.

"Really?" He seemed surprised. "Then, I guess you haven't been to that many weddings, huh?"

"I've been to a few," I said defensively, trying to add up my wedding experiences in my mind.

"Sure, everyone's been to a few, and I agree with you that nobody does it like Adair, but . . ." He let his words trail off.

"What's up?" I asked before I could help myself. I was getting a weird vibe off Nathan. This conversation was stilted and lacked substance. We weren't really getting anywhere. I felt like he wanted to talk about something, but instead of just coming right out with whatever he was thinking, Nate was intentionally holding back.

"Nothing." He shrugged casually. His brow wrinkled and I could tell he hadn't just stopped talking in the middle of his sentence because his brain was still addled by the copious amounts of alcohol that he'd consumed the night before.

Nate's hiding something...

I'd known him for a long time, and we'd been friends for what felt like ages. So, I could detect when he was feeling a little off. But when the silence stretched between us and he still didn't elaborate on his thoughts, I grew uneasy.

Maybe he's not hiding something. Maybe he's just confused about what happened between us last night...

And I didn't blame him for having a truckload of questions. Now that I was contemplating it truly, the whole event had my mind spinning.

What did we do? Could any of this even be close to a good idea? We've obviously been together, but what does that mean? Did we get all hot and messy because we care about each other or was it a little more noncommittal than that?

I cringed at the way my thoughts were spiraling out of control.

This is exactly the sort of thing that sent Nate running for the hills in the past.

He never wanted to talk about anything serious and as far as having a relationship status update chat, that was surely a discussion he'd rather put off until another time.

But time wasn't on our side today anyway.

I snuck a quick glance at the alarm clock which sat behind the water glasses on the nightstand, then asked a question I'd been dreading, "Nate, what time do you have to leave today?" Suddenly, the idea of having this laborious little talk, spinning out the finer details of the evening, discussing what our actions all meant in the long run seemed rather exhausting and like an enormous waste of time and energy. Even though just a few seconds before I'd been convinced that I wouldn't let him wiggle away this time without talking things through with me, just as abruptly, I changed my mind. We *didn't* need to talk about last night. We needed to focus on what was happening right now...in the present.

His eyes fluttered shut and he squeezed them closed for a full ten seconds before answering, "Why? Please tell me it's not already the middle of the afternoon."

"It's not so late in the day yet," I murmured, reaching out impulsively, and tracing my fingertip over the curve of his mouth.

My movements must've surprised him because his eyes flew open, and he gazed at me, tipping his head to the side slightly and gifting me with the most adorable grin. "Thank goodness. 'Cause I need to shower and we've gotta talk about…" He paused and waved his hand at me, then gestured to the rest of my bedroom. "…all this."

I gulped. "Do we need to talk…really?"

"Come on," he said, perking up once more, then nodding at the closed door to the bedroom. "Let's get cleaned up and go for a walk."

"You wanna…"

"I want to talk to you, Missy," he interrupted. "Seriously." He leaned forward and brushed the tip of his nose against mine. "Don't you think we ought to have this out…once and for all?"

Frankly, I didn't love the way he posed that last statement. Even though I knew we ought to have a candid discussion, I wasn't keen to answer any questions about what happened last night. Every few seconds I bounced back and forth between wanting to say what was on my mind and determining that we'd be better off letting our little escapade go down in our shared history as just another tryst we didn't talk about later. But now that Nate was asking…really asking…me to take this leap with him, I found that I couldn't resist the exquisite temptation of finally getting the answers to all my most pressing questions.

Chapter Two

What Will it Be...Love or Money?
Nathan

"What do you wanna do today?" Missy asked. As my hostess for the weekend, she'd insisted that I take the first shower, but now, as she reentered her bedroom, with a baby blue towel wrapped around her body and tucked neatly underneath her arms, it was disconcerting to see the frown on her face and the way her eyes went directly to the clock. I'd noticed her checking the time every few minutes since we'd both awakened and it made me feel a little nervous. I was almost certain she wasn't trying to get rid of me or making the mistake of wishing away our time together, but the way her pretty, bluish gray eyes kept drifting back to that clock on her nightstand made me itch to get out of her bedroom and away from the wretched timepiece that seemed to be dictating just about everything.

"I've got almost an eight-hour drive ahead of me today, so I'd probably better be on the road early this afternoon."

"Right," Missy agreed. "I know you've gotta get up early for work tomorrow morning, and I don't want to even think about you overdoing it by staying out too late tonight."

I smiled affectionately at her.

This was one of the things I loved most about Missy. She was always thinking four steps ahead...trying to figure out how best to take care of everyone else in her life...including me.

"Let's not worry about what I'm doing at work tomorrow or even think about my drive later. Let's just go have some fun while we can."

"All right." Missy sauntered to her chest of drawers and pulled out a simple, white cotton T-shirt. "Did you have anything in mind you wanted to do?"

"I could think of a few things," I murmured, eyeing her closely as she plucked a pair of black athletic capri pants out of another drawer.

She turned and gave me a slow, easy grin. "I thought you said you wanted to talk?"

"Yeah, yeah." I waved my hand dismissively at her. "I guess that's something we oughta do." I was sitting on the corner of her mattress, watching her get dressed and that alone made it difficult to concentrate. I'd known Missy Lawrence a long time, but from my vantage point, she'd never looked more beautiful.

Oh, she'd always been pretty in a girl next door kind of way, and when we'd first dated in college, I'd been smitten by her good-natured, amiable smile. But now that we'd both been out of school for a few years and hadn't seen each other in person for longer than I wanted to admit, I had to admire all the ways she'd changed.

Her hair was longer than it'd been a few years ago. It skimmed her shoulder blades and fell in one long, straight curtain. If I wasn't mistaken, her locks were a slightly different shade, too. They were darker, maybe a little more caramel hued than the platinum tint they'd been before. But Missy's smile was still the same. As she yanked on her clothing, grabbed a pair of white athletic ankle socks and a set of blue and gray sneakers, then plopped on the bed next to me to tie up the laces, I found myself getting distracted by her gorgeous grin. It wasn't just that she had straight, white teeth, or full, cupid's bow lips. It was the way Missy's mouth turned up at the corners…as if she was smiling just because I was there. This smile…Missy's smile…was unique and she'd conjured it up just for me.

"What?" she asked, meeting my gaze, while also fiddling with the tongue on her left shoe. The thing wouldn't lie flat, no matter how much she smooshed and prodded it with the pads of her fingers.

"I've got an idea." I hopped off the bed and she immediately gave up on fixing her shoes so she could join me.

"You know what you wanna do today?" she ventured.

"Come on," I said, taking hold of her hand and leading her out of the bedroom. "We've got places to go."

Missy giggled as she skipped right behind me. "Yeah, you've gotta go home and…"

"I do," I said, cutting her off. "But I'm not ready to go yet. And besides, there's someplace special I'd like to take you."

She jerked my hand, pulling us both to a stop. "Someplace special? What'd you have in mind?"

Now that I was excited by the idea, I didn't want to spoil the surprise by telling her all about our destination before we got there. So, I just squeezed her hand and nodded at the door that would lead us out of her apartment. "Do you trust me enough to stop asking questions?"

Her eyes widened to the size of golf balls, but I could tell she was giving my words some serious contemplation because her lips pursed tightly.

"Hmm…" she hummed. "I'm not real sure what's going on here, Nate, but I'm trusting you."

I laughed, then tugged her hand, pulling her along.

"But I need my purse," she said as we passed the counter that separated the kitchen and dining area from the living room. "And I've gotta grab my keys." She didn't let go of my hand, so when she leaned over the countertop, making a racket as she rummaged in the tiny, ceramic heart shaped bowl for her set of keys, I nearly toppled over.

"Missy, come on, would ya?" I said, righting myself and yanking her along with me. Now that I had an idea of how I wanted to spend my day with her, I was reluctant to hang around the apartment, missing out on what was sure to be a glorious late morning and early afternoon.

She snatched her keys from the bowl, tucked them into the purse she'd slung across her body, then patted her sides. "Do I need anything else for this little excursion?"

"Nope," I assured her, then, as her enchanting smile once more lit up her features, we exited her apartment and raced down the stairs. At first, it was awkward because we were still holding hands, but both Missy and I had competitive natures and once we recognized that we could race, rather than walk, we both took off.

Missy darted ahead of me, elbowing her way by me on the stairs, sprinting to open the exterior door to the Fountain Park apartment complex, then turned and gave me a triumphant grin.

"Where to now?" she asked. Her blue eyes were dancing with mirth, and I wanted, more than anything, to see her smiling like that at me not just for today…but for all the rest of our days.

"We'll need to go for a short drive," I said, motioning to the parking spot my little truck occupied.

"All right," she agreed, skipping toward the passenger side of the vehicle. She beamed at me, and slowly my own grin slid into place. It was a gorgeous day. Late August tends to be one of two things in Charlotte: really hot or really spring-like. There's a joke around town that the four seasons of the year are spring, almost spring, late spring, and construction. It's corny, but usually accurate. Today, thankfully, the weather was cooperating and peaking at just around seventy-five degrees. The sun was shining warmly, and even though I was wishing

I'd remembered to bring my sunglasses along with me, I couldn't deny that I was truly happy.

It didn't take long to drive across town and reach the outskirts of the University of North Carolina's Charlotte campus. After parking the truck, I skirted around so I could open Missy's door for her and when I offered her my hand to help her out of the vehicle, she took it.

"I'm not letting this hand go for the rest of the day," I promised, leaning over to brush a quick kiss across her knuckles. Even though I'd been sincere, Missy chuckled.

"Sure," she muttered. "You'll hold my hand until it's time to race again."

"No more racing today. I think I pulled a hamstring coming down those stairs," I quipped.

"You want a massage?" she teased.

"Maybe later." I smiled broadly at her. "But for now, let's just agree to stick together."

Missy shrugged her slender shoulders daintily and squeezed my hand. "Sounds good to me."

We walked along companionably for a few minutes, not saying much, simply meandering down the gravel pathway, heading toward the special spot I wanted to share with her.

"Sometimes the weather's nice in Pittsburgh, but we never have days like this," I said after a spell before lifting my chin and gazing upward, embracing the sunlight.

"I know," she agreed. "There's no other place in the world that has weather quite like Charlotte."

"Absolutely." I nodded, then turned to glance at her. "Maybe I should move back here . . ."

"Move back for the weather? That seems a little impulsive . . ." I was sure Missy meant to keep talking, but then her face turned bright crimson and her words just evaporated.

It was apparent she was hiding something, maybe concealing some of her thoughts, so I pushed ahead and let her know what I was thinking, hoping that by being transparent, I might urge her to do just the same. "There're plenty of reasons for me to move back to Charlotte. There are lots of things here that I love." Gently, I drew a heart shape with my thumb onto the soft part of her hand.

I was sure she'd say something then, cave to her journalistic instincts, and ask a follow-up question, but Missy stayed quiet.

When the silence engulfed us so fully that I almost felt like I was suffocating, I whispered, "You okay?" while rubbing my thumb across her hand again, massaging her smooth skin.

"Yeah," she breathed.

I waited for her to say something else, but she didn't. I was used to Missy having a bubbly personality, the kind that couldn't be hampered or contained. She was a bit of a question box really, always peppering people with queries, wondering what they were thinking, then being bold enough to come right out and ask the questions others might not. But today, she was unusually quiet and that made the place I was about to share with her seem even more special. I was glad I'd asked her to trust me and allow me to lead the way.

"We're here," I said softly, nodding for her to follow me down a winding pathway.

"Where?" she returned, twisting her neck slightly, slowly surveying our surroundings. There were tall conifer trees lining the pathway, obscuring the sunlight a little. As we stepped into the wooded area, the path was no longer made of small pebbles, but it became a dusty, dirt-covered trail. There were a few trees off to one side of the forest that needed clearing away. I couldn't tell when they'd fallen, but the branches hung limply and those that were closest to the ground were covered in ferns, ivy, and moss.

"This is one of my favorite places," I explained, squeezing her hand tighter. "I maybe should've brought you here a long time ago, but it seems appropriate to come today."

"Appropriate how?" she questioned and for the first time, I caught a hint of trepidation in her voice.

"We're almost there," I replied. "Then, you'll be able to see for yourself."

As we came through the woods, I scanned the small, luscious park which lay before us. The grass was a spritely green and trees ringed the area. There were a few stone benches within my line of sight and just up ahead there was a concrete bridge.

"This bridge used to be wooden and rickety," I explained, taking her hand, and leading her forward. "But in recent years, especially as the water started to recede, and this became more of a tourist attraction, the city rebuilt the bridge."

"How do you know that?" Missy asked, tipping her head to the side, and giving the whole place a pensive stare. "You haven't lived here in a few years, Nate, and even if this is one of your favorite places to go when you do come back to town…"

"Welcome to Blessed Creek," I interjected. "Even though I don't come here as often as I used to, I keep my eyes on the place."

"Really?" Missy snorted. "And what sort of superpowers do you employ so you can keep a watch over this park?"

I laughed lightly, then gestured with my free hand to a brown and white sign which sat prominently to the left of the bridge. "They've got a camera over there. And the ranger who takes care of this place posts updates directly on the regional parks and rec. department's website from time-to-time."

"Too bad," Missy joked, sighing softly. "I was sort of hoping you might possess some secret abilities you've been carefully concealing all these years."

"Oh?" I took a step closer to her, inhaling the tea tree scented shampoo and conditioner combo she'd recently used to wash her hair. "If you're looking for magic…then I've brought you to the right place."

Missy's left eyebrow crooked sardonically. "I was just joking around before. I don't believe in people possessing superpowers and as for having magical capabilities…" She stuck out her tongue, lifted her free hand and turned her thumb down, then blew out a raspberry, showing her disdain for the topic quite clearly.

"You should," I coaxed, nodding toward the bridge before leading her to the center of the structure.

"Really?" she challenged, giving another appraising look around us. "Tell me why."

I must admit at this point that there was nothing remarkable about the bridge or its surroundings. The park had been a sweet little spot and the idea of an enchanted meeting place for lovers was intriguing, but the view from the bridge itself left much to be desired. There was water and trees, but very little else to recommend it.

I glanced at Missy quickly then released her hand so I could lean forward and wrap my fingers around the railing that was right in front of us. I leaned forward and looked down at the water which burbled underneath the bridge. She followed my example, but then I heard her sigh dramatically.

"Am I missing something here?" She asked. "Is this a science thing and I'm just not appreciating it the way I should be?" She continued leaning forward, bending at the waist, tucking her upper body around the bar, and making it seem like if the safety feature wasn't there, she just might dive straight into the creek.

This was another thing I adored about Missy—her spontaneity. Most of the time, she was willing to plunge right into the thick of things.

"It really is a beautiful day," I murmured. My words seemed to spark something in my companion because she righted herself slowly, then turned to look me fully in the face.

When our eyes met, I saw something that I'd been missing before. Missy was looking at me the way she used to do, when we were dating in college, and she trusted me fully and completely. We didn't need to say everything we were thinking or feeling because with just one look, we knew what we had. I didn't want to be the first to break the stare because my insides were thrumming. My blood was pumping heatedly through my veins, and I felt renewed, as if I could do anything at this moment, so long as Missy kept looking at me.

Maybe that's what's magical about this place...the way it turns friends into lovers.

"So..." she said at last, breaking our silence, and pulling out the word long, "does the park ranger come through here and give a talk soon or...?"

"This is Blessed Creek," I said softly, "and there's a legend surrounding this place."

"Uh-huh," Missy grunted. "What sort of legend?" She rocked back a little from the railing and crossed her arms over her chest, now giving me a skeptical look. I liked this pose almost as much as I did the last because this one reminded me of the way Missy used to behave when she was hot on the trail of tracking down a lead. She might be willing to jump into a situation with both feet, but then, before pushing forward, she wanted answers.

I took a deep breath, then unfurled the tale. "The way I heard the story was that years ago a sailor and his crew were lost on these shores. A beautiful woman happened to be walking along the shoreline, and when she figured out that the men needed help, she was able to lead the captain in the right direction."

"Wait." Missy held up her hand. "What shores? How did a sailor and his crew get *here*?" She gestured that same hand around us, indicating how this was just a creek and we were surrounded by trees.

"It's a story," I replied. "Just go with it."

Her little nose wrinkled, and a slight humming sound buzzed from the back of her throat as she was clearly thinking over whether she'd prefer to just stay quiet and keep listening or continue to probe further.

When she didn't interject, I proceeded, "As payment for her assistance, the man offered her a bit of treasure." I stopped talking and dug around in my pocket, pulling out a dingy penny. There was nothing astounding or stunning about the coin, but when I held it up for Missy to inspect, the sun glinted off the worn edges, giving it a bit of luster. "He had a gold locket around his neck, a cherished item, but since the woman had saved his life and helped his crew out of a tight spot, he wished to repay her the best he could." Missy cocked her head to the side and gazed at the penny. "Since the man and woman didn't speak the same language, communication was stilted. It took some time for her to realize he meant to pay for her assistance and while he was gazing at her, he admired her beauty. So, he decided to offer her an alternative form of payment." Missy's eyebrow ticked a little higher, showing her intrigue. "She could take the coin, or she could kiss the sailor."

"Hmmm . . . interesting choice," Missy murmured thoughtfully. "Which did she pick?"

I stared at her expectantly. "Which would *you* want?"

"A kiss or some money?" she returned.

"Yeah," I breathed slowly and steadily, willing her to make her choice, the obvious decision, the one I was sure we both wanted.

She leaned forward and brushed her lips against mine. The kiss was soft and sweet and while there wasn't much heat behind it, my heart still managed to skip a beat in response. My hand clenched around the penny and my eyes fluttered shut. I wanted this moment to last for a very long time. Just as I was reaching for Missy, hoping to wrap my arms around her waist and tow her even closer, she pulled away. Slightly chagrined, I opened my eyes and saw that she was smiling broadly. That grin swept away all my less than satisfied thoughts immediately.

"I was hoping that'd be what you picked . . ." I admitted. Then, I opened my palm again and presented her with the penny. "Here," I said, nodding at her to take the money. "Now that you've chosen me, you can throw the money in the creek and make a wish."

"I get the treasure *and* the kiss?" she questioned.

"Yep, but only because you made the correct decision."

She took the penny from my palm and looked at it carefully for a second. Then, she unzipped her purse and dropped the coin inside.

"What're you doing?" I asked. "You're supposed to throw it away and make a wish."

"I think I'll hang onto my wish," she said, smiling in a contented way. "'Cause right now, I've already got everything I want."

Chapter Three

Missy
Will You Meet Me There...Please?

A half hour later, we were sitting at my kitchen table eating a very late breakfast. It was past lunch time, but when I asked Nathan what he wanted to eat, he'd suggested waffles. So, I'd grabbed the waffle maker off the shelf, put some sausage in the oven, and even whipped up some scrambled eggs. Now, we were shoveling breakfast foods, drenched in syrup, onto our forks and then into our mouths. I smiled at him every few seconds, thrilled with the day that we'd spent together.

"Morning," Hope said lazily as she waltzed into the kitchen still wearing a pair of fuzzy pink bedroom slippers and a cotton candy pink bathrobe.

"Morning?" I joked, flicking my eyes toward the digital clock on the oven range. "It stopped being morning hours ago."

Hope yawned broadly while reaching for the Carolina Panthers coffee mug she'd gotten last fall as part of a promotional giveaway at the Bank of America Stadium. "I can't help it if I like to sleep late."

"Late?" Nate spoke around a mouthful of waffles. "We waved bye-bye to *late* hours ago."

My little sister shrugged, then leaned her hip against the kitchen countertop so she could turn and look at us. "The two of you make it sound like I was sleeping the day away. Didn't you guys bother to sleep in a little bit this morning?"

"Sure," I replied as I dipped my sausage link in syrup then took a big bite. "But we've been up for ages and already ventured over to Blessed Creek."

Hope drummed her thumbs on the countertop, collected her mug that was now brimming with freshly brewed French roast, and plopped into the vacant chair next to mine. She reached over and snatched a sausage link off my plate. "Never heard of it."

I nodded at Nathan, and he quickly explained the little legend surrounding the place. When he was done, Hope took a long sip of her coffee, then shot me a confused look. "Is it just me or are there a few details missing from that story?"

"Like what?" Nate asked, scooping eggs onto his fork then taking a hearty bite.

Simultaneously, I said, "I know, right? Like what happened to the princess?" I picked up my glass of orange juice, drank a bit, and swished it around in my mouth while waiting for him to answer.

"What princess?" He countered before shoving a piece of waffle into his mouth. I watched as a trickle of syrup dribbled over his lips.

"The princess in the story—you know. What happened to the princess? Did *she* choose the kiss or the treasure?"

"She wasn't a princess. Who said she was?" He had his head tipped to the side, looking for all the world like a silly little doggy that was begging for scraps at the dinner table. Judging by the quizzical expression that was stamped across his face, he was surprised I'd added details to the story which just plain didn't exist.

"I guess I thought that she was . . ."

"I made that assumption, too," Hope added, leaning over, and grabbing hold of my fork. I pushed my plate toward her.

Apparently, we're sharing my breakfast.

And that was all right with me, but I didn't want her to have to keep reaching over top of me to get at the food. She took a quick bite of the scrambled eggs, made a disgruntled face, then snatched the pepper shaker from the center of the table. "I think the story'd be better if the lady were a princess," she said before covering the breakfast food in a thick layer of black pepper.

"Would it?" he asked teasingly, straightening up his head, while winking in my direction. "I thought the way I told it was just fine and the ending was pretty nice, too."

I groaned. "But you *didn't* end the story, Nate. So, just tell us. Because I can't take it anymore. What did she decide?" I leaned as far across the table as I could get without knocking over Hope's coffee cup, my glass of juice, or jostling the breakfast plate we were sharing.

Nate's eyes danced with glee. "The woman in the story took the gold and threw it into the water. She kissed the captain just seconds before she walked out of his life." He smiled a little as he finished the story, but I was dissatisfied.

"Why did she leave him? Weren't they in love? I mean, you made it seem like *he* loved *her*, so maybe, because she kissed him that signified that she had the same feelings, too." I felt grief rush into the room like an unwelcome visitor. "When you love someone, you don't leave them!" I cried.

"Who said they were in love?" Nathan asked me, putting down his own fork.

"No one, I guess," I huffed discontentedly, crossing my arms over my chest. "I just assumed it."

"And who said that you're never forced to leave the person you love?" He continued as if I hadn't spoken.

"I guess that happens sometimes, too."

We both stared at each other and this time he was the first to break the silence.

"But what if you didn't have to give up the person you loved? What if you could stay with that person forever?"

It was Hopey who answered him. She blew out an exasperated sigh while nibbling at the mound of eggs. "Wouldn't that be something?" she snorted. "You could find somebody you really liked and then…*wham*! You just got to spend the rest of your life with them?" She rolled her eyes, as if we hadn't been able to pick up on her sarcastic tone before. "It'd almost be like getting marr…"

"What if we did that?" Nate interrupted.

"Did what?" I returned.

He leaned forward so that we were nearly nose-to-nose. "What if we got married, Missy?"

"Wh…what?" I squeaked.

Hope dropped her fork. For a second the only sound in the room was the noise the silverware made when it clattered against the tabletop.

"Did you just…are you serious?" she asked, taking the words right out of my mouth.

"Come on," he cajoled, sitting back a little so we had some breathing room lingering between us. "Think about it. We could get married. We could have a big party just like Adair's and Wesley's or we could run down to the courthouse and make things official right now." He licked the corners of his lips where some of the sweet, sticky syrup had collected, then continued to rattle off possibilities. "I could move here if that's what you wanted. And we could have a whole bunch of kids. We could …"

"Kids?" I gulped.

Nate snickered. "Sure. We could have loads of them."

"Loads?" I parroted, unable to come up with anything else because I was totally dumbstruck.

His smile broadened. "Well, maybe not loads, but I guess I always figured we'd have six or seven babies and…"

Hope guffawed loudly. "Why do you want so many kids? You thinkin' of starting a family band?"

Nathan's grin turned lazy as he sat back a little way in his chair, stretching his arms high over his head. "Maybe," he joked.

I sucked in a sharp intake of breath and jumped up from my seat at the table. I wasn't sure what to do, but my instincts were telling me to get moving. I started to walk out of the kitchen and head to my bedroom, but Nathan was right behind me. He grabbed ahold of my elbows and spun me around so that I couldn't go anywhere. Once again, we were stuck, gazing into each other's eyes, but this time my nerves jangled and jounced, making me feel uncomfortable. I wanted to walk away, but I also wanted to stay. I *needed* to hear what he was going to say next.

"Missy," he whispered and suddenly the lackadaisical expression he'd worn back in the kitchen was gone. A more serious, temperate man gazed earnestly back at me. "I know I'm not perfect. I've never been before, and I know I'm certainly not now. I'll never be the kind of guy who shows up at your apartment carrying a bouquet of flowers and I won't ever be able to say the right thing at the right time." His eyes darted quickly back and forth, and I had the feeling he was searching my face, trying to read my expression. "But I love you, Missy and you love me back. I know you do. Despite everything we've been through and the distance between us, I can feel how much I mean to you, because you hold the same special place in my heart, too. We…we've got something amazing here and…"

"But you're leaving," I interceded, stepping away from him a pace, allowing my nostrils to fill with the aromas of waffles and syrup, rather than the strong masculine scent that distinctly belonged to Nathan. "In just a few minutes, in fact. Your bag is already packed and…"

"Say you'll marry me," he pleaded. "I know we don't have everything worked out right now, but isn't this what you want? Don't you think we ought to be together all the time?"

I couldn't answer. There were times, over this last year, when my friends were getting on with their lives, moving in with boyfriends, finding new jobs, and even, in the case of Jessica Adair, weaving their way to the altar, when I'd dreamed of having Nathan ask me precisely this question. And, ninety-nine percent of the time, in my fantasies, I envisioned accepting his marriage proposal. Because the truth was that I did love him. Of course, I did. But now, with him standing right in front of me, asking the question...the reply wasn't sitting right on the tip of my tongue as I'd always expected it to be.

"Don't answer right now," Nate suggested, taking his hands away from my arms and cupping them both underneath my chin. He leaned forward and pressed a quick kiss to my lips. The sensations that rippled through my body at that moment were so potent that my knees knocked together in reply. "Before I leave, I'm dropping by the UNC campus for just a few minutes. I promised some of my frat brothers who still live in town that I'd try to see them if I got the chance. So, I'll go to the house, but..." He paused and shot a quick glance at the wall. I knew he was looking at the clock which hung just to the left of the door. "In an hour...meet me at Blessed Creek."

"What?" I breathed. "Why there?"

"You picked love, Missy," he whispered, then a soft smile cracked his serious veneer. "You got to keep the money, too. But when you were given the chance, you chose to love me...to kiss me. If you want to be my wife, meet me at Blessed Creek...please?"

Chapter Four

Should I Call?
Nathan

I waited.

As soon as I left Missy's apartment, I drove straight to the little parking lot that would lead me to Blessed Creek. Even though I'd said I was heading to the frat house on campus, I didn't want to run the risk of overstaying my time there and being late to meet up with Missy. She was, as a rule, supremely punctual and the thought of making her wait even one second, wondering where I was, had me running down the pathway, sprinting toward that concrete bridge.

But she never showed.

I didn't have all the time in the world to waste, standing around, waiting for her, but time moved slowly that afternoon. As I stood there and watched the sun arch its way leisurely, heading downward, coasting toward the horizon, I was transfixed by the golden rays, the fiery orange splashes of color, and the burnt red ring that encased the glowing orb right until it dropped behind the fluffy white and gray clouds for the evening. When I realized, truly, that she wasn't going to show up, I pulled out my cell phone and glared at the screen, willing it to ring. I told myself not to worry—something had just come up. I knew that sometimes Missy got called away by her boss, Ross, so she could cover a breaking news story, and I tried to content myself with thinking that must be the case. But the longer I stared at the screen, the more I understood the situation clearly.

Missy wasn't coming to Blessed Creek. She didn't want to be my wife. And the only thing left to do was go home and try to forget I'd ever been so reckless.

Thirteen years elapsed before I returned to Charlotte. In all that time, I never spoke with Missy even once. She didn't call. I didn't text. We stopped sending each other those quirky little email messages. Even though I wondered what happened to her that day, I didn't...I *couldn't* be the one to make the call. Every time I thought about the way she'd left me standing there that day, the old wound of rejection tore open anew and I couldn't bring myself to ask the one question that most needed answering.

Why had she left me at Blessed Creek?

But now...standing in the kitchen area of the Flora Gardens Hotel suite, waiting for a cup of coffee to brew while clutching my cell phone tightly in my hand, I couldn't help but think about giving her a call.

I need to see her. I've been thinking about doing this for so long and it's time we finally talked through everything. My plan...my plan hinges on reconnecting with her, but it's been thirteen years. Maybe she changed her number.

I hadn't given up *my* old number, but that was beside the point. Anything could've happened to Missy these last few years and I had no way of knowing what she was doing nowadays.

Eh...that's not exactly true. If I wanted to know what was going on with Missy, I could've done a quick search online. I'm sure there's plenty of hits under her name and all I've got to do is...

Knock! Knock!

I jumped because the sound of someone hammering on my door startled me. Without giving what I was doing much thought, I sauntered out of the kitchen and slowly opened the heavy hotel room door.

"Oh...hey," I grumbled, seeing my friend Sean Bell. "It's just you." We worked together at Morgan and Fosters Laboratory in Pittsburgh and had both been sent to the same conference here in Charlotte for the week. He was already dressed and ready to head down to the lecture hall. Sean had on a charcoal gray pair of slacks and a crisp white button-down shirt, but he'd chosen to cap off the rather bland ensemble with a screaming electric blue tie. In one hand he carried a yellow legal pad but with the other he skimmed the top of his freshly shaven head while casting a quick glance over his shoulder.

"Yeah," he grunted. "Were you expecting somebody else?"

"No," I muttered, stepping aside, and beckoning for him to come into the hotel room. "Not expecting...but maybe just hoping an old friend might stop by."

Sean ducked around me, and I closed the door behind him. "That's right," he said slowly. "I forgot you used to live here." He nodded at the phone that was still in my hand. "You callin' up some of your old friends?" He paused and checked his wristwatch. "Maybe it's a tad early for that."

"Ah," I said, waving away the comment. "The person I was thinking about calling would've already been up for hours by now. She tends to wake up with the sunrise...sometimes before."

"*She?*" Sean's heavy black eyebrows drifted faintly up his forehead. "You got an old flame still burning bright in Charlotte?"

"Something like that," I grumbled before tucking my phone deep in my back pocket and figuring that ought to put an end to my inclinations to make the call. "Come on," I urged, "join me for a cup of coffee."

"All right," Sean agreed, "but you know they're serving us a full breakfast before the keynote speaker gives his address this morning. I don't think we ought to stand around here all day, drinking this coffee, when we can just go downstairs and get…what's wrong?"

While he'd been talking, spouting perfectly mundane facts, I'd drifted off into my own little world again. I was just staring at the coffee maker, and he'd caught me. Because Sean and I had been friends a long time, I didn't feel the need to keep anything from him. "I can't stop thinking about Missy."

"Missy…right. I think I remember you mentioning her name before." He nodded thoughtfully. "The one who got away."

"Sorta."

When explaining what'd happened between me and Missy, I usually got the details wrong. Not because I hadn't been fully present or because I wanted to exaggerate or alter our situation, but because, for me, it was all still a mystery. One minute, I was sure she was the girl I was going to marry. But a few hours later…everything changed.

Sean reached forward and grabbed the cup of coffee that had been sitting there for a few minutes, just waiting for someone to consume it. "Give her a call, man," he urged before taking a small sip. "If you think she'll be awake already, there's no harm in calling or sending a text and letting her know you'll be in town all week. You can take her out to dinner or something."

"Maybe," I agreed halfheartedly, "but it's been thirteen years. Should I just pop up like that…right out of the blue?" I'd dreamed of doing just that, but to say it out loud, to admit this part of the plan that had taken root a few months ago felt daring…and slightly ludicrous.

Before taking another swallow of the coffee, Sean shrugged. "I dunno. But sending her a text message couldn't hurt, could it? I mean, if you wanna talk to her so much that you can't even focus on getting dressed and ready for this conference…"

"Hey," I interjected, waving my hand at my business casual attire. "I'm ready to go."

Sean snorted. "Okay, but you're not wearing any shoes."

I pulled my phone back out of my pocket and checked the digital display, searching for the time. "I'm still in my own hotel room and I figured we had a few minutes. See..." I turned the screen to share the time with him. "It's not even eight yet."

"Yeah, but if we don't get goin' soon, we'll miss all the good pastries."

I chuckled. "All right...all right. *Sheesh*...you and this continental breakfast. If I didn't know better, I'd swear that you hadn't eaten a drop in at least three days." Sean said something, but I didn't hear his retort because I was already walking back to my bedroom in search of my dress shoes. Since we were going to be in town all week, I'd packed more than usual opting to bring both my sneakers and a pair of brown loafers. As I slid my feet into the dress shoes, I eyed the sneakers, wishing I could do up the laces on those and go for a run. I needed to clear my head, but I also wanted to get out some of this nervous energy that was roiling around inside my body, making me feel like if I didn't do something, didn't just break down and call Missy, I might not be much good at these conference sessions this morning.

When I walked back into the living room area of the suite, I found that Sean had taken his cup of coffee and plopped in front of my television. He'd turned the volume up loudly and it looked as though he'd made himself right at home. "I thought you wanted to go get breakfast..." The words had just sprung out of my mouth when I came around the side of the sofa where Sean was sitting and caught sight of the program he was watching. "Missy?"

My mouth dropped wide open in surprise.

I'd just been thinking about her...then suddenly, she appeared.

"Is that *your* Missy?" Sean asked, sitting forward, placing his hot beverage on the coffee table in front of him, then leaning on his elbows. "She looks good."

Slowly, I relaxed my jaw and my mouth sprung back into place. While my outward appearance might've looked mostly normal then, my insides were jumping. The queasy feeling in my stomach that had been there moments before disappeared and was replaced by a thrum of energy. Just seeing Missy on TV again made me feel alive. "Yeah," I breathed. "Missy always looks good."

That wasn't just lip service or me being agreeable for the sake of it. The woman gracing my TV screen was ravishing. Her blonde hair wasn't so long anymore. It hung in a blunt cut so that the ends just kissed the tops of her shoulders. The color was like what I recollected, but the stiffness of her locks was new. Gone was the bounce and swish that had once accompanied a signature Missy head toss. She wore a chocolate brown suit with teal pinstripes and stuck to her lapel there was what looked like a large, overgrown daisy.

"It's a good thing you didn't call her, huh?" Sean's question pulled me out of my reverie.

"What?"

He turned in his seat and fixed me with a square gaze. "If you'd have called, it'd would've gone straight to voicemail."

"Maybe," I answered slowly. "But that's only if I have the right number still."

While we'd been conversing, Missy's male co-host had been talking, but when it was her turn to take over, I clammed up immediately. Leaning forward, pressing my hands to the backside of the couch, I listened to the words Missy was telling her audience.

She beamed brightly, gifting her viewers with one of her most radiant smiles. "And now we need to say goodbye." She paused, as if for dramatic effect. "But before you leave…let's take a moment to breathe." She stopped once more and made a show of closing her eyes and taking a long, deep inhalation. Then, her eyes popped back open, and she continued grinning. "I'm Missy Lawrence."

Her co-anchor said, "And I'm Steve Martin."

Together, they chorused, "Now, go get that day, Charlotte."

With that, some jaunty music played, and a series of credits began rolling. I watched as Missy's name disappeared and a few seconds later, the DieLou Records logo floated to the center of the screen. An announcer's voice proclaimed, "This news program was filmed before a live audience at DieLou Records Studio right here in the Queen City."

"Huh," Sean grunted. "Do you know where that is?"

I nodded numbly. "Missy's friend, Adair, owns that studio."

"Maybe your girl could get us tickets to the show sometime this week," Sean commented casually, hopping up off the couch, then bending forward to collect his coffee mug. "I think we've got some time available on Wednesday morning. If you ever get around to sending Missy a text, maybe you could ask her to…"

"I don't want to text Missy," I blurted. My eyes were still fixed on the TV screen mostly because the camera had continued filming, showing Missy and her cohost chatting cordially to one another. "I've gotta see her."

"All right," Sean said, shrugging lightly as he walked by me and headed toward the kitchen area. "So…you'll set up a time to see her."

But that just wasn't good enough.

I knew where Missy was…right now…and that meant…

I was out of that hotel room in a flash.

Chapter Five

What are *You* Doing Here?
Missy

"Good show today," Steve said, nudging me gently with his shoulder.

I laughed. "Ya think? Or did I hold the breathing part too long there at the end?"

Steve snickered as he patted down the collar of his shirt, working to remove the mini lavalier mic that was clipped there. "You always hold that beat too long."

"Really?" I whined a little. "But I've been practicing, trying to get it just right."

He laughed loudly. "Oh yeah...I can just imagine your version of practicing that schtick. Sitting in your apartment, going over and over the same line, trying to make it all seem practically perfect." He rolled his eyes delicately. "You're really overthinking this, Lawrence. It's just a breathing exercise. No need to..."

"It's *not* just a breathing exercise. It's our catchphrase," I reminded him. "Our whole show revolves around those few seconds and..."

"I'd like to think our program revolves around the news we report and the guests we interview, but..."

"Stop teasing." I swatted at my friend playfully. "That long breath is part of our brand and if I don't nail it just right every day..."

"Yeah, yeah," Steve interjected, "I already know all of this." He stood slowly, taking a moment to button his suit coat. Today was another winning ensemble for my pal. Steve was tall with a rather lanky build. Most all his clothes were tailored to meet his specific needs and style, but today he'd outdone himself by piecing together a gorgeous sienna brown blazer, buttercup yellow dress shirt, and a coffee brown tie that was threaded with hints of turquoise. The hues were like my own wardrobe choice for the day but weren't close enough that anyone could accuse us of matching each other intentionally. "Before you leave...with Missy and Steve." He paused and pointed to the logos that were stamped on the identical coffee mugs which sat prominently in the center of our desk. "Sometimes, I wish I hadn't come up with that gimmick all those years ago."

"Hey," I said with a laugh, pulling off my own microphone and handing it politely to one of the assistants, a young man named Edward, who was buzzing around the set. "I seem to think it was *my* idea to call our show…"

"You're right," he agreed, arching his back, and stretching a little, letting his head tip backward so that his long blonde locks grazed the tips of his stiffly starched collar. "You are the mastermind here. I'm just lucky you let me come along for the ride."

I grinned at him, then reached for his arm, looping my hand through the opening, and tucking it around his elbow. "And what a ride it's been." I sighed dreamily. "When we first started that vlog all those years ago, who'd have ever thought we'd still be working together so many years later?"

"I did," he answered, giving me his most dashing smile. "Once you had your hooks in me, I knew you were never going to let me go."

"Ha!" I laughed. "Is that the way you remember the beginning of our friendship?"

"Yep," he confirmed cheerfully. "But I owe you everything, Miss. If we hadn't started doing this show together, we wouldn't be celebrating our two thousandth episode today."

"Two thousand? Can it really be that many? Already?"

Steve nodded. "Two hundred episodes…ten years on the air, in the studio. You do the math."

I swiveled and glanced slowly around the set. "All right, so if we're celebrating an anniversary today, where's the cake?"

"Tom promised to bake us a cake tonight."

"Chocolate?" I asked, smiling at him hopefully.

"You know it."

"Ah," I sighed contentedly. "Your husband really is the best."

"I'm glad you think so because Tom and I have been wanting to ask you a favor. We…"

But Steve didn't have the chance to finish his statement. At that moment, there was a flurry of activity near the back of the room. I could hear scuffling feet, which wasn't so unusual, since the studio audience needed to vacate the area and the production assistants were tidying up our set and preparing for the next show that would film almost an hour later. But this bit of commotion was out of the ordinary. It sounded like people were trying to come back inside rather than make their way toward the exit. "What's going on out there?"

"I don't know." I dropped my hold on Steve's arm and stood on my tiptoes, straining my neck to get a better peek at what was happening.

"Wouldn't it be funny if..." Steve started, but once again his words were whisked away when a shout resounded through the room.

"Missy!"

I recognized the voice immediately.

"Nathan?"

I lurched forward and Steve put out a hand to stop me from tripping over one of the large, thick, ropelike cords that lay on the ground, leading to one of the cameras just ahead of us. "Careful there, girl."

"But I think that was Nathan," I murmured.

"Nathan...like *the* Nathan?" Steve questioned me and I nodded.

Just then, I heard Nate call my name again. "Missy? Are you still here?"

At that point, I couldn't stop myself from acting, even if I'd wanted to try. I leapt over the robust cord and raced toward the fire doors. There, standing on his tiptoes, in much the same way I'd just been doing a moment before, was Nathan Hamilton.

My heart jumped into my throat and my windpipe constricted, making it difficult to catch my breath or utter even a single word. It was the same way I felt when I was riding a roller coaster. For the first few seconds, I screamed with delight, but then, after the cart slid down the first, most treacherous hill, I could never regain my breath. I was stuck in a sort of limbo, waiting to express my excitement and elation, but incapable of uttering more than a squeak.

He looked much the same as he always had, with his fluttery brown locks combed into a slightly messy fashion and his deep blue eyes gazing at me, piercing me with their intensity. We were too far apart at first for me to see the changes that had been brought on by age, but I remedied that at once by striding toward him.

"Hello," I said softly, feeling my whole body relax as the words flowed. "Fancy meeting you here." Nathan huffed a little and it was then that I realized he was breathless. His right hand was clutching his side, near his belt loops, and when he smiled at me, I could see that he was doing his best to calm his erratic breathing. "Did you run here?"

His grin twitched. "I didn't run, but I walked quickly."

"He ran." A man appeared at Nate's elbow then. He was shorter than Nathan, but not by much. His frame was slim, but the way he doubled over, as if he might never be able to regain his bearings, I figured that he was either telling the truth and the two men had run to the studio this morning or he was horribly out of shape because he'd been unable to keep up with Nate's speedwalking. Either way, the spectacle of seeing these two men, dressed in obvious work attire, but panting madly, made me turn and share a smile with Steve Martin.

"Well, this is a surprise," I said, coming right out and saying exactly what I was thinking. "I didn't expect...Scratch that, not in a million years would I have expected..."

Nate sucked in another quick breath, then interrupted, "We caught the tail end of your show."

I chuckled. "If you did, you'd know how you ought to be breathing right now."

Almost as if I'd given him a direct order, rather than dropped a joke into the mix, Nate straightened up, let his hand fall away from his side, and breathed deeply in through his nose, before releasing the exhale through his mouth.

"See?" I prompted. "Isn't that better already?"

"Yeah," Nate said as a blissfully relaxed smile stole over his features. "I'm feeling a lot better now."

"Good."

There was a slight pause as everyone seemed stumped regarding what to say next. A whole bevy of questions rolled around in my head, but I didn't jump in with any of them, mostly because I figured it might be considered rude to come right out and ask Nathan what he was doing in my studio and why he'd felt the need to run here.

Fortunately, Steve didn't allow the silence to last for long. He offered his hand to Nate.

"Hey," he said smoothly. "I'm Steve Martin, Missy's best friend and co-host. I'm glad you caught our program this morning."

Nathan accepted the proffered hand and pumped it twice courteously. "It's good to know ya, Steve," he said, smiling more confidently, evidently feeling better now that introductions were being made properly. "I remember Missy talking about you years ago, but we never had the chance to meet back then."

"That's all right," Steve said slowly. "It's like my granny always used to say, 'better late than never.'" He paused and nodded to Nate's companion. "And this is...?"

"I'm Sean." The man stepped forward and shook Steve's hand. "Nathan and I work together. And we're in town for a conference this week." He rolled over his wrist and glanced for a long second at his watch. "Matter of fact, we're supposed to be having breakfast right now and getting ready to file into the convention center in a few minutes so we can listen to the keynote speaker give the welcoming address."

Steve laughed brightly. "If you're supposed to be there, what're you doing here?"

Sean exhaled slowly. "I'm not sure. One minute we were watching TV, and the next, Nathan was barreling out the door. I've known him a long time, but never seen him be so…"

"Missy," Nathan said my name softly. During this whole discourse his eyes had never left my face. If anyone else had looked at me in such an appraising manner, I might've felt a shade uncomfortable, but with Nate, I didn't mind so much.

"Yeah?"

"Do you wanna go out to dinner with me tonight?"

"I…umm…"

My gut reaction was to accept his offer, but then immediately, before I had time to blurt the words, my heart began thumping rapidly in my chest. My palms went slick with perspiration and the rush of sensations all at once made my tongue tie. "I…just…"

"It's so nice to see you again," Nathan pushed forward. "But I know you're busy right now and as Sean said, we've got to get back to our conference. So, maybe we could meet up a little later…what do ya say?"

My eyes flicked toward Steve and then I remembered the conversation we'd been having before Nate and Sean arrived. "I'm supposed to have dinner with…"

"Cancelled," Steve chirped, cutting me off completely. Then, he directed his warm smile at our visitors. "My husband and I were planning to host a little celebratory dinner at our place tonight, but we can put that off 'til the weekend."

"Oh…uh…are you sure?" Nate's eyes skipped anxiously from Steve's to mine.

"Absolutely," Steve assured him. "And if I text Tom right now, I can tell him not to bother with making the chocolate cake."

I pivoted and gave my friend a quick look. He blinked at me innocently.

We'd known each other for more than thirteen years and worked side-by-side most of that time. So, we'd gotten pretty good at having these silent, mental conversations.

He wants me to go out with Nate.

That much was obvious. Steve was grinning to beat the band and he even gave an enthusiastic nod in Nate's direction. His approval of this situation was so over the top all that was missing was him leaning over and giving me a gentle shove, physically pushing me in the direction of my old flame.

I inhaled deeply, drawing energy from the practice that had become mine and Steve's trademark then turned to face Nathan.

"So…?" he asked, posing the question once more. "Dinner…tonight? What do ya think?"

Chapter Six

You Don't Want to See Me?
Nathan

I may have just made a colossal mistake.

As someone who works in a laboratory, I've been trained to make wise, judicious decisions and never act without thinking about all the consequences. When I was in college, I made terrible choices. They piled up one right after the other. But I tended to blame most of those indiscretions on my youth. Now that I was older, I liked to think that I'd learned my lessons. And most of the time, I acted pragmatically. But that wasn't true…not entirely. Not today. And certainly not when Missy was involved.

Employing my deductive reasoning skills, I could see that I'd just made Missy uncomfortable. It was one thing to show up at her place of business unannounced. Another, to ask her to accompany me on a date this evening. But by pushing ever so slightly, I wasn't just tossing the ball in her court, hoping she'd bat it back. I was putting her in complete control, making it so she had the power to crush me. And for a long moment, that's what I was sure she was about to do.

Missy locked eyes with her friend, Steve Martin, and the two stood there, not saying a word. The silence thickened and I shot Sean a quick glance, wondering if he was feeling the awkwardness of the moment, but he'd already pulled out his cell phone and started thumbing through his calendar, double checking our itinerary for the morning, presumably making sure this little impromptu visit elsewhere wasn't keeping us from listening to the keynote speaker or participating in the first breakout session of the day.

Her eyes skittered back to mine and I could see the indecision there. This struck me as odd. Missy had a lot of personality quirks, just like everybody else, but lacking confidence had never been one of them. And she certainly had always known her own mind.

So…why the hesitation?

If I had to venture a hypothesis, I'd say she was vacillating between accepting my dinner invitation and sending me away as quickly as possible because she simply didn't want to be with me.

Yikes…that hurts.

A question sat on the tip of my tongue.

Is it possible you don't *want to see me tonight?*

But I didn't dare utter it, mostly because I wasn't ready to hear the answer. If she rejected me again outright, that'd be it. I'd know for certain just how she really felt about me. And while I'd never understand what had brought her to this point, why she wouldn't even want to have one meal with me as her companion, I'd have to accept it. But hanging here, doing this odd balancing act, was excruciating. My heart was beating frantically in my chest and a stiff staccato beat was drumming in my head.

Say something. Do something. End the suspense.

Finally, mostly because I just couldn't take the quietude any longer, I stepped forward and said, "If you've got other plans, Miss…"

"It's fine," she interrupted. "I'd love to go out with you tonight." Her words were exactly what I'd been hoping to hear and while they managed to calm the racket in my head, they did little to soothe the thudding of my heart.

"Yeah?"

"Sure." She chuckled lightly and just like that the genial sound broke all the tension. I let out a massive sigh of relief, which only made her laugh louder. "And since I'm the one who still lives around here, I'll even pick the restaurant."

"Great," I said, tucking my hands into my hip pockets, hoping to conceal the way they were trembling with excitement. "Do you know where you wanna go now or…?"

"I'll text you the name of the place and the address later," she replied.

I tipped my head to the side and eyed her dubiously for a moment. "You didn't change your phone number?"

She shook her head as a small, secretive smile crept onto her lips. "And I guess I already assumed you didn't change yours…"

"That's right." I gave her an understanding nod. While this might not seem like a very big deal, the whole interchange had my temples pounding again.

We could've called each other. We could've been talking this whole time…all these years.

But it was no use pursuing that line of thinking. The past had come and gone and now…with Missy standing in front of me and a date etched loosely into our shared calendars, I felt grateful. Not that I'd missed out on spending so much time with her, but that I had the chance…this opportunity…to give it all another try.

After saying a few hasty goodbyes, I followed Sean down the stairs, and we exited the DieLou Records building. We hadn't made it very far down the block on our way back to the convention center when Sean said, "So...tell me about Missy. I'm pretty sure you've only ever dropped her name into our conversations a couple of times, mostly when we were younger, but she's gotta be important to send you running like that."

"I didn't run," I countered, taking a moment to unbutton my shirt sleeves then roll them to the elbow. It was going to be a pleasant fall day and with the sun already shining brightly and the thrill of what felt like victory singing through my veins, I was feeling warm and exuberant.

"Maybe not," Sean chided, "but you had me running to catch up with you."

"Sorry about that," I apologized at once. "I guess I should've told you what I was thinking, but I also reasoned there wasn't any time to waste. Since I knew where Missy was, right at that second, it seemed fortuitous. I'd just been thinking about her, wondering what she was doing, then...there she was...letting me know exactly where I could find her."

"So, tell me about her," my friend urged. "I assume the two of you dated in college?"

Over the next several minutes, I gave Sean the barebones version of my history with Missy. The dating...the cheating...the way she forgave me so we could carry forward as friends. And I ended my story with telling that final tale...the last time I saw her...on the day I asked her to marry me.

He let out a low, appreciative whistle, then said, "Now, correct if I'm wrong, and I might be because the timeline is a little wonky here, but did you ask that girl to marry you before or after..."

I cut him off right there. "This all came before...that."

Sean nodded slowly. "So, I guess you could say a lot has happened since the last time the two of you saw each other."

"Yeah," I agreed. "And I assume that's why things were so awkward between us just now. We've both changed quite a bit."

We'd reached the hotel and conference center by that time and the bell hop held the door, politely ushering us inside the cool, clean, air-conditioned lobby that smelled faintly of citrus. Sean led the way toward the ballroom, where the breakfast buffet was supposed to be laid, but before entering, he turned and looked at me squarely. "If things are so strained between the two of you, why was it so important for you to see her immediately and why'd you push to have that date tonight?"

I shook my head slowly, pondering the answer before giving it. "I don't know. All I can say is that I've got to see her again. I needed to hear her voice. I can't just be in town, knowing she's here too, and pretend like it doesn't matter."

"Does it...matter?" He prodded gently. "I mean, if she'd have stuck to her guns back there, and said she really needed to keep her dinner plans with her other friends, would that have wrecked you for the day?"

I laughed dryly. "I'm already a wreck. Whenever I'm around Missy, I start acting like a madman. Couldn't you already tell that much?" Sean snorted but had the decency not to answer.

I knew what he was thinking though. My life was very different from the way it'd been thirteen years ago, when Missy and I had last laid eyes on each other. But just the thought of seeing her again...the idea of spending another long moment in her presence...had lit a fire underneath me. I might've changed. My world might be drastically different. But if I thought I'd get to see Missy again, I was willing to do just about anything to make that happen.

Chapter Seven

How Much Does He Deserve?
Missy

"So…" Steve said, pulling out the vowel sound much longer than was strictly necessary, "that was Nathan."

"Yeah," I grunted. "The one and only." The security guards who'd been manning the doors, trying to shepherd our audience members out of the building when Nate and Sean had attempted to come rushing in the opposite doors nodded discreetly at me, then took their leave. As they wandered away, Steve leaned laconically against the doorframe, making it so I couldn't exit the studio, unless I pushed my way around him. "And…?"

"And I suppose I always pictured him being shorter," Steve said, leisurely crossing one leg over the other.

"Why?" I laughed.

He shrugged nonchalantly. "You told me about him, a long time ago, but you never let me see pictures. And since I wasn't a guest at Adair's wedding, I'd never met the man in person before right now."

"Okay, but why'd you think he was short?"

"*Shorter*," Steve corrected, slowly straightening himself up to his full height. "But I have no idea how I came to that conclusion." He fiddled with the knot on his tie. "You've always been drawn to the tallest men in the room."

I pinched my pal's arm playfully. "Is that all you've got to say? You only want to make jokes about my type of guy?"

He arched his right eyebrow cynically. "You know I want to say more, Miss, but I'm trying not to overstep."

"I appreciate that."

"But that doesn't mean I want you to hold out on me," he continued. "Was that the first time you've seen him since he proposed?"

I squeezed my eyes shut tight, wishing I could just push away the memories from that day, as well as all those that came directly after. "Yeah."

"And did you ever call him up and tell him about…?"

"Nope," I broke in, speaking over top of him, making it so he couldn't utter another word on the forbidden topic.

Steve's expression grew very serious. He gave up on his laidback façade and fixed me with a quizzical stare. "When all that happened, you never…not even once…called him up and told him about it?"

I shook my head emphatically. "What you just saw was our official reunion."

Frown lines appeared at the corners of Steve's mouth when his lips tugged downwards.

"How is that possible? Why didn't you call when…?"

"I couldn't," I said, speaking around a lump that had suddenly risen in my throat. Tears sprung to my eyes, and I blinked rapidly, hoping to dismiss them. "I didn't call Nate because I couldn't tell him what happened. I couldn't stand to hear the disappointment I was sure would be there and…"

"He might've been disappointed, but he wouldn't have directed those feelings at you. What happened wasn't your fault, Missy. You couldn't do anything. You made the logical choice. But Nathan? He should've factored in somewhere. He could've…I don't know… made a difference somehow. Made things better for you." He paused and shook his head, plainly agitated by the situation. "Don't you think he deserved to know what happened?" Steve pressed.

I whimpered as a soft sob escaped my lips, causing the tears I'd been trying so valiantly to keep at bay to slide down my cheeks. "How much does he deserve? What amount of pain is too much?"

"You should've told him…everything."

"No." I shook my head vehemently. "Everything Nate needs to know about our relationship, he already does. When he asked me to marry him, we were just a couple of kids."

"But you wanted to be his wife," Steve reminded me in the gentlest possible way, using the tone he reserved for reading out the most horrific and troubling news stories. "I know you did. Back then when he asked you, I know that you wanted to marry him, so why…?"

"I was scared," I blurted. "Scared he was acting on a whim…afraid he'd change his mind…or I'd think better of being so hasty and change mine. I thought the whole thing might be a joke…something he'd just said that would make us both laugh later. I was worried he'd cheat on me again and then…then…"

"Shhh…" Steve hushed, taking a step forward and wrapping his long, strong arms protectively around my shoulders, pulling me into a fierce hug.

I buried my head in his chest but continued mumbling. Now that I'd begun, I couldn't seem to stop the torrent of words or my free-flowing tears. "Then, long after Nate was gone, I lost...well, you know what happened. I just lost *everything* and that was how I knew...for certain... that letting him go had been the right thing to do."

"How do you know?" Steve whispered. He stroked his hands through the ends of my hair. "I saw that man just now and while I might not be an expert on love, I could tell that he still had strong feelings for you. If you'd have called him...Explained what happened...Maybe he'd have run down here back then, just like he did today."

"No," I sobbed. For so many years, I'd managed to push down my emotions, to keep them guarded and locked up tight. The way I hustled through my daily routine was by forgetting about Nate and our shared past and just breathing through the pain. But now that I'd seen him again and was stuck rehashing all my feelings, the keen sting of old wounds smarted and made all my senses throb in a raw and aching manner. "I couldn't be the wife Nathan wanted. I couldn't give him everything he needed. I...I..."

I sucked in a deep inhalation and forced myself to do the breathing exercises Steve and I were constantly encouraging our viewers to try. Blessedly, the technique worked, and I was able to get a grip on my emotions. Slowly, I wriggled away from Steve slightly and looked up into his deep, liquid brown eyes.

"What?" he urged gently.

"You asked me a minute ago if Nate deserved to know the truth of what happened. Well...from where I'm standing, he got exactly what he deserved. A life without me."

Chapter Eight

Let's Check in with the Gang…Shall We?
Nathan

I was a fidgety, nervous wreck by the time I arrived at Anne Marie's Bakehouse. Just as she'd promised, Missy had sent me a text around lunchtime, letting me know where to go for our dinner date and asking if I could meet early, around five, because she still got up at the crack of dawn for work and needed to turn in at her regular hours. I'd been all too happy to oblige. I was so keyed up over our arranged date that I barely paid attention to any of the lecturers who spoke at the convention, so meeting sooner, rather than later, suited me just fine.

Except that I couldn't stop fussing with my hair. Our last session had concluded at four, so I'd had a few minutes to freshen up in preparation for this date, but no matter what I did, no amount of pomade I added to the locks, I just couldn't get that stubborn cowlick in the back of my head to lay down right. It was because of that unyielding cowlick that I'd always worn my hair in a messy fashion, but tonight, I wanted to seem more put together than the man Missy surely remembered. I wanted to look like the person I was now…not the man she'd left alone all those years ago.

Surreptitiously, I glanced around the restaurant, inspecting the décor. The place was situated in the middle of Tryon Street, but it looked a lot like some of the old-fashioned diners that I'd visited back in Pittsburgh or stopped by on one vacation I took to New Jersey. The tabletops were made of white and silver flecked linoleum. The seats of the booth were draped in red plastic leather. On each table, there was a stack of laminated menus stuffed right next to the gleaming silver napkin dispenser and the ketchup and mustard caddy. And, of course, near the back of the shop, there was a fully functioning juke box. It wasn't the sort of place I thought would thrive in Uptown Charlotte, and definitely not the restaurant I would've imagined Missy picking out for our get together, but it was cozy and cute, so I figured I had no reason to argue.

But as the minutes dragged on and I watched the waitress named Yvette flounce from one table to the next, taking orders, refilling coffee mugs, and placing large platters of food in front of her customers, I started to wonder what I was doing, sitting all by myself, in this little place.

She's late.

Quickly, I checked my watch and found that my inclinations were wrong. It was five minutes to five, so Missy was, decidedly, not running late.

Well, then she's not coming. Too much time has elapsed since we saw each other last. If she wanted to have dinner with me, she'd have shown up early, too.

That was absurd, but I entertained those notions, just the same. And since I was permitting my thoughts to spiral in that direction, I took it a step further.

We should've talked years ago. I should've been the one to call and explain everything. I could've…

But then, I heard Missy's laughter and turned to see her walking through the diner. She was wearing the same brown and teal suit she'd donned this morning, which made me feel marginally better because I hadn't changed out of my work attire, either. She was being led to our table by a woman with long, black hair, enormous gold hoop earrings, and a deep, throaty voice. I only knew that much because I could hear her laugh mingling with Missy's creating a sort of melodic counterbalance that was pleasing.

"Nate," Missy said, gesturing to her companion. "Meet Anne Marie."

I stared at her in surprise. "Anne Marie? As in the owner of this bakehouse?"

"One in the same," the lady said, sweeping her hand wide and gesturing for Missy to take the available seat in the booth across from me. Anne Marie reached between us and plucked two menus from the rack. She gave me one first, then started to offer one to Missy, but was quickly waved off.

"Oh, I already know what I'm having," Missy said as a sweet little smile tickled her lips.

"But you always order the same thing," Anne Marie simpered, pooching out her lower lip a little in a faux pout. "Don't you wanna try something new?"

"No, thanks," Missy replied, still beaming at her friend. "I like what I like, and I don't have any reason to be adventurous."

Anne Marie fixed her eyes on me then and continued in that same slight pleading tone, "Order one of my new menu items, please.

And make Missy take a taste. I keep telling her she's got to expand her palate...try something new so that she exercises her taste buds."

Missy giggled and when my eyes slid to hers, she gave me an encouraging nod, so I answered, "I can't make Missy do anything, but *I'll* order whatever you recommend."

Anne Marie laughed lightly, and crinkles formed around the corners of her bright, black eyes. "I like this one, Missy. I'm glad you brought him by."

Because I just couldn't help myself, I asked, "Does Missy bring all her dates here?"

Missy snickered and Anne Marie cackled delightedly, then she shot me a teasing wink. "Wouldn't you like to know?"

Now that the concept was dangling out there, I had to admit that I was curious. So many years had come and gone, and I was sure in all that time, Missy had been on dates with her fair share of beaus. But now, I wanted to know everything—all the stories I'd missed, all the men who'd been a part of her life. I was even eager to learn about the usual order she placed here at Anne Marie's Bakehouse. A few moments before, I'd been so uneasy, but now, with Missy sitting across from me, giving me a comfortable, carefree smile, I allowed myself to relax, too.

"I'd like to know more about those specials you mentioned," I said, searching for a good way to segue out of our current topic.

Anne Marie nodded approvingly, then pointed to a small section of the menu. "Last month, I started experimenting with my hollandaise recipe, so I've got a new version of the Eggs Benedict on the menu now and a friend gave me a hint about adding some different ingredients to my waffle batter so..."

"This place serves breakfast?" I interjected.

Anne Marie gave a perky, little laugh. "We're a full-fledged diner. So, you can order a burger and fries if you want, but it's our breakfast that's put my little spot on the map."

I gazed across the table at Missy, and she shrugged nonchalantly. "I seemed to recall just how much you loved eating breakfast...no matter the time of day."

We shared a long look, and I was sure our thoughts had drifted in the same direction. The last time Missy and I had breakfast together, I'd asked her to marry me. It couldn't be a coincidence that she'd brought me here tonight.

"I'll try those waffles, please," I said while handing Anne Marie the menu, but never taking my eyes off Missy. "And a cup of black coffee."

"And you know what I like," Missy said, breaking eye contact with me long enough so she could glance upward at Anne Marie. "But I think I'll have a cup of coffee, too."

"And the water?"

"Yes," Missy said simply. "I always need an extra glass of iced water."

Anne Marie stuffed my menu back in its holder, then turned away, allowing her long, flowing black skirt to swirl as she moved. I turned to watch her go and noticed the way she stopped by other tables to chat. That made me chuckle. "So, she's not real worried about placing our order, is she?"

Missy shrugged. "If we wanted speedy service, I wouldn't have suggested coming here." She sat back a little in the booth and unfastened the top button on her blazer. "I hope you don't mind waiting a while for your food." Her forehead scrunched in consternation. "I guess I didn't figure time would be an issue, but if you've got somewhere to be tonight or if Sean was expecting you to come back so you could…"

"Miss," I interrupted, "I'm good right here. I've got nothing to do tonight except spend a little time catchin' up with you."

"All right," Missy said, motioning with her hand, twirling it in the air between us, and prompting me to continue. "What do you wanna know?"

I chortled. "Jumpin' right in with the questions, are ya?"

Her shoulders lifted and dropped delicately in a noncommittal manner. "We may have all night to sit here, but I don't think we ought to beat around the bush. Do you?"

I wasn't so sure how to answer that. While there were hundreds of questions that I wanted to ask Missy, I wasn't ready to dive right into the deep end of the pool so quickly. So, instead, I asked her something that I knew would please her to no end. "I guess not." I plucked a napkin from the dispenser and laid it on the tabletop in front of me, then questioned, "How are the girls?"

Missy beamed. For once, I'd said exactly the right thing. She rolled her shoulders, then sat back, evidently fully relaxed. "I don't even know where to start."

"Wherever you want."

She tapped her long fingertips on the tabletop, then said, "Well, since you already know Steve and I do a morning show at DieLou Records, I probably ought to tell you all about…"

"Adair," I interrupted. "How is she?"

"She's great." Missy laughed. "She and Wes are still married and working for her has been a dream."

"Yeah," I murmured as Yvette appeared, carrying our drink order. She deposited the mugs of coffee in front of both of us, then slid a glass of water that was already dripping with condensation toward Missy. "I thought Adair didn't like working with her friends, so how did you and Steve manage to…"

"When he went back to law school, we started our own news website. It wasn't anything special, really. Just a couple of blogs featuring the top news stories in the area. And we vlogged at least once a day, too. But before long, we got this idea to start a podcast and that's when Adair stepped in and rescued me."

"Rescued you? How?"

"You know I liked my job as a field reporter for WSTA, but I had a difficult relationship with my boss, Ross. I wanted an anchor position, but with Melody on the desk, I was sure that was never going to happen. So, Jess offered to help Steve and me produce our podcast. In exchange, we had to agree to host a morning show."

"That's interesting," I said before taking a slow sip of my coffee. The liquid was boiling hot, and it tasted of cinnamon, which was kind of unexpected. "But I'm still not sure why Adair presented you with this opportunity after spending all those years letting Jack go without a record contract…"

"Ah," Missy sighed. "Poor Jack."

"Why'd you say it like that? What happened to her?"

"I'm not really sure," she returned as her lips twisted into a tortured grimace. "The last time I heard from her was years ago. She'd reinvented herself as Jackie Rose and then…" Missy lifted her hand and wiped it through the air, as though she were dusting away a thin film of cobwebs. "She just disappeared."

I nearly choked on my next sip of coffee. "Jack disappeared?"

Missy smiled ruefully. "No. But, I haven't heard from her in a very long time, so I guess you could say the two of us just fell out of touch."

"That happens," I murmured.

"Yeah," she agreed. "It sure does."

Our eyes locked and I held her gaze.

If someone had asked her about me before tonight, she might've given the same answer. Nate and I lost touch years ago.

That notion made me feel awful.

Not wanting to wallow in that heartbreaking thought, I prompted her to continue. "But what about the other girls? Tell me about the ones you still see all the time."

Missy sipped from her water for a second, then said, "I guess I don't see the old gang that much anymore. Oh, I work with Adair, so she's always around, but the others have all moved away."

"Everyone left Charlotte?"

She nodded. "Eve and Savanna play on the World Poker Tour full-time now, so they both moved to Vegas. Hope married Skeeter...err, Scott."

"Little Hopey got married?"

Missy's gorgeous smile reappeared when she was talking about her younger sister. "They met while she was working at the Lob. He was a customer and boldly asked her out." She paused and chuckled. "And I guess you could say the rest is history. They got married...ten...yeah, ten years ago, then they moved to Georgia. She's got three kids and..."

I snorted a quick laugh. "It's hard to imagine Hopey settled and taking care of three kids."

"Who said she was taking care of them?" Missy joked. "She lets those kids run the house. Hopey likes to pretend otherwise, but her kids are her whole world and she'd do just about anything to make them happy."

"That's the way it should be," I said softly, which coaxed another smile from Missy.

"Yeah," she murmured, "I think so, too."

Yvette returned, this time carrying plates of food. She placed an enormous stack of waffles that were covered in cinnamon apples and whipped cream right in front of me, then deposited a platter that featured a gigantic omelet in front of Missy. The last item on her tray was the largest chocolate chip muffin I'd ever seen. It was maybe the size of a small pumpkin or gourd, and the shape was irregular too, almost like there were so many chocolate chips stuffed in the batter that it couldn't be bothered to conform and stick to its proper size.

"Wow," I whispered admiringly nodding at the array of foods that covered our table. "How are we gonna eat all this?"

"We'll manage," Missy said, leaning forward and dipping the tines of her fork in my whipped cream. "If we share, I figure we'll be able to make a pretty big dent here."

"Who said I wanted to share?" I asked, playfully grabbing the edge of my plate, and towing the waffles away from her.

She rolled her eyes. "Once you get a taste of this omelet, you'll be begging me to split it with you fifty-fifty."

"All right," I agreed. "Anne Marie did say she wanted you to try something new, so I guess I'd better carve you out a bite of these waffles, then, huh?"

"Yes, please." Missy licked her lips and leaned further forward. "They smell amazing."

For the next few minutes, we talked only of our sumptuous meal, taking turns cutting off huge chunks of food and sharing them with each other. When it was time to try a bite of that gargantuan muffin, I was surprised by the bursts of flavors that exploded in my mouth. I only expected to taste chocolate chips, but there was something else there, too. "What is that?" I asked.

"It's Anne Marie's special recipe," she replied while using the back side of her fork to smoosh a bit of the muffin before popping it into her mouth. "She's sworn me to secrecy. And you know me…I'm the kind of reporter who never reveals my sources."

"Fine," I said, using my fork to stab at another bite of the sweet baked good. "Don't tell. Let's talk more about the girls."

Missy nodded. "I still see Hope regularly, because either she comes here with Skeeter and the kids or I travel there during the holiday season, but it's not enough."

"Sure," I agreed. "You two were always so close. I imagine it's tough not to see her all the time."

"I might cope with the distance better if some of the others had stayed in town, but…"

"Who else left?"

"Well…" Missy paused and tapped the tines of her fork on the rim of her plate. "Brooklyn and Duke got married about a dozen years ago. But they divorced within the first year, after Brooklyn discovered Duke was cheating on her. She didn't waste a whole lot of time mourning their relationship though because about six months after the divorce was finalized, she moved to Minneapolis."

"Why there?" I just had to ask.

Missy smirked. She sat forward, leaning dangerously close to the plates that were still piled high with food. "Remember how Duke wanted Brooklyn to find a career of her own?"

I shrugged. "I guess."

"Well, she followed his advice. She took some evening classes for a few years and eventually got a degree in nursing. Before we knew it, she'd been offered a good job at a prestigious hospital in Minneapolis, so she moved there. I think she's dating a football star who plays for the Minnesota Vikings now and…"

I couldn't help but laugh. "Good old, Brooklyn. She sure made the best out of a bad situation."

"Too true." Missy leaned back a little way, then continued, "Benson lives in Wilmington now. She still teaches kindergarten students and has four kids of her own."

"Four kids?"

She nodded. "And Autumn moved to Rock Hill just a few years ago. She got an offer from an accounting firm that sat just across the South Carolina state line and the job was too lucrative to pass up. She's been married twice, but I think she just finished signing the divorce papers with Nigel last week."

"Woah," I breathed heavily, taking a long moment to digest all the food, as well as the onslaught of information. "So…all the girls have moved on, had babies, or got married." I paused before asking the one thing I really wanted to know, and Missy had somehow conveniently left out of the conversation up until this point. "What about you? Have you ever been married?"

Chapter Nine

Can We Go Back…for Just a Second?
Missy

I knew this question had been rattling around inside Nathan's brain for at least the last ten minutes or so. As soon as I'd mentioned Hope's marriage to Skeeter, I could see that he wanted to ask me about my dating life or sneak a query in there about my own marriage prospects, but he'd waited. Whether he did that because he genuinely wanted to hear what had happened to my tight-knit group of friends or because he was hoping I'd give him the perfect opening, as I'd just done, in which to pose the question, I couldn't be sure. But I didn't leave him hanging in suspense.

With one good, stiff shake of the head, I answered, "I never did manage to find the right guy."

Nate put down his fork and one of his hands drifted absentmindedly to his chin. He stroked the spot where he'd once tried to grow out a goatee back when we were in college. The patch was clean shaven now, but I remembered the way the little feathery light hairs used to tickle my chin when we kissed all those eons ago and had to look away from him momentarily. "How is that possible?" he asked softly.

His question drew me back to the present. "I don't know," I answered honestly. "These last few years, I've had two serious boyfriends, but each time it looked like one of them might want to take the next step, I just…I guess you could say I just backed away."

He shook his head slowly, evidently still pondering my situation. "I never would've guessed. I mean, I always just assumed you'd get married." His blue eyes drifted so that they locked onto mine. "It seemed like getting married…having a husband…maybe having a few kids of your own… I thought that was all something you really wanted."

I stared at him, lost for a moment in his words, but also vividly calling to mind the proposal he'd laid at my feet just a shade over thirteen years ago. He'd been so sweet, so hasty. He'd simply said the first things that had popped to his mind, and it had been evident, even then, that he'd acted without thinking through matters fully. I pushed aside the plates of food that were dividing us from one another, then leaned forward, resting my arms onto the now open tabletop. "Why?" I whispered. "*Why* did you think I wanted to get married?"

Immediately I regretted presenting him with this question because his cheeks turned scarlet. He tugged on the collar of his dress shirt, pulling it away slightly, making it so I could see the way he gulped nervously.

"I…uh…" He was clearly scrambling. "Just because you didn't want to marry me doesn't mean you didn't want to marry someone eventually," he quipped. "I'm not narcissistic enough to believe that I was the only one out there who was right for you."

I narrowed my eyes and continued gazing at him, trying to gauge just how serious he was being. But then, deciding it wasn't worth the time or energy, because I'd never be likely to figure it out, I waved my hand through the air between us dismissively. "You were joking then, just like you're kidding around with me now."

"Joking?" His heavy eyebrows lowered, and his lips pulled into a taut, thin line. "What…You thought I was joking when I asked you to marry me?"

I shrugged one shoulder delicately, hoping to convey how that was exactly what I'd thought.

"That's why you didn't show up? You never came to Blessed Creek because…"

"I didn't think you were being serious, Nathan," I said softly. "We hadn't seen each other in a few years. And, the last thing I knew, you'd just broken up with yet another girlfriend. You showed up at my apartment and stayed for what…like twenty-seven hours? But then, before you left, you said you thought we ought to get married." I huffed. "What was I supposed to think? Was I really supposed to just assume that you were being serious and…"

"I *was* being serious," he interjected. His voice came out in a low, husky way, and I could see, when I dared to meet his eyes once more, that my recollection and rationale for what happened between us had pained him. "Those words I said to you…when I asked you to pick me…to be with me…I meant all of it. I *wanted* to marry you, Missy."

My chest ached suddenly, and it wasn't because he and I had just worked our way through a mountain of breakfast foods. My heart hurt because somewhere, deep down, I'd always wondered. While what I'd just said had been the truth, I hadn't known what to do with Nathan's proposal when he made it, I could see the sincerity clearly etched on his face now. When I didn't show up to Blessed Creek that day, I'd destroyed him…and that made the fact that we'd waited thirteen long years to have this conversation seem even worse.

I inhaled deeply, then exhaled slowly through my mouth. Having regained my composure, I decided that we'd talked just enough about my life and motivations, so when I opened my eyes and met his stare, I asked simply, "What about you, Nate? What have you been doing since we parted?"

Chapter Ten

But Wait…is There More?
Nathan

I licked my lips nervously, stretching out the relative silence. It wasn't as if we were in our own little cocoon, after all. The restaurant was abuzz with patrons, coming and going, exclaiming over the sizable portions, and talking enthusiastically with the owner, Anne Marie, who was still sashaying around the diner, greeting everyone like an old friend.

Where to begin…

I'd known that Missy was about to turn the tables on me in such a manner. It was inevitable. Once I asked about her relationship status, there was no avoiding the follow up questions that would put me and my situation in the spotlight. But I didn't want to go there…not yet. We were having such a nice time, catching up with each other, learning about all the changes life had wrought, and I was loath to put a damper on the evening.

"I've mostly been devoted to my work," I answered, steering as far clear from the messier aspects of my life as I possibly could.

"Right," Missy said, nodding thoughtfully. "You're here on business, so I guess I can assume things are going well?"

Since she'd pushed aside her food, I didn't have to reach far to snag another bite of that delicious muffin. I stuffed a bit into my mouth, chewed for a second, then said, "My company has been very good to me."

"Okay," she said slowly, "so tell me about it."

And so, I did. For the next ten minutes, I explained how even though I'd started at the lab testing company right out of college and only planned to stay there for a few years, I'd ultimately decided to hang around much longer.

"You mean you still work for SaniTest?" She seemed surprised, but also intrigued by this information.

I shrugged. "The company has changed names quite a few times. It's called Morgan and Fosters now, but yeah, it's still mostly the same place, located in the very same spot where it's always been. And I really can't complain about the work I do there. They pay me well and…"

"But your hours were atrocious," she intervened. "I mean, I know I've got to get up bright and early, beating the rooster to the punch, but that's the nature of my job—waking up before the news cycle has a chance to spring to life. But you...You aren't still going in for work at four in the morning, are you?"

"Naw," I drawled, cutting off a hunk of waffle and trailing it through the gooey apple cinnamon concoction. "I worked that shift for a long time, but as I got older and gained more experience, I kept earning one promotion right after the next. And that put me in a good place to choose when I wanted to work."

"You pick your own hours?"

I shrugged. "Let's say I'm required to work so many hours a week, but how I manage to do it is mostly up to me."

Missy nodded. "That must be awfully nice."

"It's been a blessing, really. When I first found out..." I stopped right in the middle of my sentence. I knew Missy was listening closely, so she'd notice how I broke off abruptly, but I had been about to spout some information that I just wasn't prepared to share yet. So, I figured it was better to have her ask questions about my bizarre behavior than come right out and say all the thoughts that were niggling in the back of my mind.

"Found out...?" She sat forward and widened her eyes, letting me know for certain that she was still paying attention and hadn't missed a beat. "What?"

It wasn't that I wanted to lie to Missy or even keep a bunch of secrets. But something about spilling my whole story right here and now didn't feel right. So, I tried to cover as best I could. "You know how I've always liked having my freedom. And now, I can rearrange my schedule any way I like. Before, I was moving through life almost robotically, but then, when my boss gave me the chance to set my own hours, I found out that I did much better...thrived really...when I got to sleep more than five hours a night."

From the way her eyes were narrowed, I could tell that she was scrutinizing my little speech and finding it wanting.

Is she about to call me out and force me to own up to the whole truth?

I put down my fork and clasped my hands underneath the table so I could utter a silent prayer, begging the good Lord not to let this meeting go south as quickly as I knew it could if I had to offer up all my deeds since we'd last parted ways.

I'm not sure if God answered my prayer or if Missy just decided it wasn't worth the hassle to pry, but a second later, her features smoothed out once more and that soft, secretive smile I'd always loved graced her lips. "All right," she whispered, "so things are good. Work's going well and you're happy?"

"Yeah," I agreed. "I've never been happier."

She slapped the flat of her hand gently against the tabletop. "Then, that's all I needed to hear."

Before I could retort or add something else, she stood.

"Where...where are you going?" I stammered, clambering to my feet in a much less graceful manner.

"I've gotta get home," she said, easing her way out of the booth and standing in the aisle that separated us from the two top tables which were bunched nearby.

"But we haven't finished eating and I didn't pay the check yet."

"If you want to take any of the food back to the hotel with you, I'm sure Yvette will box it up. And as for the check, I've got that covered."

I stared at her in disbelief. "How?"

She waved her hand at the clunky, old-fashioned cash register that sat toward the end of the counter where almost a dozen bar stools were filled with customers. "I keep an open tab here. Anne Marie just puts whatever I order on the bill, adds a nice tip, and we call it even."

"You...you trust Anne Marie to do something like that?"

She tipped her head to the side and gave me a sympathetic look. "She's my friend. Of course, I trust her."

I shuffled out into the aisle, blocking Missy's path, making it so if she wanted to leave the restaurant in such a hurry, she'd have to push me aside. "But...so...that's it?"

Her smile broadened and she leaned forward to give me a hug. When her arms wrapped around me, I scented the chocolate from the muffin she'd just eaten, as well as the coffee that still hung on her breath. She whispered in my ear, "It's been so good to see you, Nate." Before I could even wrap one arm around her waist and pull her in for what I considered a proper hug, she wriggled away. In a careless, almost flippant manner, she said, "It's been good catching up. And don't be a stranger going forward."

"Yeah," I mumbled, "let's not wait another thirteen years before seeing each other again."

"Right," she agreed. "Please, whenever you've got the time, shoot me a text, or pick up the phone and call. I forgot just how much I missed our conversations."

Missy might have forgotten but I hadn't.

She'd always been athletic and lithe, so when her words caught me off guard and I stood there pondering them, she managed to slip around me without causing a commotion or even jostling the couple who were sitting at the table next to us. I turned to watch her walk out the door. She lifted a hand and waved at Anne Marie, then called out a cheerful 'thank you' to Yvette before pushing through the glass doors and exiting the restaurant.

No!

It felt odd to dash out of the place without paying the bill, but since Missy said she'd already covered it, I tried to content myself with that knowledge. Because as awkward as it felt to leave a tab unpaid, that was nothing compared to the way my heart sank when I watched the wind whip through the open doorway and carry Missy right out of my life again.

She can't leave...not like this.

I knew now that she hadn't just ended our dinner date early because she was tired and had to get up with the sunrise. No, no, she'd known that I was hiding something and instead of delving deeper, she'd chosen to let me keep my secrets. But I didn't want to be so elusive. With Missy, I wanted to tell her everything.

Seized by the urge to do something, for the second time that day, I took off, not quite jogging, but walking so quickly that it might've seemed that way to a casual onlooker.

I burst through the exterior door and was greeted by a rush of lukewarm air. Even though fall had descended on the city, the temperature was still pleasant. The wind might be tousling my hair, but it wasn't enough to make me shrink back inside or want to hustle to my hotel and get out of the elements. I wanted to find Missy and that's exactly what I meant to do.

Fortunately, she hadn't gotten very far. She tended to walk everywhere with a purpose, never just lazily loping along, but moving at a brisk pace, so I needed to lengthen my stride to catch her, but that wasn't an insurmountable feat by any means. When I fell into step alongside her, she gave me a sidelong glance.

"Did I leave something back at the restaurant?"

I cracked a smile, wondering how she could be so nonchalant when my heart was racing. "Yeah," I grunted. "Me."

That pulled her up short. Her eyes flicked back and forth between mine and I wondered if she could see all that I was feeling.

Does she know what being so close to her again is doing to me?

"Was there something else you wanted to tell me, Nate?" she asked, taking a step back, and creating some space between us.

But that, I could not abide. I reached across the divide and touched the sleeve of her suit blazer. It was made of fine, soft fabric and the material felt almost silky underneath my fingertips. "Only about a million things," I grumbled.

She chuckled lightly. "We've got time for all that later." She paused and sighed. "Now that we're friends again, we can talk whenever you feel like it. And, when you're ready to tell me about all the things we've missed sharing, I'll be eager to listen."

"How did you know I was holding back?" I asked and her smile widened. The streetlamp overhead cast a warm, tangerine glow on Missy's face, so I could easily see it when her expression went from curious to amused.

She stepped closer and reached up to tap her finger on the tip of my nose. "I just knew."

The touch had been cute and playful, and certainly not designed to thrill me, but just being so near to Missy was making all my senses jump with agitation. I wanted her to touch me again, to stay this close and allow me another long moment to peer into her eyes. "And you don't mind? I mean…you're not mad because I was being a tad evasive?"

She shook her head gently. The minute movement allowed me to get a whiff of her tea tree scented shampoo and I stared at her, wondering if she could still use the same hair care products after all this time. But then, I reasoned how that made sense. Missy was loyal—to her friends, to her shampoo and conditioner brand, even to her breakfast order. "I don't blame you for keeping a secret or two, Nate."

The understanding and sense of calm that was threading through her voice relaxed every bone in my body. It wasn't just the fact that she was accepting of my faults or that she was so reliable and predictable, even after all these years. It was the knowledge that she understood me. She got where I was coming from and didn't push me to be someone I wasn't.

I'd been tense while chasing her down the street and even when I reached out to touch her arm, I'd been doubting if doing as much would be crossing a line. But now, Missy was doing what she'd always been able to do best—comfort those around her and make me feel like I was the most important, most cherished person in her world.

The urge to kiss her came over me all at once. I wanted her to know how much she meant to me...even after all this time had spread itself between us. And I wanted to show her how, for me, very little had truly changed. She was still the girl who understood me better than anybody else and would forever be the one lady who managed to calm my nerves when I got unreasonably agitated.

But I couldn't do that.

She was smiling at me, but the grin was friendly, amiable, and obliging. She wasn't beckoning me forward and leaning nearer, tempting me to kiss her perfect mouth.

I squeezed my eyes shut for a second, willing myself to stop looking directly at her lips and focus on her eyes.

We can't cross this line...not yet. Not when we're just rekindling our friendship.

When my eyelids fluttered open, I was captivated by another desire. "I need to see you again." Quickly, I amended my statement, "I mean, you said before that we *could* see each other again. Did you really mean that or...?"

"Of course," she said, keeping her tone as light as the air around us. "Whenever you're free..."

"How about tomorrow?" I interceded.

Missy snickered. "Oh, I don't know. Meeting up two days in a row? What will people think?"

"I don't care what they think," I answered honestly, ignoring the fact that I knew she'd been trying to make a feeble joke. "I'd like to see you and I'm only in town this week. So, let's make the most of this time we have and spend it together."

I'm not sure what I'd said that surprised her so greatly, but Missy's eyes widened for a moment and her eyebrows jumped up her forehead before returning to their normal way. "That all sounds really nice, Nate. It does. But I can't cancel plans with friends two nights back-to-back."

"Are you...did you reschedule with Steve and his husband?" I ventured.

"No…" A sly smile stole over her features. "I'm supposed to go over to Wes and Adair's apartment for dinner tomorrow, but…"

"Perfect," I said, jumping at the chance. "I'm not trying to invite myself along, but do you think the happy couple would mind if I crashed their little get together?"

She chuckled. "I'm sure Adair would be more than willing to see you again. And I know you didn't get to spend much time with Wes, but I think you'll like him." She shrugged and it was then that I let go of her arm. "I'll talk to Jess and ask if it's okay that you tagalong." She paused and eyed me closely. "But I'm sure it'll be fine."

"Great," I said, nodding enthusiastically. "Dinner with friends…tomorrow."

"Tomorrow," she echoed, then pivoted on her heel and strode away, leaving me standing right in the middle of the sidewalk.

Watching her walk away and not racing after her took a tremendous amount of fortitude. Having dinner, catching up…that was great and all, but I wanted more.

I stood there and stared after Missy, watching until she turned the corner and disappeared.

And that's when I realized the truth of the situation.

Even if I was in a position to offer Missy something more…she might not be inclined to take it.

Chapter Eleven

Are You Going to Tell Him?
Missy

"Are we done for the day?" I asked while taking off the headphones and setting them off to the side of the control console.

"Everything looks good," our producer, Vic Thomas, murmured, not looking at me, but directing his comment at the sound board. "I think everything went smoothly enough."

Steve, who sat at my side, ran his hand through his hair, fluffing the ends of his locks. "Was it just me or was that show a bit off-kilter?"

I turned to give him a hard stare. "What's that supposed to mean?"

He sat forward in his chair and met my gaze. "You can't keep anything from me, darling. I know that you went out with Nathan last night. And we've spent the whole day together, but you've yet to utter a peep about what happened between the two of you. Were things really so bad?"

"No," I groaned. "Things were fine."

"Just fine? If that's true, why are you groaning?" Steve bunched his lips up near the corner of his mouth the same way he always did when he wanted to showcase his disbelief without coming right out and being contrary. "You hadn't seen the man in more than thirteen years. I expected a little better description than *just fine*."

"What can I say?" I returned, standing, and smoothing down my skirt. "I guess our little dinner date just wasn't as eventful as you were hoping it would be."

Steve stood, too. "Were *you* hoping it'd be eventful?"

I snorted. "No. But..."

"But what?" he prompted when I showed signs of hesitating.

"Hello, my pretties!"

Before I could even consider the way in which I wanted to finish my previous statement, Jessica Adair waltzed into the glass studio compartment. As always, she looked flawless. Today, her whitish blonde hair was twisted into a loose chignon so that tiny tendrils wrapped lovingly around her face and cascaded beautifully down the back of her neck. She was wearing a satiny cranberry colored blouse that was held together by pearl in-laid buttons. Her slacks had been expertly tailored so that they nipped in precisely at her ankles, making it so her lovely brown suede boots were fully on display. Even though I thought my work style was appropriate and even a tad stylish, I'd never been able to match the cool comfort that Adair brought to the office. Everything about her screamed that she was the boss of this place from the way her diamond earrings sparkled to the way she strode into the room, breaking up and putting an effective end to all previous conversations.

"Good show today," she continued, sidling forward to stand between me and Steve.

"Really?" I cast a long look at Steve while waiting to hear Adair's answer.

"I'm not sure how it could've been better," she said, leaning forward to flick a miniscule bit of dust off the counter.

Steve scoffed. "You're just pleased because we managed to slot in Zacharias Hoover today."

Adair turned her chin to the side, then shrugged her shoulders prissily. "I can't be faulted for doing a little self-promotion. What's good for my record label is good for your business, too. Never forget that. We're all in this together."

"And Zacharias has real talent," I interjected, remembering the way I'd heard him play on the day when Adair decided to offer him a recording contract. "Right now, he's an unknown, but in a few months, once his album is released, we'll be glad he made time to appear on our show early in his career."

"Exactly," Jess said, nodding her head approvingly. She paused then and gave Steve an appraising look. "Is it just me or do you look a little more spiffed up than usual for the podcast?"

Steve wiggled his shoulders, standing up straighter. "You expect me to be a slob just because our listeners can't see us?"

Adair snorted. "Of course not, but..." She flicked her index finger up and down, motioning to his dashing navy blue suit. "You look fabulous this afternoon."

His grin broadened. "I try."

"And?" she prompted.

"And Tom got us tickets to the theatre tonight. We're going to see *Chicago* and I must admit that I'm excited. I'm not sure how it's possible, but I've never seen that show live before, so I'm sort of chomping at the bit to get out of here. But..." His words trailed away as his eyes drifted toward mine.

"What?" I asked, clueless as to his meaning. "What'd I do?"

"I feel like you need to talk," he said plainly. "You haven't said even half of what you're feeling, and we all know that if you keep your thoughts bottled up, you'll eventually..." He cut himself off right there, brought his fingertips together, then made this motion as if a ball of energy was exploding. "And we can't have that."

"I'm fine," I assured him. "Better than fine, really."

"Not possible," he retorted. "You just went through a major..."

"Steve," I interjected, "enough. Okay? Just for now, let me sit with my feelings. And I promise...later, I'll tell you everything I'm thinking."

"I'm going to hold you to that," he said, wagging his finger at me, almost as if he were giving me a sound scolding.

"I know." I sighed. "But for now, you've got a date with your husband and I've gotta get out of here."

I set to work tidying up the studio. Steve and I weren't especially messy people, but while we talked and interviewed Zacharias, we pushed a few papers and notes across the desk at each other. I could hear Steve and Adair whispering feverishly and figured there was a strong possibility they were discussing me and my situation, but I persevered, carrying out the task of cleaning away our debris and tossing it all in the waste bin.

When I turned back around, I saw Steve striding out the door, but Adair was standing in the same spot, looking at me expectantly. "Well?" She urged tapping the toe of her designer boots. "Are you going to tell me about your dinner date with Nate or do I have to pry the information out of you?"

I sighed in a beleaguered fashion. "Did Steve just tell you what happened yesterday?"

Adair laughed prettily, tossing her head as she did. "You're joking, right?" She lifted a hand and held it up so I could watch her count off using her fingers. "When Nathan and his friend first appeared outside the studio, I heard a call come over the walkie talkie because one of the security guards wasn't sure what to do about the uninvited guests. Then, about ten minutes later, Steve called me, telling me to expect to hear from you. When you didn't send any communication my way, I was a little concerned, but decided not to press the issue." She took a deep breath before continuing. "Then, last night, Anne Marie sent me a text. She said you were having dinner with a handsome man, then suddenly, you hopped up from the table and practically ran out of the place. So…" she huffed. "What happened?"

"Nothing," I returned, aiming to add a bit of breeziness to my voice. "We had dinner. That's it."

"Did you kiss him?"

"Of course not," I answered hurriedly…perhaps a shade too quickly because my hasty refusal made my insides prickle and I instantly felt it when my cheeks flamed with color.

Adair's eyes widened marginally, and she leaned forward. "Did you *want* to kiss him?"

"We're not discussing *that*," I said, putting special emphasis on each word in that phrase. "If you wanna talk about the date or the food we consumed, that's fair game, but…"

"But how are you feeling?" Adair asked, changing tactics apparently while gesturing toward the vacant chairs Steve and I had given up just a few minutes before.

"Don't you have someone coming in here later to do another podcast recording?"

Adair shrugged, making her indifference on the subject plain. "We can talk here or take this to my office. It's your choice. But Missy…you're gonna tell me how you're feeling about this whole thing with Nathan just popping back into your life…one way or the other."

"Why?" I challenged. "Why do I have to talk about it?"

My friend seemed taken aback and maybe even a little wounded by my reaction. I hadn't meant to snap at her, not really, but I'd also wanted to shut down her prying, too. The longer I'd sat with the events from last night, the more I'd come to regret all the secrets that lingered between me and Nate. And while I was sorting through my emotions, I didn't want to have to spell them out for someone else.

"You don't *have to* do anything, Missy," Adair said after gently clearing her throat. "But I thought, given the circumstances, that you might *want* to confide in someone. And well…I'm here, you know."

I groaned, then lifted my hands so I could massage my temples. My fingertips were frosty cool to the touch and while it felt good to have the little ice blocks caressing my throbbing pulse, I couldn't help but remember how warm Nathan's hand had been last night when he'd reached out and grabbed my sleeve. Even though he'd merely been touching me through the material of my blazer, I'd still been able to feel the heat flowing from his fingertips.

We'd been standing dangerously close together and there had been a moment when I'd stared at his mouth, wondering if I ought to take the plunge and plant a quick smooch on his lips. But that had been only a fleeting thought, one I was glad…well, sort of glad, I hadn't acted on last night.

"What am I doing?" I moaned. "I can't believe I just barked at you and Nate…Nate…what am I gonna do about him?"

"So," Adair chuckled wryly, "is it safe to say Hurricane Nathan just blew into town again and managed to wreck your whole world in the span of a day?"

"No," I whispered, "it's not like that."

"Is it not?" she countered. "Then tell me. What is it like?"

She perched on the countertop, then crossed her arms over her chest, giving me the sign that she was ready and waiting for me to unload my burden. But I was still reluctant to go there. That's when I recalled a facet of my evening with Nathan that I probably should've shared with Adair right away. I winced. "Okay…don't think I'm a total flake for bringing this up so late, but I sort of invited Nathan over to dinner tonight."

"You're bringing a date tonight?"

"Not a date," I corrected her. "Just Nathan."

Adair rolled her eyes. "Uh-huh."

"Yikes," I groaned. "I know I should've asked before I even made the offer. But he wanted to see me again and I didn't want to break plans with friends two nights in a row, so I just thought it'd be best if he came with me to your apartment. But now…is that okay? Do you mind having him around?"

Adair blinked owlishly. "Do *you* like having him around?"

"I do." The words flew out of my mouth. As much as I wanted to keep all my feelings to myself, once I started sharing them, it was difficult to hold back from revealing everything. "I missed hearing his voice. And his smile…Oh, Adair, it's just as warm and inviting as ever. And…I can't believe I let this happen."

"What?" She sat up a little straighter and her eyes widened in surprise. "I know I already asked if you kissed but did you do… more?"

"No, no," I answered quickly. "Once we left the restaurant, we said goodnight and that was the end of it. But…I just can't help but wonder…how did we ever manage to lose touch with each other? There are so many ways for people to stay connected nowadays and it's hard to figure out how people just let friendships expire. How could I ever let go of someone like Nathan? How could I have gone thirteen long years without speaking a single word to him again?"

Adair snorted derisively. "Rejecting a marriage proposal will put a strain on any relationship," she quipped.

I gave her a knowing stare. "But this is Nathan we're talking about here, not just some random guy. He and I…the two of us…you know there was more at play."

She nodded. "And I also understand how when the two of you drifted out of each other's lives, a gaping hole was left in your heart." She reached out and grabbed ahold of my hand. "But you don't have to go on like this, Miss. You can try to mend the breach. He's here in Charlotte, isn't he? And he ran all the way to the studio just so he could spend a few minutes talking to you again." She squeezed my fingers tightly. "I know it might hurt initially to share your story with him, but don't you think you should tell him about…?"

"No." The word flew from my lips. I'd never been so ornery and obstinate in all my life. I was normally a rather obliging sort of person, but since Nathan had rolled back into town, I found myself saying 'no' a lot more than 'yes' and that was slightly disconcerting. "It all happened such a long time ago," I tried to explain. "And I don't want to have to relive any of those painful memories."

"But think about it," Adair said, giving her head a sympathetic tilt. "Don't you think Nate would want to know what happened?"

"*Argh*…" I grumbled, "I cannot be having this same conversation again, Adair. Steve harpooned me yesterday, trying to convince me to spill my secrets, but…"

"But what?" Adair urged.

"I already understand that my story is one Nathan would want to hear, but that doesn't mean he needs the information. Because, let's face it, even if he knows the full truth, the outcome remains the same. There's no changing the way things are at this point, so why talk about something that can only bring us both a whole lot of sadness?"

"Yeah," she sighed, "but sometimes, it helps to share our grief with others."

"That's why I've got friends like you," I jested.

"Okay," she agreed halfheartedly, "but Nathan's always been different. You said so yourself. He's not just some guy you picked up on the street. Don't you want to confide in him a little?"

I shook my head and lowered my chin so I could look at the blue, black, and gray carpet that was underfoot. Tears were stinging the corners of my eyes, blurring the pattern, making it look like one swirling mass of thunderstorm clouds. "You should've seen Nate last night," I murmured. "I could tell that he was hiding something, too. And Adair...all those secrets...his...mine...Wouldn't it just be better for the both of us if we kept them to ourselves?"

Adair let go of my hand and sat back on the desk. She tapped her nails idly on the countertop right next to her hip. "I don't understand your relationship with Nathan, Missy," she said softly. "I never have, and I fully admit that, but from my point-of-view, the two of you were better together than you've ever been apart."

I guffawed as tears leaked from my eyes and slowly trickled down my cheeks. "How can you say that? He cheated on me years ago and..."

"And you forgave him," she interceded. "You did, Missy. You recognized that he made a mistake...slept with some other girl one night when we were like twenty..." She dismissed that thought with a wave of her hand. "But you decided to move on after that. You let him back into your life and the two of you cultivated a baffling friendship. You were always texting or sending him emails. And when you wanted a date to bring to my wedding, no one would do but Nathan Hamilton." She stopped talking and silenced the incessant tapping of her fingernails which had accompanied the duration of her speech. "So...now that the two of you really need each other and he's here, why can't you find a way to be honest with him?"

"I don't know," I whimpered.

"Think it through, Sweetie," Jess said, scooting off the table, and rising into a fully standing position. "If Nate's only come to town for the week and the two of you are just hanging out once or twice, then maybe, you don't need to say everything I'm sure you've already got on your mind. But if you think there's more...or there could be more there...then don't you owe it to yourself and to him to speak?"

"But what about his secrets? I know he was hiding something last night and..."

"You can't control his behavior," she interjected, "and I don't think you'd want to, either." Her tone softened even further. It grew so quiet that had I not been standing directly in front of her, I might've missed some of her advice. "But I can tell you this much: if you want him to deal straight with you, you've got to be willing to afford him the same courtesy. If you want a relationship, a friendship, or even just a pleasant conversation with a man who once meant so much to you ever again, you're going to have to trust that the truth needs to come out. And maybe, if you put your faith in that, you and Nathan will be able to see your way through all this."

"He's just here for a week though, Adair. What if…?"

"Precisely," she whispered. "What if…?"

Chapter Twelve

Can an Old Dog Learn New Tricks?
Nathan

I wasn't nearly as anxious tonight as I'd been yesterday. The conference sessions had been slightly on the boring side throughout the day, but that was fine by me. It gave me lots of time to recall all that had passed at Anne Marie's Bakehouse and to consider what I might say tonight, when I had the chance to see Missy again.

Right around three o'clock, she sent me a text containing Adair's address and once I'd punched the apartment numbers into my GPS, I was off and walking toward my destination. Since we were meeting a smidge later tonight, the sun was dipping low already, racing toward the horizon as I strode down the street. Neon lights and street lamplights were flickering to life as I passed them and when I sauntered by a flower shop, I decided to pop in for a second and pick up a little something for my hostess.

Now…what kind of flowers did Adair carry at her wedding?

I could recollect vividly Missy's pool blue bridesmaid gown and yet, when I tried to picture everything else, nothing poignant floated to mind. So, when the florist smiled at me genially and asked what I'd like to purchase, I shrugged and answered, "Something nice. Classy. Elegant."

"I've got just the right thing," she said, before turning, rummaging around in a cooler behind her and pulling out a display of simple white roses. The vase was overflowing with flowers that were in various stages of their blooming process and while they were rather plain, they were also lovely and eye-catching. "They'll last for days, and they look splendid. Don't you think?" The woman's voice was chipper as her fingertips floated to the edges of the vase, so she could primp and prod the petals that had already opened, revealing the heart of the flower.

"I'll take two bouquets, if you have them," I said, slapping my credit card down on the countertop. "But the second batch doesn't need to be in a vase. It can be…"

"Coming right up," the lady said in a sing song voice. She worked hurriedly, gathering a second bundle of flowers, pulling a bit of butcher's paper from an enormous roll, and neatly wrapping up the gift in less than a full minute. I paid for my purchases, thanked the kind woman, then balanced everything so that I could continue the walk toward Adair and Wesley's place.

It didn't take long to reach their apartment, mostly because they lived in a building that was near the center of uptown. The doorman greeted me cordially and once I checked in with the clerk in the lobby, I was pointed toward a bank of elevators that lifted me up to the tenth floor.

I whistled at the extravagance of the place. Every part of the elevator gleamed and when I stepped off and entered the hallway that would take me onward to Adair's apartment, I was welcomed by the faint scent of vanilla. There was a large end table in the hall and a pot of white orchids sat there, also perfuming the air. Rocking back and forth on my heels, I glanced down the hall and realized there were only really two options because there were just two apartments on this floor. Even if I walked in the wrong direction, it'd take less than a second to swing around and find the appropriate place. But then, before I could make my decision, I heard Adair laugh. The sound was musical and fluttery, and I knew, at once, that this evening was going to be an adventure.

Juggling the flowers from one hand to the other, I managed to ring the doorbell and a half second later, Adair appeared. She looked just as I remembered, with her fair skin, pretty eyes, and smirking hint of a smile. "As I live and breathe," she muttered, looking me over without a bit of self-consciousness, "if it isn't Nathan Hamilton."

"Hey, Adair. How's it going?"

She snickered, then gestured for me to come inside. "I can't complain," she answered flippantly.

"These are for you." I offered her the vase as I stepped across the threshold and immediately, she lowered her head and sniffed the blooms.

"Gorgeous," she said as her smile ticked up at the corners. "And I assume those are for…?"

"Missy," I breathed in response, but also because she appeared in the archway that led from the foyer to the rest of the apartment. Like yesterday, it was apparent she had continued wearing her work attire, rather than changing into something more casual, and I was glad that I'd chosen to keep wearing my tie and dress shirt combo. For a long second, before leaving the hotel this evening, I'd eyed my sneakers and considered putting on some more relaxed clothing but was glad now that I'd made the right choice. She looked glorious dressed in her black pencil skirt and robin's egg blue button-down shirt and because I just couldn't stand to be this close to her without holding her in my arms, I strode forward and presented her with the flowers.

"For me?" she whispered excitedly, as if my actions had taken her by surprise.

"I wanted to bring something for my hostess, but when I got a look at those flowers, I just knew you'd like to have some, too."

"How thoughtful," Missy said, sniffing the petals dreamily. Her smile broadened. "But you didn't have to do any of this. We're all just friends here, so there's no need to make a big deal out of nothing."

"Speak for yourself," Adair huffed, flouncing by us as she headed toward the kitchen. "I happen to like it when people bring me gifts."

I snickered and Missy laughed lightly. "Good old Adair," I muttered. "I'm glad I did something to make her happy."

Missy turned to give me another surprised look. She pursed her lips together as if there was something she wanted to say but was busy pondering exactly how she ought to come out with it. After what seemed like way too long a pause, she finally murmured, "This might shock you to know, but Adair's slightly fond of you."

"Is she?"

Missy shrugged and a beguiling smile slid into place on her face. "She didn't say that in so many words, but she definitely let me know she was on your side."

I shook my head and gave Missy my best fake baffled expression. "Are we picking sides here? Because if we are, I want to be on your team."

She giggled, then cocked her head to the left, indicating we should trail Adair down the hall. I followed along in Missy's wake, marveling a little at the opulence of Adair's apartment. The walls were mostly neutral tones—eggshell, white, and ivory—but there were large paintings and gold records hung just about everywhere. The living room was an impressively large space and there was a rather enormous office on the right side of the hall. But when we got to the kitchen, I saw a much more cramped spot. The appliances were all bunched together near one end of the room. They were glittering and stainless steel, of course, and because they were nestled right next to one another, it almost seemed like that part of the kitchen was gleaming. There was a long breakfast bar taking up most of the rest of the space.

And as I rounded the corner, I saw Adair place the vase of white roses right in the middle of the island.

"What's all this?" her husband, Wesley, asked. He was maybe a full three inches shorter than me, but our build was remarkably similar. He had blonde hair, much like Adair's, but his eyes were a sharp green hue, so much so that I could see the intense color from my vantage point. He was hovering near the stovetop and wearing a simple black apron tied around his waist.

"Nathan brought gifts," Adair explained.

"Well done," Wes said, putting down the wooden spoon he'd been holding in his right hand, then offering to shake with me. "I'm glad somebody came ready for a celebration."

"Are we celebrating something?" I asked, stepping further into the kitchen, and lifting my head high so I could smell the aromas that were permeating the atmosphere. I detected something sweet, but there was also a bit of spiciness lingering too and I wondered what Wes was making for dinner.

"The gals are celebrating," Wes returned. "Missy and Steve's talk show has been running for a full decade now and they've racked up quite the number of news programs in that time."

"Ten years?" I shot Missy a speculative look and she just shrugged. "I imagine they've accomplished a lot in that time."

"You wouldn't believe what our girls have been able to do," Wes said, nodding at a drawer off to his left side. "Grab yourself an apron and lend me a hand here, would ya, Nate? Once we get cookin', I'll tell ya all about it."

I liked the way he'd already taken to me, not just by inviting me into his home, but asking me to join him in doing some of the meal prep. If there'd been any bit of residual nerves floating around inside my belly, they were all flying away because of Wesley's warm, welcoming attitude.

Missy laughed. She and Adair were perched on bar stools, seated around the island and as I pulled a thick white apron out of the drawer and started expertly tying it around my waist, I turned to see an astonished look on her face.

"What's so funny?"

She continued staring at me. "I don't believe it. You don't know how to cook and…"

"Sure, I do."

"No, you don't," she argued. "The only thing you've ever been able to do is boil a bunch of hot dogs and even then…" She stuck out her tongue and made a disgusted face. "Let's just say that you're no master chef."

I finished tying the apron, then walked purposefully to Wesley's side so I could peer over his shoulder. It looked like he was making beef enchiladas, as well as all the trimmings…fresh guacamole, salsa, seasoned rice, and refried beans. Without waiting for him to give me orders, I picked up a pair of ripe, red tomatoes and selected a knife from the wooden container, then carried them over to the butcher's block and got to work on dicing.

"This is unreal," Missy breathed.

"What?" I asked, without looking away from my task. "You didn't think I could chop a tomato?"

"I didn't think you knew what a tomato was," she retorted, chortling a little as she did. "Back in school, you ate nothing but pizza and pasta."

"And there's tomato sauce on both of those." I looked up to see her smiling at me.

"Yeah…but I just figured if you weren't popping something in the oven or microwave you were more of a go out and pick up food kind of guy."

Showing off a little of my knife wielding skills, I flipped the tomato on its side and completed several even cuts, all perfectly satisfactory. "I eat out—just like everybody else. But, these last few years, I also learned how to cook."

"Why?" Missy questioned.

When I glanced in her direction again, I saw that the question was sincere. My showmanship in the kitchen, as minimal as it was, had baffled her, and now she wanted to know what happened that had prompted me to teach myself how to do some simple cooking-related tasks. "It was a necessity," I answered honestly. "I can't afford to go out to dinner every night and as for eating boiled hot dogs and flimsy chicken patties all the time…well, that might not have been the healthiest thing for me."

"Ya think?" Adair joked.

The next few hours passed in the same, lighthearted manner. Wes and I served the ladies dinner, as well as a sumptuous dessert featuring chocolate mousse. The conversation was mostly bubbly and bright, with loads of questions and answers flying back and forth across the table. Any time Missy really doubled down on her inquiries, Adair was quick to jump in with a joke or anecdote of her own, keeping the atmosphere lively and cheerful.

I enjoyed spending the evening with Missy and her friends, and it was good to talk with Wes. We had a lot in common and even exchanged phone numbers. He was mightily interested in the work I was doing with Morgan and Fosters and wanted to hear more about my job responsibilities as well as the conference I was attending this week.

When it was time to bid the couple adieu and take our leave, I was wary of going. The night had just been so carefree and deliciously friendly. I'd smiled and laughed more than I had in years. And I knew that a large part of that was the fact that I got to sit across the table from Missy. Her smile, like always, enchanted me. Seeing it there, gracing her lips, made me want to be happy too, and it was difficult to think of having to part ways with her again at the end of this evening.

Once Missy and I were out in the hall and waiting for the elevator, I felt a tick of worry scuttle through my stomach.

What comes next? We've already stayed out much later tonight than we did last night, so I know she needs to get home and go to bed, but…

I didn't want our time together to end.

The elevator dinged and a second later the metallic doors slid open. Missy led the way inside the compact compartment and when we both glanced into the mirror that made up the back wall, our eyes met. I could see something brewing behind her eyes and held perfectly still, hoping that she'd tell me what was on her mind.

"Do you…should I…" Her words came out in a flustered manner. She sucked in a deep breath, switched her bouquet of flowers from one hand to the other and as the doors to the elevator slid closed, she asked, "Can I walk you to your hotel tonight?"

"Uh…"

"I'm the one who lives here, after all," she added hurriedly, "and I'd hate it if you got lost trying to find your way there."

"I could go for taking a walk around the city," I suggested. "That is…if you've got some time to spare."

Tentatively, I reached for her free hand, and she jumped.

I knew I hadn't startled her. I'd moved slowly and barely made a gentle connection with the tips of my fingers and yet…she'd backed away. The happiness which had been surging through me all night dissipated, and like the elevator we were riding, my spirits plummeted.

Chapter Thirteen

Who Was That?
Missy

"Did you feel that?" I questioned, stepping away from Nathan, still staring at his hand. When he touched my bare skin, I'd felt a jolt race up my entire arm before it tickled my spine, causing my whole body to feel electrified. The sensation was powerful and almost painful, the way I felt if I ever had occasion to experience a friction shock when touching a metal doorknob after scuffing my feet across the carpet.

"Feel what?" I could hear something, slightly like confusion, tinging Nate's tone and when I finally glanced up at him, I saw a stricken look on his face.

Ah…He thinks I jerked away because I didn't want him to touch me. He's feeling rejected again.

It seemed nonsensical for him to even entertain such a notion. We had just enjoyed a splendid evening. Every minute we'd spent in Adair and Wesley's apartment had been merry and *I* was the one who suggested walking back to his hotel together.

How could he misinterpret my reaction so badly?

But I reminded myself, it had been a long time, much too long since we'd interacted with one another. And Nate was entitled to feel on his guard. I'd broken his heart once before and even though I hadn't meant my actions just now to seem off-putting, that's exactly what I'd done.

"Hey…" I said softly, reaching out to take his hand of my own accord, "I just experienced a little shock. That's all."

"Huh," he muttered. "It's funny that I didn't feel anything then."

I shrugged and towed him out of the elevator. "Then we're all good. Now, let's get to walking." As we exited the building, I paused and glanced up and down the street. It was full dark, but because it was Tuesday night and there were several pubs and bars in town that hosted live music on their patios this time of year, the city streets were abuzz with noise and life. No matter which way I turned, we were bound to walk right into a pack of people, so I left the decision up to him. "Where do you wanna go?"

"I don't know," he answered slowly, holding my hand loosely. "To hear Adair and Wes talk, it sounds like almost the whole city changed since the last time I was in town. I'm afraid to mention a place only to find that it's not there anymore."

Nodding to our right, I indicated we should walk that way. "I get it," I commiserated. "There for a while, it felt like all my favorite spots were closing up shop." We fell into step with one another as we coasted down the street. "That's actually how I found Anne Marie's."

"Huh?"

"Adair and I used to go to a restaurant called Humphrey and Hubert's for lunch." I paused and tipped my head to the side. "This would've been like five or six years ago. We went to H & H because it was close to the studio and since we were regulars, they'd seat us quickly. But then, one day, they shut their doors for good."

"And Anne Marie moved in?"

"It didn't take long for her to gobble up that prime bit of real estate," I replied. "She made a lot of changes to the interior, as you can imagine, but I found, after giving the menu a test run, that I liked her food better than I ever cared for H & H's, so I was happy with the switch."

"What else has changed around here?" he asked conversationally, slowly turning his head and glancing around the busy sidewalk.

"Pretty much everything." I nodded to a building that was a few steps ahead of us, near the corner of the street. "Do you remember the place my friends and I used to go called Hunter's Saloon?"

Nate shrugged. "You might've mentioned it once or twice."

I snickered because I was sure I'd talked about that particular establishment a great deal back in the day. "Well... Hunter's has been gone for years. It's changed hands two...maybe three times. Every few years, a new owner buys it up, hoping to reinvent the place and bring in a new crowd."

"Dance Hall?" We stopped right in front of the club and Nate lifted his head to read the small electric sign overhead. "That's not a very inventive name, is it?"

"I guess not," I said, smiling at the group of people who were queued up to get inside the place. They were all dressed to the nines and my heart went out to the gaggle of young women who were prancing from one foot to the other, clearly trying to find a comfortable way to stand while wearing high heels. "But the crowd doesn't seem to mind."

"All those people do know it's a Tuesday night, right?" Nate asked, nodding at the long line. "Don't any of them have to work tomorrow?"

I sighed wistfully. "I remember...not too long ago...when I'd have been one of their number, going out with my girls, trying to find some guy to dance with for the night."

Nathan's eyes slid toward mine. "Do you miss that?"

"What? Hanging with the girls or going out to clubs every night?"

"Both? Either?" he replied.

"I miss the girls all the time," I confessed, "but the clubbing? *Eh*...not so much."

We continued walking and once we'd reached the end of another block, I pointed across the street at a building which now sat vacant.

"What's that?" he asked, scrunching up his nose and squinting in the distance. "Is it...No..."

His reaction mirrored much the way I felt. "Yeah," I murmured, "That's The Pond."

"But it's closed," Nate whispered reverently. "How can that be? Didn't you and the crew throw enough money their way to help them weather any financial storm?"

"I'd like to think that was true," I said, staring at the restaurant which had been the site of so many get-togethers with my girlfriends over the years that I'd lost track ages ago. "But sometimes things happen that are just completely out of our control. The owner got sick a few years back and since she didn't have any family close by to help her through or pick up the slack at the business, there was little she could do. She had to shut the doors because she just wasn't well enough to keep going on her own."

"Do you ever feel that way?"

I'd been so wrapped up, thinking about Loretta, the owner of the Pond, that I nearly missed Nate's question.

"What's that?"

"I asked if you ever felt like that," he reiterated. "Do you ever feel like it's tough...being on your own all the time?"

"I'm not alone." I squeezed his hand. "I've got Steve and Tom and Adair and Wesley. And there's my job…which keeps me busy. And…"

"But when you get home—to your apartment, don't you ever feel lonely?"

He was peering at me with wide expectant eyes, almost like he thought I might break down crying right then and there. But I wasn't about to do that. I simply let go of his hand and gestured to the buildings surrounding us. "I'm never alone when I've got the Queen City to keep me company."

Nate heaved a long sigh, and I watched his shoulders slump. He'd been so high-spirited earlier in the evening, it was interesting to see this turn of his countenance. So, I held still and waited for him to speak.

Maybe whatever was troubling him last night has drifted back to the forefront of his mind. Maybe he's finally going to tell me what he was thinking about yesterday during dinner.

I shuffled from one foot to the other as the silence stretched on interminably. Then, mostly just to get the conversation flowing again, I reached for his hand once more and gave it a gentle squeeze. "So much has changed since you were here last."

He looked up then and met my eyes. "Not everything's changed."

My heart leapt up into my throat. I could tell, from the look in his eyes, that he wanted to lean in and kiss me and, I'm almost ashamed to admit this, but I was praying he'd be the one to make that move. I needed him to be the one to break and reveal his feelings for me, so I stood there, breathing heavily…waiting.

But the kiss never came. Instead, Nate just tugged my hand, then nodded, gesturing for the tour of the city to proceed.

We wandered slowly down the city streets then. He said very little, while I continued to fill in the blanks, reminding him of places we'd visited so long ago and telling him about the new hot spots that had cropped up later. When we reached our destination, the place I'd really wanted to share with him, a small gasp escaped his lips.

"What is this?" he asked, letting go of my hand and spinning around, slowly taking in the new environment.

"Welcome to Charlotte's newest park," I said, placing my bouquet of flowers on the nearest bench and gesturing to the water features and statues that surrounded us. There were couples lounging nearby on the grass, people riding electric scooters, zipping along at a brisk pace, and a few pigeons were waddling near the water, possibly trying to get a thirsty sip. Even though it was getting late, the place was thrumming with life and activity.

"What is this...? Why is this place even here?"

I laughed at Nate's questions. "People seem to like it," I replied. "You already know how nice the weather is and it's torture being cooped up indoors all the time. So, the city built this park near the banks and other high rises that way businesspeople could pop outside during the day and get their dose of vitamin c."

"Do you come here?" he asked.

"All the time," I answered promptly. "Or...as much as I can," I amended my statement just as hastily. "On Saturdays or Sunday afternoons, Steve and I come here, or Adair and I go for a walk down the trails. It's..."

"I wish we could do that," Nathan interrupted, swinging around to look at me squarely. His eyes were full of the same intensity I'd only ever seen there once before...on the afternoon when he'd asked me to marry him.

My insides squirmed, so I tried to lighten the mood. "Well, why didn't you say so?" I smiled broadly, even though I could feel my cheeks shaking with the effort of putting up a good front. "If you want to rent bikes or go for a walk, we can always meet here sometime instead of going out to dinner."

Changing the subject or veering us off this track didn't work out as I planned. Instead of reacting to my words, Nate took a step forward, narrowing the distance between us. "Miss," he whispered, reaching for my hands, "I want to do all these things with you. Go for a walk, ride those bikes, have a picnic. We ought to be doing all of this together."

"We...we are," I said tremulously.

It's not that we hadn't been walking hand in hand before, but when we were side by side, I didn't have to gaze directly into Nathan's eyes. Now...with him standing right in front of me, I was captivated. I couldn't look away, but I didn't want to, either.

For a split-second last night, I'd thought there was a possibility he might want to kiss me, and I hightailed it away from him as quickly as I could without running. I wasn't ready then. I couldn't be. I knew he was keeping secrets, and I was too, so the thought of kissing him just felt plain wrong.

Even a few minutes ago, when we'd taken that pause on the sidewalk and stared deeply into each other's eyes, I'd been waiting for him to initiate contact. I wanted him to be the audacious one. But now…I wasn't worried about our festering secrets. All I could think about was the thrill that had lanced through my body when he'd tried to hold my hand in the elevator and I knew that if he even brushed his lips against my own, my whole world would be set aflame.

I inched closer to him, smelling tinges of spicy enchilada sauce and sweet chocolate mousse lingering on his breath. I was fully invading his personal space, but he didn't seem to mind. Instead, he reached out and placed both hands on my waist, leaving them there for a second, allowing us both to adjust to this proximity and the feelings that accompanied it. The sensations were both new and old. I'd stood with Nathan hundreds of times, in just this same way, more than thirteen years ago, so much about our pose was familiar. But there were new things to notice, too. I saw little crinkles near the corners of his eyes and there was a faint smattering of gray threading through his sideburns. Brazenly, I lifted my hands and ran them through his messy locks, feeling a slightly sticky substance and sniffing a woodsy scent that was likely his gel or other hair product.

"Nate," I whispered, leaning forward, wanting to kiss him, needing to feel the rush of excitement that was sure to follow when our lips finally collided, but then, before either of us could make that daring move, his phone buzzed.

He had evidently set the ringer to the lowest setting because the noise it emitted was nearly drowned out by the hammering of my heart. I'd been so intent on kissing him that I might've ignored the call and proceeded, had he not backed away.

"Who could that be?" I asked teasingly, but Nate didn't reply right away.

Instead, his lips pursed so tight they nearly disappeared and his eyes hardened. "I'm not sure," he returned.

"Well," I prompted, nodding at him. "You can answer it if you want." Now that the mood was broken, I didn't see any need for him to miss taking the call.

"I…uh…" He hesitated. "Just let me see…" He fished the phone out of his back pocket and even though I hadn't really been meaning to look at the caller ID when the name flashed on the screen, I saw it anyway.

Incoming Call…Jordan…

Jordan? Who's that?

It occurred to me then that even though I'd asked him about his relationships last night, Nate had avoided the question. Instead of telling me about the women in his life, he'd talked about work. And I'd been so interested in what he was saying that I didn't force him to get back to the original thoughts.

He could have a wife or a girlfriend…and she could be the one calling right now.

I stared at Nathan, waiting for him to answer the call. But he seemed perplexed, almost stunned by the enormity of the situation.

Who is Jordan? Why's she calling at this time of night?

I knew it wasn't exactly late, but if this were just a courtesy call from a colleague or a friend giving him a ring, it would be a breach of etiquette to phone at this hour.

All these questions and ideas battled for the prominent place inside my head and my tongue cramped because I had to put in a real effort to restrain myself from spewing out everything I was thinking. But I held strong.

Too much time has separated us. If Nathan is married or he has a girlfriend, it's none of my business.

Chapter Fourteen

This Can't be Happening…Can it?
Nathan

Ever since the wheels of the airplane had skidded to a stop after touching down in Charlotte, I'd been considering how it would feel when my two worlds collided. The old world meeting the new. The people who were part of my present mingling with those of my past. These last two days, I'd allowed myself to be swept up in the romance of not just finding Missy again but rekindling some of what we'd had before. But now…with Jordan's name illuminating my phone screen and Missy taking a big step back, giving me space to take the call, I felt our flame of passion flicker.

This wasn't what I expected at all.

I watched the screen flash Jordan's name repeatedly as the phone kept vibrating and bouncing in my hand and I knew that I had to make a choice.

Do I take the call and consequently spill every remaining secret I've held locked away all these years or do I let it go to voicemail?

It was a cowardly thing to do, I know that, but I was inclined to go with the latter option.

Quickly, I shot Jordan a text message, making it clear that I was busy now, but would return the call as soon as I got back to the sanctity of my hotel room. With that managed, I turned my full attention back to Missy.

Uh-oh…the damage might've already been done.

Even though I hadn't taken the call, she still seemed irritated. She put not one pace, but several between us and was standing there with her arms crossed over her chest protectively, as if she was anticipating the worst and already bracing for it.

Her senses are on high alert, as always. She knows when something's not quite right.

"Are you okay?" I asked, striding forward, and reaching out to gently touch her forearm.

Missy didn't jerk away, as she'd done back in the elevator, but her expression faltered, and I saw a distinct grimace cross her pretty features.

"I…I'm fine," she whispered.

"No, you're not," I countered, stepping nearer. "Just a moment ago, we were so close. And now, I feel like you've drifted worlds away."

She shook her head slowly. "That can't be helped," she breathed. "Things changed...our situation changed...in the blink of an eye."

I gazed at her, wondering if she was talking about what had just occurred or thinking of how we'd parted all those years ago. One minute, we'd been hugging and kissing and the very next, I'd exited her apartment only to never hear from her again. If I hadn't seen her on the TV screen yesterday, our story might've ended on that unpleasant note. But here we were. And that had to count for something.

"I know that was awkward," I said, trying to come up with an explanation that might suffice. "But it was just a phone call. I'll return it later."

"Sure." She shrugged. "Whatever."

"Missy..." I pulled her name out long, laboring over it, trying, just by using the one word, to convey all the things I needed her to know.

"No, no," she continued, flapping her hand at me in a flippant way. "It's really not a big deal, Nate. You got a call, and you know what? It's probably a good thing it came in when it did. I was this close to kissing you and I'm pretty sure that would've been a mistake. So...yeah, I guess I'm grateful that your friend broke us apart."

"My friend? A mistake?" I fumbled to carry on with this conversation. She'd put everything so bluntly that I didn't know what to do now that things between us lay so wide out in the open.

She ignored my faltering speech and picked up the bundle of roses from where she'd deposited them on the bench earlier. I watched as she sniffed the bouquet yet again, then shrugged her shoulders despondently. "I promised I'd walk you to your hotel, but I'm exhausted. Do you mind if I just head home, Nate?"

I had no idea where she lived. She could still have that little apartment in Fountain Park, or she could be in one of the buildings nearby. I had no way of knowing and her words didn't allow for wiggle room. She was ready to go home, and she certainly wasn't inviting me to join her there.

"Sure, Miss. I know you've gotta turn in early." She gave one last wistful look around the park and I felt slightly uncomfortable still, so I added, "Do you want me to rent you a scooter?"

Thankfully, she laughed. The sound thawed the icy chill which was slowly creeping over my heart. "Maybe another time."

"How about tomorrow?" I suggested. I'd never been this persistent in all my life. But I found that each time Missy started to walk away and leave me behind, I was filled with this sense of urgency. I had to keep making these plans with her. I wanted not just to stretch out the time we spent together, but I needed it to last for as long as possible. And she had said that we should ride the bikes or scooters together *sometime*, so it stood to reason not to put off the outing.

She snorted. "You *want* to see me again?"

"Yeah," I said softly. "We can do whatever you want. I'll meet you wherever. You just name the time and place and…"

Her eyes narrowed and I could feel the way she wasn't just absorbing my words and analyzing them, but also concentrating on my actions, scrutinizing them too, searching for any hidden intent. But I wasn't trying to trick her. My affection was genuine and my need to be next to her was sincere. "You sure you want to get together again tomorrow?" she asked. "You don't have other people pressing for your time and attention?"

I waved off that comment. "There will always be other people vying for my attention, but I don't care about any of them. I just want to spend more time with you."

My words weren't entirely truthful. They were partially true, of course. I *did* care about quite a few other people, and I knew that I owed them my fidelity. But because I was so reluctant to see Missy turn away from me, I'd said the first thing that had popped to mind.

She scoffed, which was a clear sign she wasn't exactly buying what I was selling, and I was aggrieved because I'd overshot while trying to lay on the compliments so thick.

"Miss," I said, taking a step toward her, "That all came out wrong. The thing is I *want* to spend time with you. That's it. That's all. If you'd like to see me too, then I think we should meet here tomorrow. We can ride the bikes or…" I broke off when she started shaking her head. "What?" I asked, fully bewildered. "What did I say?"

Chapter Fifteen

What's With All the Plans?
Missy

"Stop," I commanded, halting his rambling speech. "Just slow down."

"What?" he asked.

My mind was reeling. Not a full minute ago, a mysterious woman had called and yet, Nate was acting as if none of that had happened. He was carrying on like it was just another night and I hadn't just observed the phone call from his significant other.

Who was that person on the phone? Why, in one breath, do you purport not to care about her, but then, ten seconds later correct yourself and acknowledge that you spoke out of turn?

I ground my back teeth in frustration.

"Missy," he ventured quietly. "You still with me?"

"I don't know," I admitted. "I'm having a tough time processing what's going on here."

"Nothing's going on," he returned, holding up his empty hands and showing them to me, as if that made some kind of difference. "I got a call and that's about the long and short of it. Right now, I think we need to get back to where we were before that interruption sidetracked us."

He stepped forward smoothly, making it so the distance I had so carefully crafted vanished. He was close enough that I could see the way tiny flecks of steel blue danced in his aqua colored eyes and this kind of nearness once again made my heart thrum in a tiny pitter-pattering way. The movement reminded me of how a hummingbird flaps its wings madly, just trying to fly and stay adrift on the breeze. Suddenly, I felt just as light as that little bird, and it didn't matter to me who had called or why Nathan had pretended for a moment that the person on the other end of the line meant little to him.

But I didn't allow myself to get bowled over by my emotions as I had a few minutes ago. The idea of kissing Nathan wasn't as pleasing or as monumental as it had seemed earlier.

I licked my dry lips. "Why are you being so insistent tonight?" I came right out and asked the big question. "Why do you keep trying to make all these plans? Haven't you had enough already?"

"Enough?" His voice came out in a rasp, and I wondered what he was thinking, what made him react in such a way. "I keep making all these plans with you, Missy, because I can't seem to get enough. We've spent too long apart and now that we're back together…"

I took a swift step backward. "We are *not* together, Nate," I said firmly.

He sighed in a way that sounded much more like a groan of despair. "I didn't mean we were *together*." He made air quotes around that last word. "I'm just saying that we've been given this gift, the chance to spend a week together and I don't think we ought to waste it."

"Yeah," I murmured, "you keep saying that, but…I don't know. It seems odd. It reminds me of the sort of thing a guy would do if he had a wife and kids waiting for him at home and he was just trying to have a fling with an old girlfriend." I stared at him, hoping he'd contradict me. "Is that what you're doing here, Nathan?"

"No," he spat out the word forcefully. "Of course not. How can you even think such a thing?"

I shrugged. "I'm trying to line up the facts, but they don't make sense," I stated flatly. "You blow into town after thirteen years without ever picking up your phone or even trying to send an email my way. You show up at my workplace and since then…you can't even let me walk out of your sight without arranging what we'll do the next day." I shook my head. "And on top of that, you say this thing about spending time with me…like I'm the most important person in your life and Nate…we both know that's not the truth. If I mattered to you at all, you'd have reached out to me years ago. You wouldn't be waiting until now to pop back up and…"

"I've been busy," he interjected to which I laughed sharply.

"Okay."

"No," he persisted, "it's true. Since the day I left Charlotte thirteen years ago, my life has been a whirlwind and now…now that I'm back here, I need…"

"Nate," I barked, "don't say it again. Don't pretend like I'm the air you breathe, and you can't go another second without my company."

"But what if that's all true?" he countered. "What if I keep asking you to spend time with me because I really and truly feel like every time you walk away, I'm left gasping for air?"

I pondered his words for a second, allowing them to sink in, and burrow their way into my heart. "This..." I said after waiting a beat, gesturing between us with the bouquet of roses, "it probably won't work out. I'm not as trusting as I used to be and you...you seem..."

"I know," he agreed automatically. "You're right. We're different from the people we were before, but isn't that a good thing?"

I tipped my chin downward and stared hard at a crack in the pavement. "I don't know," I muttered. "I'm so tired. I can't tell anymore."

Nate hurried forward. He placed the tip of his finger underneath the curve of my chin and tipped it slightly so that I just met his eyes. Sweetly, he leaned forward and brushed his lips over mine, sending a shock wave rippling through my entire body. The kiss had been quick, but it didn't lack substance. Regardless of what my head was screaming, my heart, as well as the rest of my muscles, was aching to lace my fingers around his neck and deepen the kiss, making it last much longer. "Get some sleep then, Missy. You don't have to make any grand decisions tonight."

"But this is irrational," I whispered. "You seem like you're here and you're fully committed...sometimes...sort of...but I just can't reason through what's happening. It's all so confusing and..."

He pressed another kiss on my mouth, this time missing the mark a little and hitting just the right corner. When he stepped back, I could see that he was smiling at his own bad aim. "Are these kisses helping clear up my feelings or do you need me to keep showing you how I feel?"

I put up a hand, then took a massive step backward, making a wide divide between us. "No more kisses," I said, "not tonight." I inhaled deeply. "For now, I think I just need to go home and process what's happening."

"What about tomorrow?" he ventured.

"We'll deal with tomorrow when the sun's shining," I replied.

Then, before he could do or say anything more, I turned on my heel and strode out of the park. The proximity we'd just shared had been driving me wild and even though my head was still swirling with multitudes of questions, I couldn't sort through any of them long enough to get them out of my mouth. And it didn't help that he'd kissed me. I'd always been intoxicated by his mere presence and having his lips on mine only served to muddle my thoughts further.

I'd only marched a few paces away from Nathan when the fog cleared, and I fully understood why I was behaving a bit like an erratic maniac.

He keeps asking to see me and I keep accepting his offers. So, we're both in this thing knee deep.

While it was nice to know my feelings were reciprocated by Nate, this thought didn't make me feel much better. Neither did the one that followed.

I want to be with him, even though I know he's hiding something or someone. Agh…what am I doing? I'm still trying to bury my own secrets and yet I can't ignore the fact that he's here…in town… and he wants to be with me, too. What a mess.

Chapter Sixteen

Are You Still Playing That Game of Cat and Mouse?
Nathan

"You know what I've always liked about our job?" Sean said the next morning over coffee and pieces of danish. The conference was set to commence in the next few minutes, but we were still seated at one of the breakfast tables. He was noshing on the pastry, taking small nibbles, saving the bit of cream cheese in the center for last and I was sipping slowly at my hot coffee, not hungry after enjoying the feast at Wes and Adair's apartment the night before.

"What's that?" I asked, drawing my focus away from my last conversation with Missy last night and trying to give my friend and colleague the attention he deserved.

"I like how straightforward it is," he replied, licking a bit of cream cheese off his fingers. "In the lab, we have certain tests we need to run, the parameters are set, and once the job's done, all we've gotta do is read down the chart and make sure all the numbers look right. If everything matches the way it's supposed to, we go onto the next test. If the results aren't what we're hoping to find, we have a whole protocol already in place, a system of routine procedures that we need to go through next, so we know how to fix the problem areas."

"I…uh…I'm not sure I understand why you're telling me all this," I said slowly, leaning forward in my chair a little and eyeing my friend keenly. "Does your story have a point that I'm just missing altogether?"

"The point is that you're making more trouble for yourself than is necessary," Sean said, popping the rest of the danish into his mouth, then giving me a long, cool stare while he chewed.

"Are you talking about the time I've been spending with Missy this week?"

Sean nodded, then swallowed the rest of his pastry before answering. "I think it's great that you decided to spend some time with a few of your old friends. But you've been distracted this week. Sometimes, during the seminars, I think you might not be listening to the presenters and…"

"I'm not," I confessed, before quickly adding, "I mean…*sometimes*, I'm listening, but other times, I'm thinking about Missy and when my thoughts start spinning in that direction…"

"Yeah, yeah," Sean said, waving away the need for further elaboration. "I get it. You're mad about her." He took a quick sip of his coffee, then after placing it on the table leaned forward and lowered his voice, so he was whispering, "But if you care so much about this woman, why'd you have to wait 'til this morning to call Jordan?"

I grimaced. "You heard that?"

He shrugged. "It wasn't like I was trying to eavesdrop on your phone conversations or anything, but when I came back to the table, I heard you talking to Jordan. You were apologizing for not picking up the phone last night. Why…"

"I know," I grumbled, speaking over top of him. "I know I shouldn't have put Jordan off while I was with Missy. But how could I tell her about Jordan? How could I possibly explain the situation?"

"Try telling the truth," Sean huffed. "That might help ya sort things out."

I shook my head and stared into the depths of my coffee cup. I'd drank almost the entire thing, and even though I'm sure the beverage had a rather potent blend of seasonings, I hadn't tasted a drop of it. I'd been so focused on dealing with this situation with Missy and wondering what to tell Jordan about all this, that I didn't bother to enjoy my first dose of daily caffeine.

"I can't," I murmured.

"Why not?" Sean challenged. "You and Missy have spent two days together and judging by the way you keep peeking at your phone, I'm guessin' you're expecting a text to come in from her at any time."

"So?"

"So…" he continued, "If you want to spark up anything with this woman…a relationship…a friendship…whatever, then you need to get the ball rolling by telling her about the other important people in your life." He paused and scoffed. "You can't even be thinking about spending another day with Missy without considering telling her about Jordan. That isn't fair to either of them."

"But she's not going to understand," I whispered. "If I tell her who Jordan is, she'll figure out the whole situation in a matter of seconds and…"

"So, let her figure it out," Sean interjected. "At this point, what do you got to lose?"

"I could lose Missy," I responded quietly.

He took another slow, measured sip of his coffee, then gently returned it to the tabletop. "Yeah, maybe. But that's only if you think she's yours right now anyway."

"What?" I'd been on the verge of picking up my own coffee cup once more, but I lost my grip and nearly dropped it when he said those words.

He shrugged. "Think about it, Nate. You've got your secrets. You told me you're pretty sure she's got hers too. Really give this some thought. What if the thing she's concealing is equal to or greater than your situation with Jordan? What if…?"

"No," I said, shaking my head adamantly. "Missy might be hiding something. She might even be reluctant to spill everything that's gone on in her life these last few years, but that's normal and totally expected. We've only been back together for two days and…"

"But you want to spend time with her again today," Sean interrupted. "Exactly how much time are you gonna spend with this lady before you decide to finally get real with her?"

"*Ugh*…" I groaned. "I don't know."

"I know you don't wanna hear this…" He paused and swiped his hand over the top of his head. "But I feel like, as your friend, I've gotta say it. If you ever want to talk to this Missy Lawrence woman again, you need to tell her about Jordan. She might not fall to her knees and thank you for sharing this news with her immediately, but in time, I think she'll be grateful to know the truth."

"And what about Jordan?" I returned.

"What about Jordan?"

"Shouldn't I be more protective of…?"

"The time for protecting Jordan has come and gone," Sean muttered, shaking his head profusely. "All you can do now is lay everything out on the table and pray Missy forgives you."

I grimaced. "You think Missy's going to forgive me?"

Slowly, Sean nodded his head. "I don't know here from Adam, but I'm thinking she just might."

"Really?" I asked, feeling a faint flicker of hope sprout in my heart.

"Once she's had time to adjust to the idea, she might figure out there's nothing really to forgive." I tipped my head to the side and gave him a skeptical glance, but Sean shrugged it off. "I'm serious, man. If your girl cares about you the way you care about her, she'll hear what you have to say, and find a way to be okay with it."

"But…" I hesitated. "This thing with Jordan…it's not a one and done deal. If Missy decides she wants to have me in her life going forward, she'll have to accept Jordan, too."

"That sounds about right." Sean finished off his coffee, then used a paper napkin to dab his lips. Having polished off his breakfast, he checked his watch. "And with that, my friend, we've gotta get moving."

We stood and after depositing our refuse in the nearest trash can, I turned to him. "So…you really think when I see Missy tonight that I should tell her everything?"

He snorted. "Man, I think you should've told her all about Jordan that very first night. It ain't right to keep a lid on something so important and this Missy lady…she needs to know what's really going on in your life."

"Yeah," I said softly, thinking of how she'd reacted last night when I'd received Jordan's phone call. "Maybe if I just tell her the truth, everything'll be all right."

"Maybe," Sean agreed and for the time being, that nonchalant conclusion had to suffice.

Chapter Seventeen

If He Were Here…Would that Make Things Better or Worse?
Missy

Come on…just cooperate, please.

Everything today, including the haphazard ponytail I was attempting to slap into shape, had been working against me.

While on air, I'd stumbled over my words and mispronounced a person's name. I thought for a moment that the torture would be over once the broadcast hit the airwaves because we weren't scheduled to record a podcast this afternoon, but that notion was blown to bits when Steve relayed a message from Vic saying one of our segments needed to be re-recorded. And now, I was planning to head out and maybe do a little light jogging around the city, but these darned stubborn bits of hair kept slipping right out of the elastic tie and clinging to my cheekbones.

What am I gonna do?

I knew none of my dilemmas would result in the end of the world, but after spending a nearly sleepless night mulling over my situation with Nathan, I was a tad off-kilter. It was nearly three o'clock and I had yet to determine if I was going to meet him in the park tonight to go for that bike ride.

I glared at my own reflection in the mirror.

Seems like I wanna go because I've already changed into athletic apparel and I'm struggling to get this ponytail just right.

But my thoughts were at war with one another, because in the very next instant, I was discarding the previous idea.

Or…I could just keep running and forget all about heading over to the park.

It irked me that I didn't know who Jordan was and that Nathan hadn't offered any sort of explanation. He'd gone ahead and kissed me, not once, but twice, even though he knew I was thrown for a loop, contemplating the bits of missing information.

So…why'd he do it?

I had to believe that Nate was letting his emotions get the better of him. He'd kissed me the night before because that's what he really wanted to do.

But was that fair to Jordan?

If he had some other woman ringing him up, while he was supposed to be behaving himself at a work conference, did it seem right for him to be planting smooches on me, giggling when he didn't entirely hit the mark?

"*Argh…*"

I growled in aggravation, then tugged on the elastic band, cinching my ponytail tighter.

"Easy there, tiger," Adair said, waltzing into the ladies' restroom and presenting me with a small smile. "You keep on like that and you'll give yourself split ends…not to mention a dreadful headache."

"I think I've already got a headache," I grumbled, leaning forward, and placing both hands on the bathroom countertop.

"You *think*? Don't you usually know when you're feeling unwell?"

I shot Adair a glance in the mirror and noticed that she was watching me, evidently trying to make up her own mind on the state of my well-being.

"I'm having a day," I groused, gripping the edge of the counter tightly. "It just feels like nothing's going right."

"Did something happen with Nathan after you left last night?"

And that little prompting was all it took. In a furious manner, I reported all the events of the previous evening. From the sincere way he looked at me to that unanswered phone call that shook my whole world, I let it all pour out. The entire time, Adair merely nodded and shook her head—whichever was appropriate. And when I finally finished the story, she pursed her lips and murmured, "Well, that's just too bad."

"Which part?" I returned.

"All of it," Adair said, sighing heavily. "The two of you seemed awfully pleased with each other and yourselves when you left last night and that got me and Wes talking."

"No," I groaned, "please tell me the two of you aren't about to start putting your matchmaking skills to use again."

I cringed when I recalled the countless times over the years that Adair had set me up with a friend of a friend or a long-lost cousin who had suddenly, and fortuitously, resurfaced. I'd gone on one date after the other with people Adair and Wes were sure would be perfect for me. But, in the end, none of it amounted to very much. I was still unmarried, living alone, and counting my work and circle of friends as the very best things in my life. All in all, I was happy with my lot, but when Adair and Wes got it into their heads that I needed more…a companion…someone to love…I just felt like calling it quits.

"We don't need to make a match," Adair said, giving her head a haughty toss. "You and Nate have already found each other. All we wanted to do was give you both a little push in the right direction. Make it so you never had to leave each other ever again."

I gawped at her. "How can you make something like that happen?"

She waved her hand airily, showing off a new nail lacquer that was a frosty shade reminiscent of a glass of wine which I guessed had a brilliant name like Sultry Sangria or Berry, Berry Quite Contrary. "This time, I'm not the one making miracles happen. It was Wes who came up with a brilliant strategy to keep you two together."

"Go on," I prompted, intrigued.

"It's really not so far a stretch of the imagination," she continued. "You know that Wes was recently promoted so that he's now the VP of Operations at his company and his team needs a health and environmental safety officer. He thinks Nate would be perfect for the job, what with his background helping run the lab and all at Morgan and Fosters. And…if I hadn't told Wes to cool his heels last night, he might've offered Nathan the job over dessert."

"What?" I was flabbergasted. "It can't be that easy."

"But it is," she returned, smiling slyly. "If Nate wants the job working with Wes, all he's got to do is say so. There'll be some interviews, for sure, but Wes will be on the hiring committee and it's not likely that any recommendation of his would be ignored. So…"

"So what? Wes is going to hire Nathan to work for him?"

"Well…" Adair lifted her hand and daintily tapped the nail of her index finger against her front teeth. "That all depends on you."

"Me?"

Adair guffawed. "I shouldn't need to explain this to you, Lawrence, but Wes and I genuinely have your best interests at heart here. If you don't want Nate bumming around Charlotte, making you panic every time he walks in a room, Wes won't offer him the job."

I frowned. "But is Nate the right man for the position? Will it be a detriment to the company if Wes doesn't at least try to get Nathan to come on board?"

She shrugged. "The job is secondary, as far as I'm concerned. You're my pal and Wes and I want to see you happy. If it'd make you happy to have your main man in town, then we'd like to see if we can help make that dream come true."

"Oh…" I moaned. "That's about the nicest thing I've ever heard, and I really appreciate the offer but…"

"But…?"

I wasn't sure how to finish my statement. The thought of having Nathan around full-time was kind of exhilarating. He hadn't lived in Charlotte since the day we graduated, and he moved to Pittsburgh. And, to my knowledge, he'd only visited that one time, thirteen years ago, in honor of Adair's wedding. The idea of having him close by made me feel slightly giddy.

I looked at myself in the mirror again.

Would I be pleased to have him around because so many of my friends have moved away and it'd be nice to have another buddy in town? Or…do I want him here because there's more to our relationship I want to explore?

Those quandaries weren't quite so easy to tackle.

Even as I was considering my true feelings, Adair butted in with more questions. She asked, "Do you want Nathan to move here? Did you guys ever discuss that option before? If he gets the job, will you be pleased knowing he'll be around all the time?"

"I don't know," I said slowly. "I'm just not sure." I sighed. "I've spent all day wondering if he's hiding a secret girlfriend, so maybe he won't even want to be here."

Adair shook her head. "I don't think he's hiding a girlfriend or a spouse."

"Oh?"

She reached out and patted my shoulder. "I saw the way he looked at you last night. The way he stared at you was the way I've seen people react to meeting their idols. He thinks you're the most amazing person on the planet."

"Yeah, well, he can think that all he likes, but that doesn't mean this Jordan person isn't waiting for him back home."

She pulled her hand away from my shoulder and said softly, "You can't keep going round and round like this, Missy. You're hiding secrets from Nathan too…keeping things concealed he'd want to know. I thought we talked about this yesterday and decided…"

"I know," I said, nodding briskly. "You think I should tell him everything but that's so…so hard."

"Do it," Adair said authoritatively as if she were making a snap decision regarding my work on set or in the studio. "I know you're tormenting yourself about this whole Nathan business, but the worry and dismay isn't worth your time. You'll give yourself frown lines." She pointed to my reflection in the mirror, indicating I should check out the deep V that was already etched between my eyebrows. Then, she continued giving orders, "Go see him tonight. Tell him everything. Get it all out in the open, then see what comes next."

"I...I'm scared," I admitted.

"As you should be," she said gently, but firmly. "Taking this kind of risk, being totally open and honest with someone, that's the sort of thing you do when you've really and truly found the love of your life." I started to protest, but she held up her hand to silence me. "No need to argue, Miss. We both know he's the one. Be honest about that much at least."

And she was right. I wanted to debate the matter, but the facts spoke for themselves. I'd been in love with Nathan Hamilton my whole life and tonight, come what may, I was going to speak the truth, bare my soul, and pray he'd be willing to accept me for the flawed, fallible woman I am.

Chapter Eighteen

This Changes Things, Right?
Nathan

"Where've you been?"

I came darting out of Conference Room C only to find Sean waiting for me in the lobby, looking bemused.

"I'm late. I know it. I'm sorry." I paused and checked my watch, verifying that indeed, I was about twenty minutes behind the schedule I needed to keep. "The speaker in that last session went way over on time. We even had to forego our break because he kept at it."

Sean snorted. "So, I'm assuming we won't have time to hit the fitness center like we planned." His comment was more of a statement than a question.

I rolled my wrist over and stared at the faceplate on my watch a second time. "*Ehh*...if we go to the fitness center, I'll be cutting it awfully close."

"Close? You got another date tonight?"

I grinned. "Yeah. Missy just sent a text. She said, if I was still up for it, she'd meet me in the park around five-thirty."

"I guess I'll be flying solo again tonight."

I started to explain or, at the very least, make an apology for leaving my friend on his own once again, but he shook his head, negating the need.

"I'm not complaining. With Felicia and the three kids at home, I never get to do anything on my own. This week, I'm kind of enjoying being by myself." He smirked. "Maybe I'll even have ice cream for dinner." Then, he gave me a sheepish look. "But don't tell Felicia."

"My lips are sealed." I shuffled the papers I was holding from one hand to the other, then took a quick peek outside. It looked like a warm, fall day. The sun was glowing bright as it headed for the horizon.

I've got to remember to bring my sunglasses this time.

"So, I guess I'll see ya sometime tomorrow morning then," Sean said, pointing at an item on the paper agenda he had laid flat against his legal pad. "Says here breakfast is served at eight."

I snorted. "Same time...all week..."

"Yeah, well, I'm a creature of habit. I like my routines."

"And yet, you're having ice cream for dinner," I joked. "What would your wife and kids think?" With that, I was ready to take off and change into some workout gear so I could book it out of there and be on time to meet Missy, but apparently, what I'd just said sparked something in Sean's memory.

I was just stepping away from him when he said, "Speaking of which, I saw Jordan's good news today."

"Yeah?"

"It's plastered all over social media."

I paused and nodded enthusiastically. "Of course it is."

"You hadn't noticed yet?"

I tapped my pocket where I'd been storing my phone throughout today's conference meetings. "I saw the text from Missy when it scrolled across my watch, but I haven't been playing around on social media all day."

Sean put on a wounded face. "I wasn't doing that, either. But when Felicia saw a post from Jordan pop up on her timeline, she forwarded it to me and…*Ehh*…forget it. I only brought it up because I meant to congratulate you."

"Thanks, man."

"No, I mean it. You've gotta be thrilled."

I bobbed my head in agreement. "This news…it's exactly what we were hoping to hear. I haven't been able to get the smile off my face all day."

"And?" Sean prompted.

"And what?" I returned.

"Does this bit of good news mean you're planning to tell Missy all about Jordan tonight?"

"That's the plan."

Sean seemed slightly taken aback and he blinked in surprise. "You sure turned around your whole way of thinking pretty quickly."

"After I missed Jordan's call last night, we spoke this morning, before all the social media posts went live, making the announcement official. I thought about that conversation and couldn't get out of my head the things you and I discussed, either. So, somewhere after lunchtime, right before I got the text from Missy, I decided that was it—this was the sign I'd been waiting for all along. It's time to tell Missy everything."

"Good for you," Sean murmured. "Being honest with her is the right thing to do, but you know this ain't gonna be easy."

"I'm counting on it," I quipped. Then, we said our goodbyes and I hurried to my room.

Even though I'd been joking with my buddy, I fully understood the ramifications of my actions. Tonight, I was going to share with Missy all that had occurred during the thirteen years we'd been apart from one another. Jordan's good news necessitated us having this conversation. And while it felt supremely satisfying knowing that I was about to unburden myself and finally say all that was on my mind, I also worried about Missy's reaction. She was a forgiving woman, but could she…nay, would she…forgive me this?

Chapter Nineteen

Why are You Crying?
Missy

He's late.

I was standing in the park, near the spot where we'd parted ways last night, staring at my smart watch.

I feel like he really should've been here by now.

My nerves were fraying around the edges. When I'd first sent him the text a few hours ago, inviting him to join me for this bike ride after all, I'd been slightly elated. I'd experienced a sort of euphoria, the kind of thing that can only occur once a person had made a decision that has the capacity to change everything. And so, while I walked to the park and found the best spot to stand in so that I might see him when he first appeared, I'd been grinning broadly.

But with each passing minute, I felt my smile twitch. Now, it felt as if I was trying to plaster a grin on my face, to put up a good front, and that sort of inauthenticity also bothered me. In my line of work, I often had to rely on my tough façade to carry me through a tricky news story or to conceal what I really thought about some boneheaded scheme one of the local politicians was cooking up for the day. But rarely, in my personal life, did I allow my phony smile to slide into place. Doing so now was making me lose my nerve.

Hold it together, Lawrence. You know he's working all week, and he can't very well come running just because you demand it.

Earlier, I'd tucked my phone into the slim pocket that was sewn into the side of my yoga pants and my fingers itched to grab for it.

I just need to take another quick look at his return reply.

I knew it had been something simple like…*okay, see ya soon*. But because I was the one stuck waiting around, my mind was playing tricks on me, making me think there was more substance to the text than there really had been.

Giving up my prime waiting spot near the center of the park, I sauntered toward the bike rack, reviewing the purchasing options. Since I owned my own bicycle, I rarely had cause to rent one of these eBikes. But since that was exactly what Nate was going to do, I figured it'd be best if I rode one as well. And I was sort of keyed up to give it a try. It looked like fun to cruise along on the lime green roadster. Whenever I'd watched other people zipping around the city on one of these things, they all seemed to be having a good time, and they were flying much faster than I was sure I'd ever get my legs to pedal. I giggled, thinking of how nice it would be just to coast through the city with Nathan at my side.

But thinking expressly about him brought my mind back to the fact that he was still not here.

Send a text. Check on him.

I'd only just tugged the phone out of my pocket when the soft calypso ringtone I'd always favored sounded.

Huh…that's odd.

I grinned at the device, this time conjuring a genuine smile, when I thought that somehow, across the divide, Nate had read my mind, and was reaching out to me at the same moment I was thinking of calling him. But then, I realized it wasn't Nathan on the other line at all. The caller ID was flashing Hope's name.

"Hello."

"Hey, Hot Stuff," she replied, "Whatcha doing? Who ya seeing? Where ya going?" This was a running joke with us, rambling out a string of questions right away. It was nonsensical, really, but also funny because it was the sort of thing only a couple of sisters would do and still find amusing after all these years.

"I'm just about to go on a bike ride," I answered, careful not to mention the fact that I was waiting for Nathan's arrival. Hopey had mixed feelings on my interactions with my ex. She'd been at the breakfast table when he'd proposed, but she, like me, had assumed he was only messing around. For the first two months after his departure, she'd encouraged me to reach out to him, but after everything fell apart, she'd stopped pushing. She was disappointed, I think, that he never made the effort himself. And because he didn't call, that only served to prove what we'd both imagined all along—the proposal had been too nonchalant, too spur of the moment to be real. But now…

What would Hopey think if I told her I was meeting Nathan this afternoon?

While I'd been off entertaining my own thoughts, my little sister had kept right on talking, telling me a story about her middle child, Faith, who had taken a spill on her bike just a few days ago and got a terrible scrape on her elbow.

"Poor baby," I murmured, commiserating with the aches and pains that the child surely experienced. "Do you think it'll leave a scar?"

"I don't know," Hope grumbled. "We cleaned it, put medicine on it, and wrapped the whole thing in a big Band-Aid. I'm not sure what else I was supposed to do."

I chuckled lightly at the way she sounded slightly harried, as if tackling this task were just one of a long list of boo-boos she'd had to manage since the last time we'd spoken. "You're a good mama bear," I said softly. "I'm sure whatever you did was just fine."

She let out an exasperated sigh and I was sure she was about to say something in response, but then I heard her youngest, Scott Junior, also known as S.J., clamoring for her attention. "Mama! Mama!" he hollered at the top of his little voice. "You gotta see what Charity just did."

"Lord a'mercy," Hope muttered. "Can't you go find your daddy and tell him all about it?"

"Huh-uh," S.J. replied earnestly. "Charity spilled a big bunch of cereal all over the floor and we need you to come quick. Faith is stompin' in it and…"

Hope groaned. "Charity's gettin' to be a big girl now. And Faith knows she shouldn't be making things worse. The girls can clean up their own mess."

"But Mama, you've gotta see," S.J. whined.

"And since you tattled on them, you oughta grab the broom and give your big sisters an assist."

I heard the shocked gasped S.J. emitted, which was quickly followed by a bit of protestation. "But that's not fair, Mama. Charity was the one who made the mess and…"

The conversation became muffled at that point, and I assumed that Hope was covering the phone with her hand, which I didn't mind in the slightest. This sort of conversation was par for the course these days, at least as far as Hopey was concerned. I couldn't remember the last time she and I got to talk uninterrupted. She was always with the kids and somehow, inexplicably, every time she picked up the phone to give me a call, one of them did something calamitous. I laughed, thinking of the mess that was surely covering her kitchen floor. Hope hated cleaning up anything, so it was little wonder she was telling her son to go take care of it or find his father and make him do his share.

"I don't know what I'm gonna do with these kids," Hope said a few seconds later. "They're driving me crazy today. Is it a full moon or something?"

I looked overhead and saw that the moon wasn't out yet. "Does that make a difference?"

"The kids go wild when there's a full moon. They're like a pack of reckless animals," Hope answered.

"I can't see the moon yet, but when it does come out, I'll snap a pic and send it your way."

"Thanks," she grumbled. "It won't do me a bit of good, but I'd sure like to see a pretty picture."

I heard her release another long exhale and my heart went out to my little sister. Once, not so long ago, she'd studied fine arts and excelled in her photography courses. The plan had been to maybe open her own portrait studio or, at the very least, travel along the coast, taking professional style beach pictures for families that were on vacation. But when Hopey met Skeeter and they were pregnant with Charity a heartbeat later, all her plans changed. Outside of snapping selfies with the kids or documenting their milestones using the camera on her smartphone, Hope rarely exercised her photography skills these days. Instead, she stayed mostly focused on her children, making them her priority.

"I'll send you a few," I promised. In the background, I heard a terrible racket and winced. When Hope didn't say anything right away, I murmured softly, "I'm almost afraid to ask, but what just happened?"

"I don't know," Hope huffed. "I told Skeeter to keep an eye on things for a minute because I really need to talk to you, Miss."

I picked up quickly on the change in her tone. Before, she just sounded tired. But now, I could detect notes of sorrow and maybe even a touch of desperation. "Aww…pooh bear…what's wrong?" I coaxed.

"I…I…" Her voice broke and I knew that she'd started to cry. And that's when a whole bunch of warning sirens began blaring in my head. My little sister was usually the jolly, happy-go-lucky sort. Oh, she had her share of woes and cried over them just like everybody else, but she didn't just lose her cool at the drop of a hat.

To try and lighten the mood, I joked, "Don't fret over it, Boo. Nobody ever cries over a little spilled cereal."

"I'm not upset about the cereal," she said between sniffles. "I…I'm pregnant, Missy."

"Again?"

She snorted at my immediate reaction. "Yes...again."

"But...but...I thought you and Skeeter decided you didn't want to have any more kids. Last I knew, he was going in for a procedure and..."

A disgruntled groan came from her end of the line, so I stopped talking right in the middle of my sentence. "Skeeter was supposed to get a vasectomy. We set up the appointment and everything, but he's not gonna go see the doctor until next week and...and...Oh, Lordy. What am I gonna do with another little one running around the house?"

"You'll manage," I replied. "Every time you first find out you're pregnant, you always react this way. You..."

"But this is baby number four, Missy. You'd think I'd be used to..." She sucked in a deep gulp of air.

"What?" I asked when silence reigned for a beat too long.

"I...I'm sorry," she murmured. "I shouldn't be sayin' these things to you. I know you can't..."

"Oh yes, you should," I snapped. "I wanna hear just this sort of news because it's something worth celebrating. You get to bring another life into the world, Hope. You get to be a mama again. If you couldn't call me with this news, who can you call?"

"I know," she said feebly, and I could still hear the soft whimpering sounds she was making while speaking through her tears. "But I feel bad...complaining and all."

"You weren't complaining and even if you did, you shouldn't feel bad about it," I assured her. "Having a baby is a wonderful thing, but we both know how many challenges come along with it. You're entitled to share your feelings—just as they are."

"So...so you're happy for me and Skeeter?"

"What kind of question is that?" I returned, thinking of how if we were having this conversation in person, I'd have given her a swat on the arm for even making that kind of comment.

"It's just that I wasn't sure...this time around...if you'd feel..."

"I'll feel however you tell me to feel," I interrupted, which made her laugh.

"Right," she snickered. "'Cause you're malleable like that."

"Fine," I consented. "I'll feel however I'm gonna feel, but when you need me to step up and be there for you, Skeeter, and the kids, you know I've got your back."

"Thanks, Miss," she whispered. "And I'm gonna hold you to that. We're expecting you to come up here for the holidays this year and…"

"I'll be there with bells on," I vowed.

I felt a tad guilty hurrying through the end of our conversation, but it was at this point that I laid eyes on Nathan. He was striding across the park, swinging his arms at his sides, giving off every impression that he was delighted to be here, walking in my direction. Just before he reached me, I said my goodbyes to Hopey and promised that I'd call her again tomorrow to check on her and the kids.

When Nathan got about two feet from the spot where I was standing, his face did this bizarre thing. He'd been smiling, but suddenly, his lips twisted, and his brows lowered. His expression was full of concern, but it also seemed as if he was puzzled.

"What's wrong?" I asked when he stopped right in front of me.

He reached out and cupped my chin using both hands. Slowly, he used the pads of his thumbs to swipe across my cheekbones.

"What are you doing?" I whispered.

"Why are you crying?" he returned.

I stared up into his beautiful blue eyes, reading the apprehension in them and answered, "I didn't know I was."

Chapter Twenty

What's Wrong?
Nathan

When she didn't elaborate right away, I stepped forward, aiming to give her a hug, but Missy was having none of that. She shook me off, backing away from me hastily, then gesturing toward the bike rack that was off to our left.

"You ready?" Her voice was even and steady and she was doing an excellent job at concealing whatever inner turmoil she might be feeling. If we'd been having a phone conversation, I'd never have known she was distraught. But since I could see her and therefore knew the way her lips drooped despondently and the tears continued to flow down her cheeks, even though she kept wiping at them, I wasn't about to proceed with our bike ride while she was in such a state.

"Not remotely," I said, striding behind her, working much harder than I probably needed to so I could keep up with her speedy pace.

"You're late, Nathan," she said tartly.

"And that's why you're crying?" She stopped right in front of the payment processing machine and pulled out a vibrant red credit card.

"No," she snapped, again making a cracking retort without giving any further details.

"I'm sorry I kept you waiting," I apologized, still uncertain what to make of this predicament. "One of the sessions ran long and…"

"I said it was fine," she said frostily, pulling her card out of the machine, then pointing to the nearest two bikes. "We've got thirty-five and thirty-eight for the next couple of hours."

"You didn't have to pay for my rental too," I said, scurrying behind her as she wove her way into the rack and started unlocking bike number thirty-eight.

"It's not a big deal," she said, shaking her head infinitesimally. "The rental only cost a couple of bucks. I'll let you buy me an ice cream later to make up the difference."

"You want ice cream?" My mind was boggled. I was still processing the fact that I'd found her crying in the park, and here she was, talking about getting sweet treats.

"Let's go." Her tone was still crisp when she wheeled her bike out of the rack and pointed the front tire toward the path. "We can ride after the sun goes down, but I'd prefer to head toward the park before it gets too dark."

"Park? Aren't we already in a park?"

Missy didn't deign to give that question a response. Instead, she just finished adjusting her seat, hopped onto the bike, then started pedaling like a madwoman.

"Wait!" I called after her. "Where are we going?"

I might've gone to college at UNC Charlotte, but I hadn't grown up around here and even if I had, my knowledge of the landscape would've made very little difference. I hadn't been in the uptown area for more than a decade. And, as was proven yesterday during our tour of the city, almost everything had changed. I wouldn't have been able to find my way around this town if I didn't have Missy to guide me. But, as she rode away, not bothering to stop or answer any of my questions, I got an awful feeling.

Maybe she's trying to ditch me. Maybe she went snooping this afternoon, tapping into all her journalistic skills, and decided to scour the internet for information about me. With Jordan posting the good news far and wide, she wouldn't have needed to look hard to uncover a whole lot that I've been keeping to myself.

Afraid that if I didn't go after her and beg to plead my case, I might never get the opportunity again, I yanked the bike from the rack and mounted the seat quickly. In my haste to get moving, I didn't get the seat adjustments quite right, but I figured I could suffer through a little discomfort, if it meant catching up to Missy and talking through everything.

I only hope she'll listen.

She'd worn a crisp white t-shirt this afternoon and lucky for me, that was easy enough to track. Since it was the fall season, most of the people in the park were dressed in maroon, varying shades of brown, or, in some cases, pumpkin orange hues. This made spying Missy a breeze. But catching up to her was a completely different story. Not only did she have the advantage of knowing where she was heading, but she also had that head start. I pumped my legs and applied the "boost" button liberally, dodging around pedestrians on the sidewalks, veering far left when I nearly collided with an oncoming cyclist.

"Sorry," I called over my shoulder after we barely avoided having a wreck. I knew I was riding this bike like a lunatic, but I needed to get to Missy and try to figure out what was going on with her.

Once we got off the main thoroughfare, we rode along the rail line for a stretch. It seemed that this pathway was designed expressly for bikes, scooters, walkers, and joggers. This made navigation a tad easier. But then, just as I was getting comfortable and nearly able to kiss Missy's back tire with my front one, she dove off to the left, taking us away from the heart of the city. It didn't take long, maybe less than a mile or two of pedaling, for enormous trees to crop up indicating we were heading for another park—presumably the one she'd mentioned earlier.

When we got to the point where it was time to traverse a hill, I hit my stride, and glided easily to her side. I saw the way she glanced at me sidelong, but instead of trying to engage with her or ask what she was thinking, I held my tongue.

Now's not the time for conversation…not when we're already fighting an uphill battle.

The road we were on just happened to be quite the hilly trek and if I hadn't been so worried about staying right in line with Missy, I might've enjoyed the thrill of pushing myself hard on the uphill stretch then coasting down the gently sloping descension.

Ten minutes later, after reaching a surprisingly flat environment, we pulled our bikes to a stop at another bike rack.

"You've gotta charge it," she said, pointing to one of the empty spots, indicating evidently that I should put my bike there.

Twilight was upon us, but the park was nicely illuminated by a series of quaint, antique-looking lamp posts. People dotted the grounds. A group of young men were trying to get in just a couple more frisbee tosses. Several people were walking their dogs. And over by the grandstand, someone was strumming a guitar, clearly warming up for a performance.

Now that I could get a good look at Missy's face again, I noticed that the tears had never really abated. Her cheeks were red, and her eyes were slightly puffy. Her lips were swollen too as if she'd been biting the bottom one, while attempting to control her emotions.

This time when I stepped forward and held out my arms, offering to give her a hug, she didn't pull away or even try to resist. Instead, she stepped right toward me, and I embraced her lovingly.

"Missy," I whispered, placing my lips close to her ear, "please, please give me a chance. Let me explain."

She'd been nuzzling her face into my chest, seeking to bury herself there, but at my words, she stopped and slowly lifted her chin. She stared at me, and her expression was inscrutable. I couldn't tell if she was peeved, dejected, or just plain bewildered. She cleared up that matter quickly when she breathed, "Explain what, Nathan?"

That was when I realized I might've miscalculated the situation. While Missy certainly could've done a bit of digging into my past this afternoon, it stood to reason that if she'd found out everything, she wouldn't have agreed to go biking with me. She wouldn't have bothered to rent a bike so I could chase after her. No, if she knew the secrets I was keeping, she'd have wanted to stand right there in the middle of the park and pepper me with zillions of questions. We hadn't just flown through the city at a record pace because she was hoping I'd come after her and explain myself. She'd beat it out of there because she was running from her own demons.

I decided it'd be best to ignore her last question and proceeded with one of my own. "What's wrong, Missy? Tell me, please…please."

Chapter Twenty-One

When Did Everything in Life Become so Serious?
Missy

Guilt clawed at my insides.

Just looking into Nathan's eyes, seeing the helpless look there, and hearing that pleading tone in his voice was enough to make me feel terrible. But knowing that all this time…all these years…I'd concealed this one big secret from him…well, that was enough to make me feel like a true villain.

These last few days, my friends had prompted me to be honest with him, but I could see now that when Steve and Adair interjected their two cents, they weren't so much concerned with Nathan or what he deserved to know. They were thinking of me. I needed to work through my grief, rather than continuing to keep it bottled up. My reaction to Hope's phone call made that much plain. Even though I liked to pretend that everything was honky dory and that I was living my very best life, there was a missing piece…a tiny hole which I'd never be able to fill. And Nathan *did* deserve to know what this awful truth had done to me.

"Can we sit somewhere first?" I asked, turning around, and searching for a spot that was slightly separated from the rest of the people in the park. If I'd known we were going to have this particular conversation, I wouldn't have come to such a crowded place. I might've taken Nate to my apartment, or we could've gone to a bar or coffee shop. But since we were here, and I was finally inclined to share my feelings, I knew that this lovely little park, with all these happy citizens milling around, enjoying the fresh fall air, would have to suffice.

"Over here," he said, loosening his grip on me just long enough to take my hand and lead me toward one of the stone benches which sat beneath a towering white oak tree.

Once we were both settled, I inhaled deeply, sucking in warm air through my nose, then releasing it slowly through my mouth.

"Miss," he said, "do you want me to get you something to drink? Or maybe you'd prefer one of those ice cream cones you mentioned earlier?"

I stifled a watery laugh, then wiped the tears that were continually forming in the corners of my eyes. "Thanks for the offer, but I'll pass. I'd like to tell you something, Nathan. Something I should've shared with you a long time ago." I squeezed his hand. "Do you think you're ready to hear what I have to say?"

"You're scaring me, Missy," he answered in a soft, reverent voice. "I'll admit that when we were riding through the city, you were making me feel a touch of nervousness, but now…" He paused and cleared his throat. "I guess you'd better go on and say your piece, 'cause whatever you've got to tell me can't be nearly as bad as what I'm already imagining."

Oh, if only that were true.

I took another deep breath and steadied myself, then plunged into my story. "The last time you came to Charlotte for a visit, you and I spent an incredible night together."

"I remember," he whispered.

I snorted, then shook my head gently. "I'm not sure you do. When we woke up the next morning, the day after Adair and Wesley's wedding, you made it seem like you'd forgotten most of what went down."

He shrugged. "I'm pretty sure I remember the highlights."

I shook my head a tad more forcefully. "I don't want to get caught up in rehashing all that happened that weekend, but I just needed to remind you that we spent the night together."

"Okay," he murmured softly. "I remember."

"What you don't know is that after you left, I waited for you to call. As I mentioned before, I was fairly certain your proposal had been nothing more than a joke, so I figured you'd call later that night, at the very least, to let me know you'd made it back to Pittsburgh safely. When I didn't get a call or text, I thought you might be ticked because I didn't play along with your little romantic game and…"

"It wasn't a game," he interjected.

I sighed wearily. "I know that now. But back then…I was young. And confused. And scared of what it would mean if…Anyway…We were little more than kids. I wasn't in any shape to make good decisions."

"All right," he whispered while slowly rubbing his thumb across my knuckles, "so after a few days elapsed, why didn't you reach out then?"

"I was going to," I replied. "I picked up the phone dozens of times and meant to send a text, but I couldn't come up with just the right thing to say. I mean, how do you apologize to someone for rejecting their marriage proposal?"

Nate's brow contracted as did his lips, all creating a slightly sour expression. "I guess that's the sort of thing that would require more than a simple text message."

"Exactly," I agreed. "But I didn't know what to say, either. So, I just held off, hoping you'd come up with something brilliant."

He grunted. "That was taking a real gamble."

"I was sure, even though I'd hurt your feelings, that you'd see your way past that and call me again. But then, after about two months elapsed, I wasn't thinking so much about making that phone call anymore."

"What happened?" he urged. "Did you...did you find a new boyfriend?"

Suddenly, my emotions surged, making a lump rise in my throat.

"I...I...I didn't get a new boyfriend," I croaked.

"Then what?" Nate asked. He was partially demanding the truth but also doing it in an imploring tone. The mixture was enough to evoke the words to topple right out of my mouth.

"I found out I was pregnant."

"You...you had a baby...*my* baby?"

Hot, thick tears congregated on my lower eyelashes, but I didn't even bother wiping them away. I just let them run their course, cascading down my cheeks before dribbling off my chin. "I didn't know I was pregnant until...until I lost the baby."

"Oh, Missy...no," Nate groaned. He let go of my hand and wrapped his arm around my shoulders protectively, pulling me closer so that I was tucked into his side. "Why didn't you call me then? I would've wanted to know about the baby...our baby...and we could've..."

"There was nothing you could do," I sobbed.

"Yes, there was," he countered. "I could've been by your side. I might not've been much comfort, but I could've tried to do something. I would've wanted to be with you."

"Maybe that's true," I sniffed. "And I probably should've called, but the...the miscarriage...was the least of my worries."

"What does that mean?" Nathan whispered.

"When the doctor performed the procedure after I lost the baby, he found something else."

"Something else?"

I could tell by the baffled look on Nate's face that he was startled by this onslaught of information. I promised myself then to forego using all the technical jargon and just stick to giving him the plain facts which he'd be easier able to digest.

"I had cysts covering my ovaries…tons of them. The doc said he was surprised I'd never complained of having horrific cramps before and I told him that I'd done my fair share of griping, but always just figured what I was going through was natural. Every woman suffers through the same thing. But he assured me my case was unique. There were so many cysts, he wasn't sure I'd ever be able to get pregnant again and…more than that…he was worried about the masses becoming cancerous."

"Oh…" Nate moaned. "You didn't…you don't have cancer, do you?"

"The doctor presented me with a few treatment options," I proceeded, knowing that by sticking to my story, I'd eventually answer Nate's questions. "And while I could've undergone several different treatments, I chose the most aggressive, proactive approach."

"What…what did you do?" Nathan's eyes had widened to the size of softballs and the way the moon was reflecting off them made the blue orbs glint. I snuck a glance overhead and saw that Hope was right. There was a full moon tonight.

"I elected to have a hysterectomy," I whispered.

"You…you…" He seemed at a loss for words.

"It wasn't an easy decision, but I also didn't want to live with the possibility of having cancer growing inside me always looming over my head."

"But, then you can't…you won't…"

"Yes," I said simply. "I can't ever have children. And that's why I didn't call you."

His expression flickered. It changed instantaneously from showcasing his stunned disbelief to a look of irritation. "I'm not following you anymore, Miss. Why did having this surgery somehow change the way you felt about me? How do the two add up?"

"You wanted children," I reminded him. "You said so during your proposal that day at my apartment. Remember? Loads of them…at least six or seven? Enough to have a family band?"

He gasped. "But I was joking."

"Were you?" I countered. "Because from the moment you came back to town this week, you've been trying to convince me that the words you spoke that day, the way you asked me to be your wife, were part of so much more than an idle joke. Just yesterday, you wanted me to believe that…"

"*Ahh…*" Nate groaned. "I know what I said. I know…Oh, I can't believe how badly things got misconstrued." He let go of my hand and lifted both his hands to cover his face. He did this strange thing then where he pressed his palms to his mouth and let out a terrible, anguished cry. "I should never have said that thing about having a bunch of kids. What did I know? I was an idiot back then. I…"

"Precisely," I whispered. "Those words…that proposal…they didn't really mean anything. Yet, after I had the hysterectomy, I knew I couldn't call you up and tell you the news. Even if you said you didn't care, I'd always know that somewhere, deep down, in the part of you that had spoken on a whim that day, you really wanted to have children. And I…well, I couldn't give you what you wanted."

Nathan peeled his hands away from his face and turned to look at me squarely. Fat, heavy tears were streaking down his cheeks. "I never wanted anything other than to be with you."

My tears renewed themselves at his words. I blinked rapidly, wanting to banish them. Now that we were in the thick of this conversation, I didn't want to stop talking, even for just the second it would take to wipe away the tears. "How can that be possible?"

Chapter Twenty-Two

Don't You Need to Answer That?
Nathan

"I'm so sorry."

I couldn't apologize quickly enough. The effusive words poured from my mouth, tumbling one right on top of the other as my head spun.

"I shouldn't have said all those things. I should've...I should've done things differently, so differently and I should've reached out to you a long time ago."

All those years ago, when I made that declaration of my love for Missy, I'd spoken what was right on the tip of my tongue. Never had I been so open, and, for a long time, I considered that the most romantic speech I'd ever delivered.

But to know now...to think that the words I'd said that day had been the reason she'd never contacted me?

I was crushed.

She thought I wanted kids because that's exactly what I'd said. That day, hanging out in her apartment, sharing waffles and sausage links for breakfast, I'd envisioned a future in which Missy, and I were surrounded by our children, munching on waffles, squabbling over who got to use the jug of syrup first, and laughing profusely. But that one dream...that one mere fantasy...and my mentioning it had been enough to scare her away from me for good.

"If you had reached out long ago," Missy said slowly, using the tips of her fingers to wipe her tears, "what difference would that have made?"

"What?"

I'd been stuck, replaying that fateful afternoon in my head, and at Missy's words, I felt like somehow, I'd missed a beat.

"If I'd called you or you'd sent me an email, how would that one little blip of communication managed to change anything? Wouldn't we still be right here...having this same conversation?"

"Of course not," I replied, doing my best to keep my voice even and not let my upset show too greatly. "You should've called me and told me about the miscarriage, but I should've picked up my phone and connected with you, too. If we'd have talked things out years ago…"

"What?" she interrupted. "We could've been together?"

I wiggled on the bench, wanting and needing to turn a bit more so I could look her fully in the face. She needed to hear what I was about to say. "If you'd have called, I'd have come running."

She scoffed and it sounded more like a ragged sob because she was still crying. "Right."

"No," I insisted, "I mean it. If you would've said you needed me, I'd have quit my job that day, packed up everything I owned, and moved down here. I could've…"

"That can't be true," she muttered thickly. "If it were so easy just to pick up and move, why didn't you do it before?"

"I didn't know you wanted me here," I returned.

She snorted. "So, you'd only have come because you thought I needed you."

"Yes," I answered honestly. "If the situation called for me to do the right thing, to stand steady, and be by your side, that's exactly what I would've done."

"But I wouldn't have wanted you to make that sacrifice," Missy murmured. "I couldn't ask you to just give up your life in Pittsburgh and your job so you could…"

"But I *wanted* to be with you," I growled, allowing myself to vent a bit of my frustrations. "That's what you keep forgetting. I asked you to marry me. I told you I loved you. I wanted to have a future with you."

There was a lengthy pause and I watched Missy fiddle with her long, spider-like fingers. She wore no adornments or jewelry this evening, but she toyed with her ring finger, as if there were an imaginary engagement ring there. "If what you just said was really the way you felt, why didn't you follow through?"

"Huh?"

"I just explained why I didn't call, but you…you could've checked in with me." She interlaced her fingers and clasped her hands together so tightly I could see tiny white marks in the places where her knuckles stretched. "It's been thirteen long years, Nathan, yet here you are, reappearing out of the blue, making one sweet overture after the other, but to what end?" She lifted her chin slowly and met my gaze unwaveringly.

I shook my head slowly. "You're reading more into our current situation than is necessary. Our whole issue stems from your refusal to take me seriously all those years ago. If you'd have accepted my proposal, we'd have figured out what to do. I'd have moved or…something. And we'd have made it work."

"No…no, no, no, no, no…" She mumbled the word repeatedly, adding emphasis to each bit by shaking her head gently. "We'd never have been able to make things work out because there was always something or *someone* who came between us. Whether it was friends, school, work, or indescribably alluring red-headed women…"

I was taken aback by the way she'd casually thrown Lana into the mix. I'd allowed myself to believe Missy had forgotten all about the way I'd cheated on her back in college a long time ago, but to hear her mention it now…as one of the reasons why we couldn't be together…well, that little insertion tore my heart into fragments.

"We're never going to get past all that if…"

My phone rang and the wretched feelings that had come over me a few minutes before intensified. I knew who was on the other end. I didn't need to pick up or check the caller ID. Only one person could come between me and Missy right now, so of course, that would be the very person who was giving me a buzz.

"Aren't you going to answer it?" Missy huffed as I allowed the second chiming of the ringer to go unchecked. When I said nothing, I saw a bit of fury flicker through her blue eyes, and they hardened. "This…*This* is what I was talking about, Nate." She exhaled an outraged puff of breath. "Another woman has come between us yet again." She paused and stared at me. "How can you keep doing this? How can you be so sweet and kind to me, all while keeping another woman dangling on the line?"

Chapter Twenty-Three

To Love is to Lose...or is it the Other Way Around?
Missy

I wanted some answers, so I sat there and waited for him to reply. While Nathan could be characterized as being charming, he'd never been roguish precisely because of this one fact... He was a terrible liar. When he messed up it was clear, from the look he wore on his face, that he knew he'd done something wrong. And while I didn't catch him in such a state often, and certainly not at all over the last thirteen years, I recognized the signs of evasion when they were right in front of me.

Nate fidgeted and tapped his pocket, as if he wanted to answer his phone, but knew that doing as much would lead to devastating repercussions. Moreover, the look in his eyes showed his remorse because we both knew he wanted to come up with a good way to answer my questions, but there was no response that would be honest, yet satisfying.

What was it Adair said... We're better when we're together?

I just couldn't see how she'd come to that conclusion. I loved Nathan Hamilton from the tips of my polished toenails to the topmost tendrils of my hair, and yet, when it came down to it, all we ever did was cause each other an immense amount of pain. I knew he wasn't to blame for my miscarriage or the subsequent surgeries and procedures that followed. But this...right now...sitting here without saying a word...this mayhem he'd created when he'd rushed into my studio on Monday morning was all his fault.

The phone sounded again and this time, perhaps because it was incessantly ringing without being answered, I felt the tone grating against my nerves. My eyes hadn't left Nathan's face, mostly because I was waiting for him to make a move and answer the call or, at the very least, try to respond to at least one of my questions, but he sat motionless, frozen into place.

"Do something," I grumbled, annoyed by his inactivity.

"I can't," he said, lifting his hand and allowing it to hover over his pocket. "I want to say the right thing, but..."

"You never say the right thing...remember?" Once more I was harkening back to his marriage proposal. On that day, he'd recognized his imperfections, laid them bare before me, and made it seem as though if I agreed to be his wife, he'd try to become a better man. But Nathan hadn't changed! My life had transformed since that day. Even our beloved Queen City had new alterations popping up around every corner, but Nathan was still the man I remembered…incapable of doing all that was necessary when the moment for action arrived.

"Missy, stop," he said softly. "Let me think through what to do next. I wanna say what you need to hear and…"

"Don't bother," I snapped, then leapt from the bench. Hurriedly, I jogged across the park, returning to the bike rack and swiftly securing myself a ride home. I didn't pay for his bicycle rental this time because I really didn't care what he did going forward.

He can sit on that bench all night if he wants…

Because I had to select a new, fully charged bike, and didn't have the luxury of hopping on the one I'd already adjusted to my height, it took a second to get moving. I fussed with the silver knobs, loosening the seat, and slapping it up and down, trying to get it aligned with my hip.

"Come on," I griped, tugging on the stubborn, sticking handle.

"Missy, wait," Nate said as he came upon me. He hadn't gone directly to the purchase kiosk but barreled straight in my direction. "You can't leave like this."

"Why not?" I challenged. "Haven't we already shared enough tonight?"

He shook his head sorrowfully, giving me a serious stare. "Not remotely."

"Well, what else do you want to know?" I exclaimed, throwing my hands up in defeat.

"It's not what I want to know," he said softly. "It's what I need to tell you."

"What could you possibly say right now to make things better?" I thundered. "These last three days you've been the one drawing me in, asking me on dates, inviting yourself along to Adair and Wesley's apartment so we could spend as much time together as possible." A dry sob escaped my throat, and I gritted my teeth, willing myself to not begin crying anew. "I…for just a moment, I thought I could trust you, so I told you about my past and I shared my story with you…letting you know…"

"I'm glad you told me," He whispered. "I needed to know what happened."

"Then why don't I get to know what's been happening in your life?" I felt an angry, heated sensation stir in my stomach and all the things I wanted to say just exploded right out of my mouth. "Do you know that Adair and Wes are working on a plan to get you to move to Charlotte? That's why Wes was so eager to talk to you about your work and the conference you're attending this week. He thinks there might be an open position at his company that'd be just right for you and…but you can't move here. What good would that do anyone? You'd just have to bring your wife along with you!"

His eyes widened in astonishment. "My wife?"

I shook my head dejectedly. "I should've known you were married, Nathan. I should've remembered how years ago, when we talked on the phone all the time, you'd be dating some girl semi-seriously, but you wouldn't bother to tell me about the relationship until it ended, or she moved in with you."

He made a low sound in the back of his throat. It displayed his displeasure at being reminded of his painful past relationships and unfortunate breakups. "I seem to recollect that you dated your fair share of men during those years, too. And you rarely told me about any of them."

"What was there to tell?" I was losing steam. All the outrage and annoyance were slowly draining away only to be replaced by steely resolution. "I was in love with you, so yeah…I didn't want to talk about the guys I was seeing in the meantime…the placeholders who never, not even once held a candle when compared to you." I sighed sullenly. "But that doesn't matter anymore. All that matters now is you've got a lady in your life, waiting for you to take her call. And…at least this time I know her name. I hope Jordan realizes just how lucky she is to have you."

Impulsively, I reached out and laid my hand gently on Nate's cheek. His eyes searched mine and I could see I'd confused him with my rambling thoughts, but I persevered, wanting to get to the end of this diatribe, so I could finally, really and truly, be done with Nathan Hamilton. "You may not be perfect, Nate. But you always tried, and I think that's what I love most about you."

He might've wished to respond, but who knows?

Not me.

As soon as I'd uttered Jordan's name, I was doomed. Just thinking of the faceless woman who kept calling Nate, waiting for him to answer the phone, hurt me in a way that I never would've dreamed possible.

I liked seeing Nathan again, and I loved spending time with him. But I'm older now and I should've known better than to let him manipulate my feelings.

Assured that I'd never make the same mistake thrice in my lifetime, I hopped on the eBike, and rode away, leaving Nate standing near the rack, staring after me.

Chapter Twenty-Four

Do You Need More Time to Process?
Nathan

"Hey, buddy," I said, returning Jordan's call. "I'm sorry I missed ya before, but..." I broke off so I could hear the excited yammering on the other end. When I was sure the call had been placed for the soul purpose of chattering exuberantly about his day, I quickly excused myself. "I've gotta run right now, but I'll try calling ya again before I turn in for the night." I took a few seconds to say goodbye and rent a bike of my own, but before a full two minutes had come and gone, I was trailing after Missy again, watching her weave her way through the people who were sauntering slowly down the sidewalk, enjoying the way the warm air wrapped around them like a cozy blanket.

I can't let her go...not like this...not without knowing the real story.

It stung to think that she'd managed to jump to so many inaccurate conclusions. And while she might not be thrilled to learn the truth, I'd promised myself, after my talk with Sean this afternoon, that I was going to tell her as much. I'd hesitated too long back on that park bench and missed the window of opportunity that presented itself, but now, I was determined to say my piece.

Missy wasn't speeding away at an unreasonable pace like she had been before, so I dared to think she wanted me to catch up with her. Even if she was irritated, I also knew she had a curious nature and probably wouldn't be able to sleep tonight without getting the answers I owed her.

When I rode to her side, she didn't stop pedaling, nor did she turn and acknowledge my presence, but I didn't take that as a bad sign. If she told me to go away, I'd feel inclined to oblige. But since she didn't dismiss me immediately, I reasoned that my summation had been correct. She wanted answers.

"Let's turn in here," I suggested, nodding at an elementary school parking lot. The place was empty, as it should be, considering we were getting close to the eight o'clock hour. The empty parking spaces were all painted in various shades of green, silver, and white, and I figured that must be the school's colors. Tiny little army men figures were painted onto some of the squares, and I came to understand that those represented the school's mascot.

Missy rode all the way to the front entrance of the school, dismounted, then walked her bike forward stuffing the front tire into the metal rack that was stationed there.

I was simply relieved that she was giving me this chance, so I did the same, then stood back and looked at her.

She'd put both hands on her hips and there was a faint scowl on her face, letting me know that the clock was ticking. She might've agreed to this short interlude, but she wouldn't stand around forever waiting for me to get my thoughts in order.

It's now or never.

I cleared my throat loudly, then began, "I'm not sure how you managed to misconstrue the situation so magnificently but..."

"So, this is my fault?" She waved a hand between the two of us and I could practically feel the agitated heat waves rolling off her body.

"No," I answered simply. "The reason we're standing here right now and you're as angry as I've ever seen you before is all my problem. But I hope you'll listen long enough to hear me out."

"Go on," she said, ladling a hefty dose of sarcasm on top of that phrase.

"Jordan isn't my wife," I stated calmly, gazing into her eyes, begging her not to snap at me or question what I was saying before I had the chance to get out the full explanation. "He's my son."

"Oh..." Missy's face fell. All the hostility that had been roiling there, just waiting to bubble over, evaporated in an instant. "*He's*...your kid?"

"Yeah," I said, smiling despite the seriousness of the situation, just because I was picturing the goofy laugh Jordan sometimes did when he was really tickled with himself. "He had a bit of good news come in yesterday and that's why he keeps calling. We've got a lot to figure out and since he just turned eighteen, he wants to be able to make some decisions on his own, but he knows he needs me to back him up so..." I stopped talking abruptly when Missy held up her hand.

"Wait," she breathed. "Did you say Jordan is eighteen?"

"Uh-huh..." I hummed, not able to produce much more. I could tell that she was doing mental math, but it didn't take a brainiac to arrive at the conclusion quickly. We were both thirty-eight years old. For me to have an eighteen-year-old kid, he'd have needed to be born around the time we were twenty. And that meant...

Missy got there in record time. "Lana," she rasped, before lifting her hand and clutching at her throat. "Jordan is...your...because you cheated...the two of you..."

I nodded and as I did, I knew that this revelation had produced exactly the outcome I'd feared. Missy now comprehended the depth of my secrets and instead of wanting to talk things through and figure out where to go from here, she was already pulling away.

Without uttering another word, she wrenched her bike out of the rack and took off, flying through the empty parking lot and racing away...far away from me.

This time, I didn't give chase. I knew she'd need to process the situation and if I went after her now, I could only make things worse.

But how could things get much worse?

The moment I heard her voice on the television, I'd felt a spark of hope leap into my heart. Missy and I had been deprived of being together for all these years and yet...I'd always imagined that we'd find our way back together. These last three days, there had been small blips, brief, shining moments in which that all seemed possible. But I think, in my heart of hearts, the reason I kept Jordan's identity a secret was because I knew how Missy would react.

She'll never be able to forgive me.

Chapter Twenty-Five

That Should be Easy Enough, Right?
Missy

I decided to forego riding back to the park in the center of town and instead opted to drop the bike rental at the kiosk nearest my apartment. Even though Hope and Eve had moved out ages ago, I'd never left Fountain Park. The three-bedroom place was much too big for little old me on most days. The spare rooms only got used when Eve and Savanna swung through town and needed a place to stay for the night, or Hopey and Skeeter brought the kids up for a weekend visit. But slinking back to my apartment, seeking solitude there, felt like the only way to move forward.

Just as I was mounting the steps and unlocking the door, my phone buzzed.

Please, Nate. No more.

But when I checked the caller ID, I saw a friendly picture accompanied by Jess Benson's name. She'd married a man with the surname Betancourt a long time ago, but I'd stuck to calling her Benson because that's what felt right.

"Hey," I answered while gliding into my home. It smelled of the vanilla scented lotion I'd used just before leaving that morning. "What's up?" I crossed the room, stopping only to kick off my sneakers and deposit my keys in the ceramic dish that was on the other side of the kitchen counter. Flicking on the light switch, I continued, "Everything okay?"

"I'm actually calling to check up on *you*," she replied. "The kids went to bed early tonight and Mike was exhausted so he hit the hay, too."

"Okay," I said slowly, "so why don't you want to turn in? I know your kids and your job have you running ragged all week long. Don't you need to get the extra sleep while you can?"

"Adair sent me a text," she explained. "I think she was tempted to notify all the girls using the group text, but..."

"This is *not* an emergency situation," I said before flopping onto the sofa.

"The way Adair made it sound, you got yourself into a spot of trouble."

"Oh…" I grumbled. "A spot of trouble doesn't even begin to cover it."

"So," she prompted, "I understand Nathan came back to town. Do you want to talk about it?"

"Are you sure you've got the time to spare?" I asked.

She sighed. "You know I wouldn't have called if I didn't. Go on," she urged. "Tell me what he did this time."

Benson had never liked Nathan. She'd dated one of his fraternity brothers back in school and when they had a messy breakup, Nathan hadn't exactly been understanding or even polite to her. He constantly took the side of his friend, even though he knew that was wrong, but it was important to him to stay loyal to his frat brother. Years ago, when Nate showed up as my date to Adair's wedding, Benson had cautioned me not to sleep with him, but I hadn't listened.

If only I'd taken her advice back then, I might've saved myself a lot of hassle in the long run.

So, I settled in and began unspooling all the most recent developments.

"How can there be so much?" Benson asked, after listening to my recitation. "The man has only been in town three days. How…"

"Wait," I cautioned, "I haven't even told you the biggest bombshell yet."

"Really?"

I inhaled deeply, then shared the information he'd just told me. "Because Jordan is eighteen that means he's not just Nate's kid, but Lana's too."

"Lana Alderman?" Benson squeaked. "Like the admissions counselor Nate cheated on you with that one time?"

I snorted. "Apparently."

"But…but how is that possible?" Benson asked. "Didn't they just hook up that one time? Didn't he swear it only happened once?"

"What difference does that make?" I returned. "It only takes one shot to make a baby."

"But…but…" she spluttered.

"I know," I agreed, "I'm flabbergasted, too."

There was a lengthy pause and I pictured Benson twirling a lock of her hair around her finger the way she always used to do when she was deep in thought. Finally, she said, "I guess it's possible that Nate's got an eighteen-year-old kid, but why didn't he tell you that right away? I mean, he didn't need to spill the beans in that first moment, when he rushed into the studio, but he could've mentioned something when the two of you went out to dinner that night. Didn't you say you gave him an opening? You prompted him to talk about what was happening in his life?"

"I knew he was holding back and keeping secrets, but I swear...never did I expect his secret to be this big." I paused, then spoke to life the fears that had set up shop in my mind while I'd been revisiting the details of the story, going over them again for my friend's benefit. "How long do you think he's known about Jordan? And why did he keep the fact that he had a son a secret all these years? Is it possible that he and Lana are married and...?"

I was spiraling out of control. I could feel my pulse accelerating, even though I was reclining on the sofa, doing little more than talking and sorting through my swirling thoughts.

"None of those things matter, do they?" Benson interjected, which sent my mind skittering in the opposite direction.

"What do you mean? You think having a kid, raising him all this time, and possibly being married is meaningless?" I asked incredulously. "We almost kissed, Benson, twice, and..."

"Stay away from him, Missy," she inserted, not waiting for me to reach the end of my sentence.

"What?"

"You know what I said, Miss," she replied. "The only way you're ever going to get over Nathan is if you cut yourself off, cold turkey."

"I...I don't know."

"What's there to know?" She retorted. "He hurt you...again. Everyone's entitled to their fair share of secrets, but this was a big one. And you gave him ample opportunities to tell you the truth." She paused and inhaled deeply. "Think of it this way...what if he is married to Lana or someone else? If you were his wife, how would you feel knowing that he's been cavorting around town with some other woman these last few days, reliving old memories, and coming oh so close to laying a smooch on her?"

I gasped.

"What?"

"I just remembered," I whispered. A pit in my stomach opened wide and the hollowness made me ache. "We didn't just *almost* kiss. Nate *did* kiss me."

Benson guffawed. "And yet you conveniently forgot about it? Must not've been much there."

"He did it twice…two quick pecks…right on the lips…or sort of on the lips…because he missed the mark the second time and…"

"Missy," Benson ordered, "come back to me. Don't allow yourself to get carried away by the cutesy things Nate did to gain your affection. For all you know, when he laid those kisses on you, he was cheating on his wife and…"

"Oh," I groaned. "This is awful. I feel awful."

"You have every right to feel this way," she said, softening her tone slightly. I recognized the voice she was using. It was one she reserved for her students, when they were being naughty or when she needed to remind them how best to be kind and share their toys with others. "But you also have the power to make things better."

"Better? How?"

"You know Nathan's only going to be in town for a few more days. And you know the hotel where he's staying. Until his flight leaves, all you've gotta do is steer clear of that side of town." She paused. "He doesn't know you still live in Fountain Park, does he?"

I shrugged. "I don't remember mentioning it, but I also didn't remember the couple of kisses he stole, so…"

"Don't go doubting your memory," Benson interrupted. "You forgot that he kissed you because those simple pecks meant very little. You were in love with Nathan for a long time, but you got over him—years ago. And it's likely he stopped loving you way back when, too. These last few days, it might've been fun to feel that old spark reignite, but really…really, where did you think this flirtation was going? Were you hoping Nate would ask you to marry him again? Were you thinking the two of you would sleep together? Or…were you sure this would be it…you'd finally get the chance to put all this nonsense to bed?"

"Honestly," I mumbled, "I don't know what I was thinking. I knew Nate was keeping secrets, but I had my own too and then…"

"It doesn't matter," she said softly. "All that happened this week is now firmly in the past. And you have the power to leave it there."

"I know." I sat up straight, hoping that by changing positions, I'd be able to dismiss the ache that was causing my stomach to cramp and twist uncomfortably.

"So…for the next few days, you simply stay away from Nate. If he calls, you don't answer. If he sends a text, you ghost him. Just pretend as if he doesn't exist anymore." She paused before adding, "That should be easy enough, right?"

The way Benson said it she made everything seem so black and white. Stay away from Nathan. Allow this moment to be the last ever spent worrying over my relationship with him. But the reality was much harder to bear. Because if this was my last instance thinking of Nathan Hamilton, I wanted my remembrance of him to be a good one, not one tainted by lies and deceit.

If this was really it for us, I wanted to be able to see him smile, hear his voice, and give him one last hug before saying goodbye. If I was truly seeking closure, that's what I needed—not to abandon him in a fit of anger, but to wish him well, and to bid him adieu on my own terms.

Chapter Twenty-Six

What Did You Do This Time?
Nathan

Because I had no desire to chase after Missy and my legs were feeling gelatinous from fatigue, I crumpled into an ungainly heap right there in the middle of the elementary school's sidewalk. I knew there could possibly be some fees associated with returning the bike late, but I didn't care much about paying a few extra dollars. For now, all I could think of was how one blunder after another had piled up until I was stuck here, in Charlotte, wishing I could be with Missy, but no closer to making that dream a reality than I'd been when I was back home in Pittsburgh.

I work out regularly at the gym, running on the treadmill, lifting free weights and such, but I'm not much for doing flexibility training. So, sitting on the hard pavement wasn't exactly an easy feat. Clumsily, I tried to slide into criss cross applesauce pose, but my legs screamed in agony when I tried to tuck one over the other. I shifted to my knees, but that seemed counterproductive as I was no longer in a resting position. Finally, I scooted forward so that my feet dangled over the curb, and I was able to bend my knees in what could be called a semi-normal position. Just then, my phone rang.

"What are you doing?" Jordan asked, chuckling at some private joke he thought he was making.

"Trying to get comfortable," I replied.

"Huh?"

"Nothing." I waved away the thought. "What's up, Kid?"

"You said you'd call me back, but I still hadn't heard anything from you, so I started to get worried."

"Hey," I grumbled, wiping some errant pebbles off the backside of my mesh shorts. "I'm the parent here. You're not supposed to be worried about me. You've got things backwards."

"Maybe I wouldn't worry so much if you called me back when you said you would."

"Fair point." I didn't get into debates like this with Jordan, mostly because he'd always win. He was a bright student and excelled in communications classes like speech and theatre, so I rarely challenged him to any kind of verbal sparring contest. "So...now that you've got me, what can I do for ya?"

"You sure I'm not interrupting anything, Dad?" He lowered his voice a little before adding, "Is Missy there with you? Is that why you didn't call before?"

There are various schools of thought when it comes to raising children. Some people keep their kids at arm's length, pretending never to have any adult issues of their own and putting on shiny, happy faces for the sake of keeping their children gleeful and protected from the real world. But Lana and I weren't those sorts of parents.

We'd raised Jordan by embracing total and complete honesty. He knew that his mom and I didn't always see eye-to-eye and he understood, because I'd told him, that I was excited to see my old flame, Missy Lawrence, when I got back to town. My son and I weren't bosom buddies, and I didn't share every last detail with him, but he knew enough to understand that I'd been with Missy these last few days and that's why I'd been difficult to reach by phone.

I blew out a tremendously weary sigh. "Missy's long gone, Buddy."

"Oh no," he said softly, "What'd you do now?"

"What did *I* do?" I retorted. "What makes you think I did something wrong?"

Jordan snickered. "Do you really need me to answer that, Dad?"

In short order, I filled Jordan in on the conversation I'd just had with Missy. I held back the part about her being upset because he, my kid, was the product of a one-night stand, but he's a smart fella, and I think he got the gist anyway. When I was done, he said slowly, "So...how does this impact our grand plan?"

"I don't know."

"Come on, Dad," he cajoled. "We need to talk about this. If I hadn't gotten into UNC-Charlotte, maybe we could just ignore the whole thing, but now that I'm gonna be living there..."

"I know I said I'd move with you, but..."

"Dad," he whined a little, "you can't let this disagreement with Missy ruin everything."

I shook my head, then lowered my chin and stared at my sneakers. I felt like a pitiful excuse for a father, laying all my burdens at my son's feet, and altering plans with him just because I botched my romance with Missy, but I didn't know what else to do. "It won't ruin *everything*," I murmured. "This new development will just change things. I'm so proud of you for getting your acceptance letter. I was sure they'd let you in, because you're a legacy and all, but college admissions can be competitive and…"

"Yeah," Jordan snorted. "You don't need to remind me. Right up until I got that email yesterday, Mom kept repeating that same phrase as if it was some sort of mantra."

"Hey," I said, "you can't blame your mom for that. She's an admission's counselor, so she knows how difficult it is to get into the school of your choice nowadays. And she's your mom. She's allowed to fret and fuss a little."

"Right," he said, stretching the word out long like it was one of those gooey gummy worms he liked eating so much just after he got home from school. "So, since your plans to get back together with Missy fell through, where does that leave us? Are you still gonna try and get a new job in Charlotte? And, when I move to campus, are you going to…?"

"Woah, Buddy," I said, putting a quick stop to his torrent of questions. "Let's not make any hard or fast decisions here."

"But we already made the decision," Jordan countered. "Months ago. When I sent in that application, you said if I moved then you'd go with me. Is that not happening now?"

My muscles felt sore, and my head ached from doing so much serious thinking. I tipped my head back, hoping to massage those aching neck muscles, but wound-up staring at the full moon instead. It was small tonight, only a tad bit bigger than an opalescent pearl. But there was a fine ring, an aura, surrounding it, casting a silvery glow in every which direction.

"Dad? You still there?"

"Yeah, Kid," I murmured. "I'm still with ya."

"Well," he prompted, "what do you think? Are you gonna make some appointments and take a few job interviews over the next couple of days or…"

"Why do we have to decide everything right now?" I asked.

Jordan scoffed. "This isn't just some spur of the moment thing, Dad. We've been talking about doing this for months. That's why the timing's so perfect. I got my letter. You're already in town. Bingo! It's time to make a move."

I lowered my head and stared at the bike that I knew I still needed to pedal back to town. The task loomed before me, creating just one more issue I didn't want to have to handle at present. "I'll talk to a few fellas during the convention tomorrow," I assured him. "I can't guarantee I'll come home with a job offer, but…" My words petered out as I remembered something Missy had said what seemed like eons ago. Wes and Adair wanted me to stay in Charlotte. Wes was prepared to set me up with a job at his company if I was interested.

But am I still interested?

It was one thing to move to town with Jordan when I thought I might have a chance at starting things up with Missy again, but why had I ever dared to dream something like that in the first place? When I came up with this brainy scheme, I hadn't spoken to Missy in years. For all I knew, she could've been married and settled with children of her own. I might've run to the studio that day only to find out that I had no possibility of even having dinner with her, because after work, she needed to rush right home to her family.

So…why had I ever allowed myself to believe otherwise?

I'm not an eternal optimist. As a scientist, I tend to view things realistically, just as they are. But when it came to concocting this dream with my son, building this vision of a future I might have with him and Missy here in Charlotte, I'd really let myself get carried away. And now, in the span of one evening, I'd messed up everything.

"You know what you've gotta do, don't ya, Dad?"

"Huh?" He'd startled me out of my deep thoughts.

"Talk to Missy. Straighten things out with her."

"That's not likely to happen, Buddy."

"Of course it's not," he said, "unless you pick yourself up, say you're sorry, and beg her to forgive you."

"But…"

"But nothing, Dad," he returned smartly. "I know that I can go to college on my own, and I guess, in a lot of ways, I'm sort of looking forward to it. But I also kind of liked the idea of having you stay close. When you mentioned trying to get back together with Missy, I thought that was some sort of pipe dream…something a middle-aged guy might try to do…"

"Hey," I interrupted, wounded by his words. "I'm not middle-aged yet."

"Okay," Jordan said, absorbing that fact quickly before continuing with his own thoughts. "So, you're not middle-aged, but you are searching for something. I know you like your job, but you don't love it. And I saw how happy you were when you were packing to go on this trip. Just thinkin' about being with Missy brought out something I've never seen in you before. Don't you want to be with her? Can't you just apologize and swear you'll never hurt her again?"

I chuckled mirthlessly. "When'd you get to be such a smart kid?"

"I watch a lot of TV," he replied dryly.

"No, really," I pressed, "how do you know exactly what I ought to do when I can't even wrap my own head around all the mistakes I've made?"

"I'm not thinking about your mistakes, Dad. I'm focusing on the remedy. And maybe, if you did the same, everything would become clearer."

Chapter Twenty-Seven

Aren't You the Least Bit Curious?
Missy

"That's all the time we've got for today folks," Steve said, leading us into the final moments of our news program. "A big thank you to our special guests, County Commissioner Phillip Dylan and folk singer, Cora Collins."

"And now we need to say goodbye." I paused for dramatic effect. "But before you leave…let's take a moment to breathe." I stopped a second time and made a big production of closing my eyes and taking a long, deep inhalation. Then, my eyelids fluttered back open, and I continued smiling at the members of our live studio audience. "I'm Missy Lawrence."

"And I'm Steve Martin," he added.

Then, together, we said in our most gung-ho voices, "Now, go get that day, Charlotte."

We both held the pose for a few seconds, and I waited for one of the production assistants, Edward, to give us the cue signalling we were free to move.

Steve performed his go-to post-show maneuver by shuffling a stack of papers. Normally, I'd talk idly with him, commenting on the show already or asking if he noticed the way the audience reacted to a particular segment, but I was distracted today, so I did none of those things.

Even though the eight o'clock hour had just struck, my watch had vibrated three times throughout the course of the taping, and I knew the only person who would even think of trying to get ahold of me while I was actively working would be Nathan. I'd wondered if he'd try to call last night, but when nothing happened, I'd gone to sleep and told myself to just forget about it. But now, I felt like the messages were burning a hole straight through my watch, stinging my wrist, and making it impossible for me to ignore them. But I persevered.

I stood and started to walk off the set, only to hear Steve call, "Where're you going? Don't you wanna give Edward your mic?"

Shaking my head, attempting to clear away the thoughts that were tumbling through there, I unclipped my microphone and held it out to the production assistant. That's when Steve strode to my side and grabbed hold of my elbow.

"Who called?" he asked, giving me a calm, speculative stare.

"How do you know…?"

"I saw your watch illuminate during our conversation with Commissioner Dylan and then, while Cora was singing you actually looked down to check the scrolling words yourself. So…I ask again? Who was calling you? Was it Nathan?"

I winced. "I don't know. But I'm sorry I did that. I hope Cora didn't catch me in the act."

Steve shrugged. "She probably wouldn't mind if you did check your watch. She's a performer. I'm sure she's had people do worse things during her shows."

"Yeah, but I'm the host and I'm supposed to be…"

"Are you trying to change the subject?" Steve asked, letting go of my arm and adjusting his paisley green and pink tie.

"Not working, huh?"

"Not even close," he said crisply, before crossing his arms over his chest and giving me his best inquisitive stare. "Adair told me she thought things might've gone sideways with the two of you, but I honestly thought that was a bit of innuendo."

I snickered. "Yeah, that does seem like something she might say."

"But I can see now that she was already prepping for disaster." He tapped the toe of his shiny brown leather dress shoes impatiently. "So, what happened? Why is he calling when he knows perfectly well that you're in the middle of recording a live show?"

"I really don't know," I answered, pulling my phone out of the pocket of my blazer, then holding it up so Steve could see the missed messages. Sure enough, Nathan's name was there, but when I saw it, my stomach performed an odd, acrobatic routine, making me feel nauseated. "And you know what? I'm not sure I want to find out."

Acting quickly, I unlocked the screen, then without listening to the two voicemails or reading the text messages, I deleted the whole chain.

Steve gasped. "Why'd you do that?"

"I told you," I returned, dropping the phone back into my pocket. "I'm not sure I want to know what he had to say."

"That's insane," Steve said, then he held up his hand and made a stop sign. "No…scratch that. It's not insane, but it's so out of character for you. How can you just pretend like you don't want to know everything he has to say? Isn't it killing you to think that…"

"Come here." I grabbed ahold of his sleeve and jerked him toward the dressing room we shared. It was little more than a broom closet, but Steve and I were grateful Adair had managed to make the space for us at all in her already cramped office building. Furthermore, having this empty space all to ourselves seemed just right, now that I needed and wanted to keep our conversation hush-hush.

"Why are you dragging me in here?" Steve protested. "What's going on with you?"

Once I had the door firmly closed behind us and Steve had settled into his chair, I plopped down on my own, then shared what I was thinking. "I can't listen to those voicemails, because if I hear Nate's voice again, I might just cave."

"Cave?" Steve pressed. "In what way?"

"Going out with Nathan over these last few days was a mistake, one I don't intend to make again. But if I answer his text or listen to his voicemails, then I might be enticed to call him, and I don't want to do any of that."

Steve pouted. "Why not?"

Succinctly, I told my friend all about Nate's deception and the existence of his eighteen-year-old son, Jordan. When I concluded my tale, Steve let out a low, appreciative whistle.

"There's so much to unpack here," he said quietly.

"Yeah," I muttered. "Tell me about it."

"All right." As if I'd just given him an invitation to go rooting around in my personal life, Steve plunged right in by saying, "I'm not sure why you're so upset, Miss."

"What?" I was shocked.

"I mean it," he returned. "I know that learning about Jordan had to be difficult, but what about all those other conjectures you made?"

"What conjectures?" I countered.

Steve tipped his head to the side thoughtfully. "Well, you probably did the math right concerning the whole Jordan's birth mother thing. We can assume Nathan only cheated on you with one woman while you were together, so…"

"Oh, thanks very much," I said snidely. "I hadn't even bothered to contemplate whether there was a third woman involved in our little romantic math equation but now…"

"Don't go spinning your wheels in that direction," Steve cautioned. "I only mentioned it because I wanted to point out how you made a wild leap when determining that Nate was married to this Lana woman. You don't know that he's married, do you?"

"No," I said slowly.

"You and I know lots of people who are divorced or are single and just happen to be raising kids on their own. So, why did you automatically assume that Nathan was married to Jordan's mother?"

"I'm not sure," I answered honestly. "It's just... I think because I originally mistook Jordan's name popping up on his caller ID as an indication that he was dating someone else or married. So, I sort of continued running with that theme."

"That means when Nate kissed you the other night, you don't know for certain that he was cheating. He might really have wanted to..."

"It doesn't matter," I interceded. "Now that I know Jordan is out there, I'll never be able to forgive Nathan for..."

"Forgive him?" Steve interrupted. "What's there to forgive? I thought you'd forgiven Nathan a long time ago for his infidelity. Years after he cheated on you, the two of you remained friends. He even came here to be your wedding date and..."

All my walls crumbled at his words. "You're right," I whimpered, gazing at him through my hot tears. "This isn't about forgiveness. It's about knowing that someone else...Lana...was able to give Nathan all the things I wanted to, but just can't. I'll never be able to have a family with him and she...she...can. She did."

"Shhh..." Steve got to his feet and surged forward, wrapping me in a comforting bear hug. "You can't think like that. You can't put yourself through that kind of torture."

"Why not?" I moaned. "He...he...he...wanted..."

"Why is it so important that you give Nathan a bunch of children? Tom and I don't have kids and we're still able to live full and happy lives. And Adair and Wes never had a whole gaggle of children, either, but you don't hear either of them complaining. They're just as much in love now as they were the day they got married and never once have I heard Adair say the life that they have together is anything less than fabulous. So, why are you so caught up in this idea? Did *you* really want to have kids, Missy?"

"I did," I admitted, "once. I thought the idea was nice, in a sort of far off in the future sense. It was something I wanted, but it wasn't the *only thing* I ever wanted, ya know?" Steve's slender shoulders moved up and down, letting me know he understood. "But we're not really talking about me, are we? You wanna know why it was so important for me to have children with Nate and the answer is simple…that's what *he* wanted. While I figured it might happen someday, he had big plans. He wanted dozens of kids…or at least six of them."

Steve scoffed and I snuggled further into the hug we were sharing. "Maybe Nate changed his mind. Maybe, after having one kid, Jordan, he doesn't want a bunch of others."

I laughed, despite the fact that tears were still streaking down my face. "What? Are you saying Jordan was such a problem child he made Nathan glad there was only one of him?"

Steve stepped back a pace so I could look up into his face. His expression still showed his concern for me. "I'm saying I don't know Jordan or Nathan, but it seems to me that this is some sloppy reporting you're doing here, Lawrence."

"What?" I snapped.

He nodded his head sharply. "If you were running down a lead or prepping a package for an upcoming segment, would you just start drafting conclusions before you had all the details? Would you cut an interview short simply because you didn't feel like listening to the other person talk anymore?" He didn't give me a chance to answer, but instead barreled ahead with his own ideas. "I know you'd never put up with such shotty workmanship in your professional life, so I hate to see you do as much when it comes to your personal affairs."

Just then, my phone vibrated, and I clamped my hand over my pocket.

Steve's eyes widened. "Read the text," he encouraged. When I hesitated, he continued, "You don't know what he's been writing to you all morning and you have no idea what's been happening in his life these last few years. But don't you want to find out? Aren't you the least bit curious to know how Nate's life has changed, what he's learned from all those experiences, and what it is he wants right now?"

For about a half hour last night, when I was really steamed at Nathan, I'd considered the ways in which he hadn't changed at all. He was slow to make decisions and preferred to say everything in his head at least once before speaking it aloud. And that kind of failure to communicate properly irritated me. But that was all before I knew about Jordan. Now that I understood Nathan had a son, I saw how things had to have changed for him. Whether he found out about his kid eighteen years ago or met him just last week, Nate's life had rocked sideways, and he'd had to scramble to stay afloat.

"Yeah," I breathed, pulling the phone from my pocket. "You're right. I *am* a little curious."

Chapter Twenty-Eight

How am I Supposed to Overcome Something like That?
Nathan

"Put your phone away, man," Sean said quietly, coming up to my side and nudging me a little with the tip of his elbow. "Unless you're sending messages back and forth with someone at work or you're setting up appointments to meet again later with a few of these vendors, you're supposed to be focused on what's happening here…not fiddling with your phone."

"I know," I grumbled, after hitting the send button, and dropping the phone into my pocket. "And I'm sorry I've been out of it this morning but…"

"Things didn't go so well with Missy last night I take it?"

Sean nodded at the nearest booth. We were at a vendor fair this morning, wandering through the aisles, stopping occasionally to talk with salespeople we recognized, learn about the newest product lines that were available, or ask about price points for those products we were considering stocking from new companies. And Sean was right on both counts. While I was supposed to be committed to this part of the conference, doing my best to get Morgan and Fosters the equipment they needed at a reasonable price from vendors who were trustworthy, I was lost in thought, not just considering all that had gone wrong with Missy, but weighing my son's words as well, wondering exactly what I could do, if anything, to make things right again.

But maybe the right situation flew the coop a long time ago.

"Nate," Sean said my name quietly, giving me another stealthy jab with his elbow. "Can you get it together, please?"

I nodded and for the next ten minutes we proceeded to have a pleasant enough conversation with a couple of people who were representing DaLabel Company. We regularly placed large orders with this firm, and they supplied us with most of our paper products and sticky labels. Recently, Sean had noticed that we might be able to get a better price point on a few of the items if we came to them with some numbers from other companies and did a bit of haggling, so I stood by his side, providing moral support, while he negotiated the best deal. When he was satisfied, I said goodbye to the salespeople, then crossed the aisle, thinking we ought to at least look at the booth for Beaker

Bros. who purported to make the best, nearly unbreakable beakers in the business. I'd just leaned forward to get a better glimpse of the product when Sean cleared his throat and said, "Excuse us. We'll be right back."

I smiled courteously at the team members representing Beaker Bros. then followed my colleague to the refreshment table that was in the far back of the convention hall.

"Are you just really thirsty," I asked, racing to catch up with him, "or do you know some reason why we should've stayed far away from the Beaker Bros. booth?"

"The Beaker Who…?" Sean pulled to a stop right in front of the tray that was lined with cookies. He plucked two from the lot using a tiny pair of tongues and handed me one. "Here," he said, "eat this. Maybe it'll make you feel better."

I eyed the chocolate chip cookie closely. It looked all right but I wasn't hungry, so I didn't feel like stuffing it in my mouth. "No thanks," I said, putting my hand out to stop him from continually shoving it at me. "You eat it."

"I'm not the one wearing a sour puss," Sean said while taking a big bite out of the cookie he'd just been offering me. "You may not want to be the point man for any of these deals, Nate, but…"

"Hey," I interrupted, "I was the one taking the lead on the Beaker Bros. negotiation. I was just about to engage with them when you pulled me away."

"Sure," Sean snorted, chomping off another bit of cookie, letting the crumbs fall to the floor. He chewed slowly, then continued, "The way I see it, we've got two choices. I can either let this day go on as is, with you sulking about, checking your phone every few minutes or I can just come on out and ask you for the details." His tone softened as he added, "We've been friends for a long time, Nate, and I hate to see you so upset. If you wanna talk through what's going on, I'm here to listen." He quickly reverted to his normal self when he rolled his wrist over, checked his watch and announced, "But if you want my full attention, you'd better make it snappy. They'll be laying out the lunch spread in an hour and a half, and I need to see quite a few of these vendors before then."

"Well," I said pausing a little so I could decide how best to begin, "You've already surmised that Missy didn't take the news about Jordan so well."

"She yell at you? Call you a bunch of lousy names?"

"No…nothing like that," I replied. "But I could tell she was hurt. Mostly, I spent half the night chasing her down on a rented bicycle and when we finally did talk, there was so much ground to cover that it left us both feeling exhausted."

"You said half the night," Sean pointed out. "What happened during the other half?"

"After Missy left me, I spent some time talking to Jordan and…"

"Man," Sean interjected, "You shouldn't be gettin' your kid involved in all this. I know you and Jordan are buddy-buddy, but there's just some things about a parent's life a kid ain't supposed to know."

I nodded. "You're probably right, but what was I supposed to do? He asked me expressly about Missy and…"

"Yeah, yeah, yeah." Sean waved his hand impatiently. "Get on with it. What did Jordan have to say?"

I hesitated. While Jordan and I had come up with this fun little scheme to move to Charlotte in a few months, after he received his acceptance from the local university, I hadn't shared any of this information with my colleagues. Even though I trusted Sean and we were friends, I didn't want to float it out there that I might be leaving soon or that I was planning to do a little job hunting while in town. If things didn't pan out and Jordan didn't get his acceptance letter, I'd have ruffled some feathers all for naught. But now…it almost seemed necessary to share this part of my story with Sean.

When I did just that, my friend reacted in a completely unexpected way. He snorted, nodded, then, said, "Jordan'll get over it."

"Huh?"

"The kid might be disappointed at first to find out that he's gotta make a big move like that all on his own, but didn't you kind of do the same thing?" I stared at him until he elaborated. "Right after you graduated from UNC-Charlotte, you moved to Pittsburgh. He's doing something similar—only in reverse."

"Yeah," I agreed slowly. "I guess you've got a point there."

"Jordan's young still. He'll probably be grateful not to have his old man hanging around all the time, anyway. If you were here, you'd only cramp his style."

"I'm not that old," I grumbled, lifting my free hand, and using the tip of my finger to stroke the part of my sideburns where I knew a few gray hairs had cropped up as of late.

"You're not," Sean said flatly, "but you're too old to be hanging around a college campus, waiting to spend time with your son when he's not at classes or chasing a bunch of skirts." He paused and took a bite of the second chocolate chip cookie. "If I'm not mistaken, your boy will soon forget all about this crazy little scheme the two of you cooked up one night. He'll be so focused on getting his things ready for the dorms and making some last-minute cash at his job over the summer that he won't spare a thought for you or the fact that you've messed up this dream of tagging along after him."

"Maybe," I said softly. "Maybe everything you said will turn out to be a hundred percent accurate. Maybe Jordan will rebound and..."

"But what about you?" Sean interjected. "Did *you* want to make this move?"

"I...I thought I did."

Sean grunted while chewing another small bite of his cookie. "Judging by the way you ditched me these last three nights so you could spend all your time with Missy, I'm guessing the two of you were well on your way to rekindling your romance. And Nate...I'm glad for ya, brother. After all you've been through with Lana and Jordan these last few years, you deserve a bit of happiness."

I curled my hand into a tight fist, thinking of how close we'd come. "There were times this week when I thought or rather, I hoped that I might get the chance to start something up again with Missy, but now..." I unclenched my fingers and gestured lamely to the phone that sat silent in my pocket. "She won't even take my calls."

"That's tough," Sean said, nodding knowingly. "Maybe she just needs a little more time to come to grips with things. You did tell her about Jordan and that news must've rocked her world. She could've been having strong feelings for you too but decided to back away for a minute just so she can catch her breath."

Flashes of images from this week fluttered through my mind. Every time Missy and I had relaxed and simply enjoyed being with each other, something had gone awry. Either I said the wrong thing, or she pulled away to preserve the secrets we were both carrying. I thought of the way she'd poured her heart out to me last night, talking about the miscarriage and all that came afterward. She'd spent all this time mourning not just the loss of our friendship, but also believing that I wouldn't want her if we couldn't have the perfect little nuclear family.

She was wrong...so wrong.

"I've got to tell her."

"Tell her what?" Sean asked.

I'd gotten so carried away reliving my memories that I'd forgotten how we were supposed to be having a serious conversation. I drifted back to the present and said, "Missy won't agree to talk to me. She won't give me a chance to explain. What am I supposed to do? How am I supposed to overcome an obstacle like that?"

"You'll think of something," Sean said, giving his shoulders a gentle shrug. "It may take you a minute to get there, but if you don't want to give up on this relationship, then the way I see it, it's far from being over."

Chapter Twenty-Nine

Don't You Wanna Know?
Missy

Silence hung in the air the way the first taste of hot cocoa lingers on the lips. It wasn't exactly unpleasant, producing only a slight sting, but it also was kind of inviting, filling the room with the promise of contentment.

The trouble was that I knew Steve wasn't going to let me bask in this quietude. He'd just prompted me to pick up the phone, to look at the text, to do something other than wipe away all memory of my most recent interactions with Nate. I stood there, in the cramped dressing room, gazing at the flat blackness of my phone screen, stretching the moment, wanting to make it last longer.

When Steve finally spoke again, his words were rather unexpected. "Tell me about Nate."

I dropped my phone on the closest countertop where our makeup artist, Filene, kept all her accoutrements, brushes, and sponges neatly aligned.

I sighed. "You already know all about him. I've probably mentioned him hundreds of times in these last three days alone and…"

"Tell me about the first time the two of you met," Steve prompted. "I don't think I've ever heard that story. Was it love at first sight or were you friends first?"

A sad smile tugged at the corners of my lips. "Friends first…for sure."

"Naturally," Steve murmured. He was still giving me his best investigative reporter stare and I knew he was exercising a well-used tactic—making it appear as if he were changing the subject, when he was just redirecting by getting me to talk about an idea that was adjacent to the original. Steve's little trick worked because with far less apprehension than I'd been exhibiting before, I launched into the recollection.

"We met shortly after we finished pledging our respective fraternity and sorority. The two were connected, as brothers and sisters, so I guess you could say my group hung out with his and so on."

"Uh-huh," Steve mumbled, which was just enough to prompt me to continue.

"I think I've told you before, but my friend, Jess Benson, dated one of Nate's friends for a long time."

"Yeah," he said, bobbing his head pensively, "you said she and her boyfriend were on and off for like three years."

I groaned. "They were constantly torturing each other. Breaking up. Making up. Having screaming matches in the middle of the frat house. They were just one massive train wreck…"

"But it was because of them that you met Nate?"

"Right," I agreed, allowing him to yank me away from my digression. "It was the simplest interaction, but it made such an impact on me. A bunch of us went over to the frat house one day. There wasn't a party—not a real party, anyway. We were only supposed to be hanging out on a Thursday night. Some of the new pledges, like Benson's boyfriend, were there and when he got around to introducing his frat brothers, there was Nathan." A dreamy sigh escaped my lips and I laughed because I hadn't expected to have quite that reaction, after all this time, especially in light of how I was currently feeling about my paramour. And yet…there it was. When I thought or talked about our first meeting, I still got goosebumps—in a good way.

"Anyway," Steve urged.

"Okay," I said, shimmying my shoulders a little to shake off the cloak of memories. I plowed ahead with the story. "So, Benson's boyfriend is introducing everybody, and Nate stands up. He walks down the line, giving everyone a great big hug and…"

"Was he intoxicated?" Steve interrupted.

"No."

"Huh," he mumbled. "If he'd already had a couple of beers, I guess I could picture a guy scooting down this line of ladies, hugging them close, but otherwise that just seems sort of creepy."

"It wasn't creepy," I insisted, suddenly ready to defend his actions. "It was…sweet."

Steve rolled his eyes. "If you say so."

"I do," I retorted, lifting my chin defiantly.

"Proceed," Steve ordered, waving his hand through the air, motioning for me to continue.

"So, Nate's walking around, hugging each of us and when he got to me, he just…" My words escaped me. I knew how I felt the first time he wrapped his arms around me, but I couldn't reproduce the sensation. Describing all the things that happened in just those briefest of seconds seemed to be an impossible task.

"What?" Steve questioned. "Did he pinch your bum or something?"

I snickered and was a little grateful to my buddy for making a joke because I'd become so lost in thought that I'd nearly forgotten the thread of my story. "No," I answered, still laughing dryly. "When Nate put his arms around me and towed me in for a hug, I felt safe and…protected."

"Were you uncomfortable before that?"

"Huh?"

Steve uncrossed his arms and pressed them to his sides, then pantomimed the reactions as he said them. "Were you nervous about being in the frat house and meeting new people?" He appeared to be quaking in his boots. "Or were you annoyed with Benson's boyfriend because they'd only recently gotten back together?" He balled his hands into fists, then scowled menacingly. I laughed at Steve's antics.

"I don't remember what I was feeling before Nate gave me that hug, but when I stepped into his embrace, really leaned in, I realized I never wanted him to let me go." I paused and tipped my head to the side, turning my own discerning stare on my friend. "So…I guess maybe it was love at first…hug." I paused before asking, "Haven't you ever felt that way? I mean, when you and Tom first met, didn't you know right away he was the one for you?"

"Yeah," Steve snorted. "I had one of those amazing moments with Tom. I knew we were meant to be together, but I was attracted to him because he made me laugh and…" He snickered and his grin broadened marginally. "We both can agree fully that Tom has the best laugh in the whole world."

"True," I conceded. "Tom does have the best laugh. But Nate…I guess you could say he was the best hugger."

Steve wrinkled his nose. "Is that a thing?"

"I don't know," I chuckled. "But at the time, when I was close to him, feeling all snug and cherished, I…" He made an odd choking sound, like he'd been about to say something, but stopped himself, so the noise he produced was more like a strangled cough than anything else. "What?"

"It's just you're making this moment seem so precious."

"It was," I replied earnestly.

"Not possible," Steve countered. "The man...or really, at that point, he was so young he was still just a boy...all he did was give you a hug. How can you count that as one of your cherished memories?"

I considered my response before giving it but found that the words which floated to the forefront of my mind were still insufficient to do our interaction any sort of justice. "I don't know," I said at last. "I guess I just do. Even after all these years, when I think back on that moment, that one simple hug, I realize that something special was happening."

"Show me," Steve said stepping forward and holding his arms out, beckoning me into an embrace.

"You want me to...hug you?"

"Yep," he confirmed. "Show me what Nathan did that day so I can understand why you've spent the latter part of your life pining for him."

"All right," I said, slowly advancing toward him, "but I'm probably going to do this wrong. I'm warning you right now that nobody gives a hug like Nate and so..." I captured Steve in a massive bear hug, swinging my arms around his neck and pulling him toward me.

"Yikes," Steve grumbled. "Either you're not very good at this or your memory has been deceiving you all these years." I tightened my grip on him, trying to snuggle in, pressing him close, just the way Nathan always did. "*Ahk...*" Steve squawked. "I feel like you're trying to strangle me."

I relinquished the hold I had on my pal and stepped back. "I warned you," I reminded him. "What Nate did that day, when he held me in his arms..."

"Does he still make you feel that way?" Steve slid that question at me so quickly that had I not been paying attention I might have given a glib answer.

But I was following his train of thought and did take my time before responding.

"Sometimes," I admitted honestly. "There are moments, like when our hands met in the elevator, and I felt an electric current fly up the whole length of my arm, when I think there's still something special about our relationship."

"But other times?" Steve pressed.

"Other times, I get so angry with him that I want to spit nails," I answered heatedly.

Steve snorted. "You know they say there's a very thin line between love and hate."

"I don't hate Nathan." I ducked my head and gazed fixedly at a spot on the carpet. Our dressing room was neat and tidy, but somehow, this little speck of fuzz or maybe it was fluff floated there. It seemed so out of place and yet there it was, drifting along, doing its own thing without a care in the world.

"But you won't take his calls," Steve said gently. "And I just watched you delete his text messages without giving them even a cursory glance. Those actions imply that you do, in fact, loathe him."

"No," I retorted. "My actions indicate that I'm upset and angry with him. I'm pretty sure there's a big difference there."

Steve shook his head forcefully, allowing the long ends of his hair to rustle against the stiff collar of his dress shirt. "You're missing my point."

"Yeah?"

"What I'm trying to make you see, Miss, is that by deleting those texts, wiping them away completely, you're doing yourself and Nate a disservice. You fell in love with the man before the two of you even had a legit conversation. All he had to do was touch you and what? Twenty years later, you still can't escape the memory of that one embrace?"

My knees buckled and suddenly I felt sick to my stomach. All the words my buddy just spoke had a ring of truth about them and it made me feel weak and slightly ill to think that I'd let so much of my life be controlled by that one moment from so long ago. I hadn't eaten anything for breakfast this morning, so when my stomach flip-flopped, the motion was accompanied by an uneasy gurgle.

Steve didn't seem to notice the sound, probably because he was so focused on driving home his point. "The thing is…"

"The thing is," I interrupted, stealing the words right out of his mouth, "I might still get a little…perturbed…when I think of my feelings for Nathan, but I've managed to make it through these last few years well enough without having him in my life. Everything's been just fine around here before he turned up the other day, so why should I…" I broke off when Steve crouched directly in front of me and fixed me with a penetrating stare. His brown eyes had darkened so greatly that they almost seemed like large, black marbles. "What?"

"How have you really been doing these last few years, Miss?"

"Huh?"

"Consider it, before you answer," Steve coaxed. He bounced on the balls of his feet, evidently trying to get comfortable in his squatting position. "You can spout platitudes all you want and pretend that you've got this amazing life and you've been able to soldier on without Nathan Hamilton but be real for a second. What's the truth of the matter?"

"Are you kidding right now?" I retorted, waving my hand around our crowded compartment, gesturing to the plaques on the wall and the trophies that were lined on top of a cabinet in the corner. "Look where we are."

Steve grunted. "Yeah, we're in a broom closet."

"A converted broom closet," I corrected him.

"Miss," he paused and rolled his eyes dramatically, "Check behind the door. The janitor still stores the mop and bucket in here."

My eyes flicked to the closed door and sure enough, tucked right near the door hinges was a yellow rolling bucket with the mop handle nestled in the crook between the door and the wall.

"When did that get there?" I murmured.

"The bucket is not the point," Steve said, tapping his index finger on my knee cap. "I want you to consider what life…your life…has really been like these past few years and…"

"I'm thriving," I interjected, not allowing him to finish his thought in a melancholy way, as I was sure he meant to do. "Our website and vlog get tons of hits every day. The morning show has been so well-received that both of us constantly get offers to go elsewhere and work for bigger networks. And the podcast—well, you already know why we've got half those trophies over there. People love listening to us report the news." I inhaled deeply. "My career is so fulfilling and I'm not sure if I've ever been happier."

Steve snorted derisively, then slowly stood. Because I remained seated, he towered over me, not in an intimidating way, but almost like he was the parent, and I was the child. He wasn't quite reprimanding me, but I felt as though he might just tell me he was disappointed in my behavior.

Instead, he said simply, "That's not true."

"Which part?"

He waved his hand dismissively at the accolades that adorned our cluttered dressing room. "Obviously, you didn't speak out of turn about the show or the podcast. We've got the hardware around here to prove just how well things have been going in that arena. But when you said you've never been happier. Now, I know that was a fib."

"We've both got very full lives," I protested.

"Sort of," Steve agreed, "but I know you, Miss. I've known you for a very long time. So, I understand that you've been happy enough, but you've never really been this emotionally charged before. The day I met you, we were both rooting through a bunch of brown paper bags, searching for someone who's pheromones would attract us and…" He broke off as we both shuddered, simultaneously recalling the absurdity of that little science experiment. "My point is, you were searching for someone back then, but you didn't have any luck…you haven't had any luck, because you already found your fella a long time ago."

"That's not…I just can't…," I faltered. "It was just a hug…like you said…a simple hug."

"This thing with Nathan isn't just another fleeting romance and nothing between the two of you has ever been simple." He sighed. "I don't need to have heard the whole of your story to know that these last few days, while he's been in town, a change has come over you. You've been infused with this new spark. Even when you're trying to reject him and deleting his voicemails, you do it with gusto."

I laughed. "With gusto?"

Steve kept talking, ignoring my snide insertion. "This guy is the one who nabbed hold of your heart all those years ago and I think you've just been biding your time, waiting for him to come back."

"To do what exactly?" I replied. "To break my heart again? To shatter my dreams? To fill my head with nonsensical romantic notions, then leave me for someone else?"

He leaned forward and tapped his finger on the top of my head, near the place where my locks parted. "Your head is already full of nonsensical romantic notions. Nate didn't need to put them there."

"But what am I supposed to do?" I groaned, feeling so frustrated that I wanted to scream. "For all I know, he could be married to someone else and…"

Steve placed a gentle hand on my shoulder and whispered, "I'm sure you don't need me to tell you this, but I feel like you're not using the reporter side of your brain again. If this were a news feature, what would you do? Would you get annoyed and pitch a fit over not having all the answers or would you prep a new set of questions then do everything in your power to get to the bottom of the story?" He paused, possibly so he could give me a second to let his words sink in fully. "You understand what I'm saying, right? You'll never know the truth if you don't ask tough questions. And really, don't you want to know?"

Chapter Thirty

Will You Come with Me?
Nathan

Dinner that evening was a subdued affair. It wasn't that having dinner with Sean was a chore. He kept the conversational ball rolling, talking non-stop about work and his family, telling me just how anxious he was to get home and see his wife and kids again, but I was the slouch. I added little substance to the talk, only nodding along and inserting a few words here and there when it seemed absolutely necessary.

The trouble was simply that I couldn't get my mind off Missy. Throughout dinner, while the waiter served me and my friend a couple of steaks with all the trimmings, I kept flicking through my mental memory bank, searching for the point in which everything had gone wrong. Remarkably, I couldn't pinpoint that moment because, instead, I kept coming back to the instance when everything had gone right.

We'd both been young, so young. It was just after pledging had concluded and she'd come to the frat house with Benson and some of her other sorority sisters. When Turtle, that was Benson's boyfriend's pledge name, took the time to introduce all the girls, I leapt right up from the couch and gave them all hugs. With some of the girls, the interaction had been awkward. They didn't hug me back or they wiggled and squirmed so that I did no more than merely give them a quick pat on the shoulders. But when I opened my arms to Missy, she'd welcomed me forward with a big smile. I'd always been drawn to that grin, equal parts cheerful and enigmatic, and during that first meeting, she'd managed to captivate my heart without saying a single word. All she had to do was look at me, and I was lost to anyone else.

When I draped my arms around her, she snuggled in close, and even now, I remember how she smelled of sunscreen and sugary lemonade. The girls had been sunbathing on the lawn all afternoon, once classes concluded, and while some had showered before coming over, Missy hadn't. Her cheeks and the tip of her nose were slightly sunburnt, and heat radiated off her skin, but it wasn't the sort of thing I wanted to shrink away from altogether. If anything, these little quirks only made me like her more. Missy wasn't pretentious or a snob. She was, from the very beginning, friendly and gregarious. She put me at ease, and so, when she didn't step away quickly or keep me at arm's length, I melted into the hug with her, embracing this new feeling of finding someone who could both make my heart thud frantically but also bring me a soothing sense of calm. It was an odd paradox, but that first initial reaction seemed to permeate the rest of our dealings with each other. Missy was always making my heart race, but also, somehow…miraculously, serving as my harbor in the storm. The place…the person I wanted to be with when nothing else was going right in the world.

Years ago, if I'd been having these kinds of thoughts, I'd have been compelled to call Missy. It didn't matter that we lived hundreds of miles apart. She'd lend a listening ear and find a way, by the end of the conversation, to make me feel better. But today, I'd tried reaching out to no avail. Missy was ignoring me. She hadn't answered a single text and as for the voicemails I'd left, I'm sure those were vanquished before she took the time to listen to them.

"Nate," Sean said, tapping the tip of a ballpoint pen on the tabletop, "did you hear me? You wanna put this on the company credit card or should I use…"

"Here," I replied, pulling out the corporate card I used to cover the meals which weren't included as a part of the conference. This was the first time I was laying down this card on this trip and thinking of how I'd let Missy cover the check on our first date at Anne Marie's made me shift uncomfortably in my seat.

"What is it?" Sean asked after handing the receipt and card off to the waiter. "Something you ate not sitting right?"

Candidly, I couldn't remember taking a single bite of my dinner. I didn't remember cutting into the steak or even plowing my way through the baked potato, asparagus spears, or wedge salad, but I must've done all these things because otherwise, Sean wouldn't have asked such a question.

"Yeah," I murmured, laying my hand over my chest. "I think I've got a touch of heart burn."

"Too bad," Sean said, tucking his own credit card in his wallet and stuffing his billfold into his back pocket. "I'd offer you an antacid, but I'm fresh out. Maybe you could stop by the shop in the lobby and see if they have something."

"Sure," I said quietly. "I'll do that."

I knew, even as I said the words, that I wouldn't do any such thing. The ache in my chest probably wasn't a result of eating too much too quickly or ingesting overly salty foods. No, I was fairly certain the reason it felt like there was a tiny boxer in my chest using my heart for a punching bag was because I was reeling over this thing with Missy. I'd lost her—for real this time—and there was nothing I could do to repair the damage.

Once the waiter returned with my company credit card and I left a hefty tip, Sean and I bid each other good night. I could tell he was anxious to retreat to his room so he could call his wife and me…well, I guess I was ready to be alone, too. But it all felt just plain wrong. The last three nights I'd gone out with Missy and while every moment hadn't been a chocolate coated treat, there had been *something* there. Whether we were sharing a plate of waffles, laughing loudly with Adair and Wes, or even when I was chasing her through the city on my bicycle, I'd felt alive. Now, I was nothing more than a husk of my former self, scuffing my dress shoes across the marble floors as I skulked to the elevator bank and took the first one up to my hotel room.

While taking a hot shower, I tried to come up with one good thing in my life. This was a common practice of mine. I didn't like to get mired down and wallow in self-pity, so whenever I found my thoughts going there, I reminded myself of the good things I had going on around me. And instantly, a pleasant reminder popped to mind.

Jordan…He's such a great kid.

But today, there was more to it.

And he just got excellent news. The days I spent at UNC-Charlotte were the best of my life. He'll get to have all those same experiences, too.

I shut off the hot water and climbed from the shower, pausing only momentarily to pat myself dry. I flung the towel in a heap on the bathroom floor then walked out into the bedroom. When I snuggled down into the bed sheets, they felt cool and crisp. Beads of water still clung to my hair, but when I burrowed into the pillow that kind of felt nice too, almost like I'd just taken a dip in the ocean and was settling back against the grainy sand, letting the water dry on its own.

Before I got to town, I made Jordan a whole string of promises.

Since the summer of his junior year, when he received a brochure for UNC-Charlotte in the mail and got it into his head that this could be a fun project we did together, we'd had many long conversations. And, it was true, I had promised him that I'd make some connections this week. While I hadn't followed through and landed any potential job interviews at the vendor fair this morning, I could, at least, visit the college campus tomorrow.

I can snap a few pics and send them back to Jordan. At least, in that way, I won't be letting him down completely.

I'd yet to bring him to town for a proper college visit. We'd done the virtual tour online and we both knew it was risky to pin all our hopes on a school he hadn't walked around yet in person, but this dream…this cool idea…had been just too good to let go.

So, I'll stop by campus tomorrow.

With my plans quickly coalescing, my fingers twitched toward my cell phone which lay on the bedstand near my head.

Should I tell Missy what I'm doing?

Goodness knows why that thought popped into my brain, but it was there, nonetheless. It was reflexive, I guess. We'd spent so many years together, traversing the campus, going to parties, and falling in love. It was only right that when I thought of returning to my old stomping grounds that I'd also associate her with those thoughts.

But would she want to go with me?

Last night…two days ago…I wouldn't have hesitated. I'd have told Missy my plans and begged her to tag along. We could've toured the campus together, stopping every few feet to exclaim over the changes that time had wrought…because I'm sure they were plentiful.

The thought of going back to campus without Missy made the assault on my heart that had been so insistent earlier return in full force. Now, that tiny pugilist wasn't just slugging at a heavy bag. He was tearing into the speed bag, making me feel like my chest was throbbing painfully.

Unable to help myself, I reached for my phone, unlocked the screen, then clicked on Missy's name so I could send her a quick text.

I'm thinking of touring UNC-Charlotte tomorrow. Do you want to come with me?

Chapter Thirty-One

Are Matters Like These Ever Really Over?
Missy

When I woke up at three a.m., I roared in disgust and was, for a second, tempted to throw my phone across the room. The alarm was a gentle buzzing sound, not harsh or irritating, but it still managed to frazzle my nerves, making all my senses feel raw and agitated.

No more...Please, Lord, just let today be uneventful.

But I soon realized that it was too late for such prayers to make any difference. I plucked my phone off the nightstand and when I hit the button to silence the alarm, a string of text messages sprung to life. There was one from Adair and another from Benson, both ladies checking up on me. There was a picture message from Steve, showcasing the fun he and Tom were having listening to live music in the plaza after work yesterday. Then, there was a text from Nathan. Because of the way my messages displayed themselves, I didn't have the option of deleting it before reading it. He'd kept it short and sweet, reminding me that he was still in town and inviting me to tour UNC-Charlotte with him.

Now, that's intriguing.

But I didn't have time to ponder Nate's words. It was three a.m. and that meant I had exactly one-half hour to shower and hustle into work. My day was about to start, whether I wanted to stay snuggled in bed or not, and I wasn't about to show up late.

Exactly twenty-eight minutes and seventeen seconds later, I strode through the doors of DieLou Records, aiming to bolt for the stairs so I could make my way toward the studio when my eyes were treated to a welcome, yet unexpected sight.

"Adair? What're you doing here?" I checked my watch. "Do you know what time it is?"

She was dressed in a fantastic outfit this morning. It was a jumpsuit, finely tailored so that it matched her proportions exquisitely and the material was made of a gorgeous royal purple fabric. Everything from the amethyst necklace at her throat to the spikes of her high heeled shoes looked polished and refined. If I didn't know better, I'd swear that Jess had gotten dressed last night, forgone sleep, and stayed right here in the lobby of the building she owned so that she could look just this immaculate when I came striding through the door in my rumpled workout gear and still damp from the shower head of hair.

"I'm aware of the hour," she said, giving her perfectly coiffed hair a supercilious toss. "But I figured that you'd need to talk this morning."

I shrugged and nodded toward the elevator. When it was just me climbing to the twelfth floor, I was going to take the stairs. But now that the boss was coming along with me, I figured we'd better go for a ride. "I'm not sure what you want me to say."

"Did you talk to Nate last night?" she asked, cutting right to the chase.

"No."

"Really?" She did this little twirl as we stepped on board the elevator. It was the sort of complicated, choreographed movement she would've made back in the day when she was a part of the college show choir and I stared at her, waiting for her to show me some jazz hands. "Even though he kept calling you, you didn't feel the need to pick up...even once?"

"He didn't keep calling," I corrected her. "But he was a tad on the persistent side." I tapped the waistband of my stretchy pants where I'd tucked my phone earlier. "When I woke up this morning, I saw he left me a text."

"And?" Adair prompted.

The elevator door slid open, and we waltzed out and into the small hallway where in a few hours the members of our live studio audience would congregate. The place smelled of disinfectant and that reminded me of the mop bucket Steve had brought to my attention tucked into the corner of our dressing room yesterday.

I frowned, then used my keys to unlock the heavy doors which led to the studio. "He wants to go tour campus today."

"Okay," Adair said slowly, "what's that got to do with you?"

"He asked me to go with him."

She marched ahead, leading the way to the dressing room and once we were safely ensconced within, Adair sat primly in Steve's makeup chair. "And do you want to go with him?" she asked.

"I...I don't know," I answered, really thinking about my response. "I can't fathom why he'd want to tour the campus." I paused while kicking off my sneakers. "Maybe he's just feeling nostalgic, which

I guess I can understand." I was still wearing a pair of white athletic socks but took a moment to curl my toes into the carpet. It wasn't soft or plush, more serviceable than anything else, but the movement felt good, so I indulged for a long second before continuing with my thoughts. "I miss the bonds I had with everyone in college and during those first few years right after we graduated." I smiled at the flood of memories that rushed upon me. "Do you remember just how close we all were?"

"How could I forget?" Adair replied. "There's nothing I wouldn't do for my girls."

Slowly, I lowered myself into my own makeup chair so that Adair and I sat facing one another. "It didn't matter what we were doing…meeting at The Pond…going to Sounds…or just hanging out at my apartment…We always managed to have a good time, didn't we?"

"Yeah," she murmured. "We were pretty lucky."

My shoulders slumped as I settled back into my chair and stared at the same speck that I'd spotted the day before. That little ball of fuzz was tough and had clung in place overnight, resisting the broom or vacuum, whatever the cleaning crew used to tidy this place. "I miss those days," I whispered. "Sometimes I wish that things had never changed."

I'd been so deep in my reminiscing and so perfectly serious that I was startled when Adair gave one of her perky, sparkling laughs. She tipped her head back and giggled with glee. "You've got to be kidding with me, Missy."

"What?" I returned. "You're happy everything changed?"

She laughed brightly again. "God, yes." She leaned forward and looked me right in the eyes. "I thank heavens every day that we all grew out of that awkward time. We were a bunch of hot messes back then, running around town carelessly, falling in and out love at the drop of a hat, going to bars and dance clubs almost every night, and eating far more brunch than any person should." Her eyes widened and I could see the way the blue flecks nearest the pupil twinkled. "I'm so glad we all grew up and became the people we were meant to be."

"So, you don't miss the girls…our friendships…our…"

"Oh," Adair interjected, "I miss the girls, but, for the most part, our friendships have remained unbroken. I just talked to Benson last night and earlier this week I…"

"Yeah, yeah," I muttered, giving her a wry smile. "I know you had the whole group text going without me. I'm sure I'll hear from Brooklyn and Autumn soon enough because you alerted them to the fact that Nate was back in town."

Adair shrugged one shoulder elegantly. "I was worried about you and like I said before, we're lucky we still have each other." She reached out and patted my knee. "Things have changed, Lawrence. There's no denying that. But I'm still here for you and so are the girls."

"So," I prompted, "what do the others think about this mess I've gotten myself into this week? If I told them all about Nate's invitation to join him on campus, what do you think they'd tell me to do?"

Adair leaned back in her chair and used her index finger, which was coated in a shiny layer of aubergine polish today, to tap her chin. "Do you really wanna know?"

"Yeah," I said, a tad sarcastically. "I don't think I would've asked if I wasn't willing to hear the answer."

She certainly took her time before responding. Using leisurely, graceful motions, as if I wasn't waiting for her to answer me, Adair crossed one leg over the other before saying softly, "I think the girls would tell you it's all right to take a walk down Memory Lane with Nate this afternoon."

"What?" I replied dubiously. "Even Benson?"

Adair chuckled. "Okay, maybe that wouldn't be Benson's advice, but all the others would tell you to go with him so long as you…"

"Yes?" I urged when it seemed like she might be tempted to leave her thought unfinished.

Adair had been speaking quietly before, but when she opened her mouth to complete her sentence her words registered just above a whisper. "You need to remember that things *have* changed, Lawrence. You're not the naïve girl you were back when you and Nate first started dating. And he's not the numbskull he was back then, either." I opened my mouth to insert my own observations, but she held up her hand to halt my speech. "I'm just saying that things haven't been perfect between the two of you this week, but that's okay. It's rather expected, I think. Because the people you were thirteen years ago or…" She paused and sighed dramatically. "…Or the people you used to be back when we first traipsed all over campus, those pretty babies are long gone. You've changed and he has, too."

"But what if I don't like the person he's become?" I said aloud the worst fear, the one that had been plaguing me since I'd done the mental math and realized he had a son because of his cheating. "What if...?"

"What's not to like?" Adair returned in an almost resigned way. "Nate's not the perfect guy, but I never took you for the type who was searching for Prince Charming. I always thought you just wanted to be with someone who made you feel...safe and protected."

It was as if Adair had been in the room yesterday with me and Steve when I'd described the first time that Nate and I laid eyes on each other. When he'd caught me up in that hug on that first day...that was precisely how I felt-safe, protected, and the possibility of falling in love had simply bloomed right then and there.

"How did you know that's how I felt about Nate?"

Adair shook her head gently. "I don't know how you feel, but I know you. When you were young, every boyfriend you ever had cheated on you and that sort of pain clung to your heart. I think it still does. So...I guess what I'm saying is that you've got to go talk to Nathan today. Have an honest and truthful conversation, one in which neither of you is holding anything back. Get the closure you're craving."

"Closure?" I was surprised by what I considered to be a turn in the conversation. Up until that last statement, I thought Adair was pushing me to reconcile my differences with Nate and move forward as a couple. But that final sentence gave me pause. "You want me to...?"

"I want you to do what feels right," Adair said calmly, leveling an even stare at me. "If you want things to end right where they started, on the college campus where the two of you met, that's one option. But there are plenty of other ways you could take this thing."

My stomach twisted into a knot, causing me to squeeze my eyes shut, grit my teeth, and breathe through the agony. "I'm not sure it's closure I'm looking for," I confessed. "Answers...sure. But with Nate, I'm not certain I ever want things to be over completely."

Chapter Thirty-Two

So…This is How it Ends…Nothing More?
Nathan

I didn't hear from Missy all day. I'm not ashamed to admit that from the minute I rolled out of bed that morning, I had my phone in my hand, not in my pocket, not tucked in a bag somewhere, but right in my hand, because I didn't want to miss a text or call. But nothing happened.

"You sure you don't want to change your travel arrangements?" Sean asked as he was wheeling his suitcase toward the elevator. I was accompanying him to the lobby because just as soon as he hopped in his cab and headed to the airport, I was taking a rideshare of my own and scooting over to campus.

"I'm sure," I replied.

"It'd probably be really easy," he said, loading his heavy suitcase into the trunk of the bright yellow taxicab.

I snorted. "Right…because when was the last time anything having to do with travel was made easy?"

"Yeah," Sean chuckled slightly while slamming the trunk of the car. "You're probably right about that. But I hate the idea of leaving you here."

I waved a hand around us. We were sheltering underneath the large stone pillars that served as an extravagant entryway to the hotel at our backs. But I could see the way the sun was beaming brightly, casting its warm glow on the smooth sidewalk pavement. Since our hotel wasn't that far from the heart of uptown, there was very little foliage to speak of, so we had to rely on the archways overhead to protect us from the autumn sun's ceaseless glare. "You might forget, but for a few years, Charlotte was my home. You're not abandoning me in a strange place. You're just leaving me here so I can get acquainted with an old friend."

"Speaking of which…" Sean's heavy eyebrows ticked high on his forehead. "Did you hear from Missy yet today?"

"Nope," I said crisply. "But I'm trying not to think about that."

"Sure." Sean nodded his head understandingly. "Don't dwell on the pain. You've got a lot going on back at home right now and it'd be best if you just spent the next few days chilling out."

"Absolutely," I agreed. "I'm a little disappointed that Missy won't be visiting campus with me today, but I'm not gonna lie--I'm kind of pumped to get over there. It's been a long time since I took a stroll through the quad, and I can't wait to send Jordan some pictures."

"Good for you," Sean said. The taxi driver turned up the music on his stereo then and I laughed.

"That must be your cue to get moving."

Sean offered me a hand to shake, and I took it.

"Take care of yourself, Nate," he said pumping my hand twice before letting go.

"You, too. Safe travels and tell Felicia and the kids I said hello once you get home."

"Can do," Sean replied, opening the door, and stepping with one leg into the cab. But then, awkwardly, he held the pose for a minute. "And Nate...really try and take this whole thing in stride over the next few days. Because that's all it is...just a couple of days. In no time, you'll be back home and..."

My phone pinged and I was caught so unawares by the pulsation that started in my palm and rippled up my whole arm that I jumped. Sean's eyes widened in surprise.

"Well," he said, nodding at my hand. "You've been clutching that thing all day like a security blanket. Aren't you at least gonna check to see who's texting you?"

I gulped, suddenly overcome by a batch of fresh nerves. It could just be Jordan or Lana or any number of people from back at the lab. But I knew...I was just sure it was Missy...finally responding to me...finally reaching out.

I held my phone up to my face and stared at the message.

"Is it from Missy?" Sean asked.

"Yeah," I whispered.

"Well, what does it say?" he prompted, adding a touch of impatience to his voice.

"She wants to meet me at the spot."

"The spot?" Sean's skepticism was apparent. "Is that all it says?"

"Uh-huh."

He huffed. "I know Charlotte's got a unique name for everything so is that a restaurant around town or did the two of you maybe have a favorite spot around campus?"

"Nothing like that," I said, lowering my phone and shoving it in my pocket.

"So, you know what she means?"

"Yeah," I whispered. "I know exactly where I'll find Missy."

Chapter Thirty-Three

What is Your Story?
Missy

  I stood on that bridge overlooking Blessed Creek waiting for Nathan for what felt like hours. The place had changed very little over the last thirteen years, which was a bit surprising, seeing as how change seemed to be the theme of the week. But this little alcove was, for better or worse, quite as I remembered it.

  When I wandered through the forested area, making my way down the path, I saw the same trees, or at least, what seemed like the same trees, lying on their sides, covered in moss and ferns, waiting for someone to clear them away. The path itself was still that dry mixture of dirt and dust and once I'd reached the clearing, I observed the brown sign with the white ring around it, announcing that this park was titled none other than Blessed Creek.

  As the seconds ticked by, I vacillated between watching the path, waiting for someone else, hopefully Nathan, to appear, and turning away so I could stare at the water that burbled in the creek bed below. It was a brownish red hue, reminding me vaguely of a tepid cup of tea, but on the surface, little crested ripples sparkled brilliantly, reflecting the glare of the sun, giving the whole environment a wholesome and pleasant feeling. The soundtrack to my long wait was provided by the babbling of the water as well as the constant chirping from a pair of mockingbirds. They flitted from one tree to the next and as one darted after the other, they turned every so often to titter. I found the whole spectacle amusing.

  They're flirting with one another.

  I didn't know the first thing about birds or their mating habits, but it was evident that the pair were going through the throes of making that first initial connection. And when I watched them finally perch on a branch together, I considered the matter closed. They'd finally reached an agreement.

  I gazed at the pair of birds and remembered the day Nate had brought me here. This spot had featured in many of my daydreams often over the years. And many times, when I drew that recollection to mind, I considered his words at length.

  He thinks this place is magical...but why?

I'd never been able to discern anything enchanting or sensational about this little park. It was a nice, out of the way spot, so I guess I could appreciate the solitude, but other than that…

"Missy…"

I heard him breathe my name and spun on the spot to find Nate running down the path. He opened his arms to me, and I copied the movement, readying myself to fall into his embrace. The gesture was so natural, so exactly what I'd been needing to do, that a sigh of relief accompanied it.

Nate draped his arms around me, and our bodies fit together, so nicely, so neatly, almost as if our limbs had been designed to do this exact function and nothing else. I snuggled my face into the nook between his chin and shoulder muscle and inhaled deeply, scenting perspiration, sunshine, and that unique masculine tang that distinctly reminded me of him.

"I've missed you." His words fell right on my earlobe because he'd pressed his cheek against the side of my head, making sure not even an inch of space lingered between us.

"How is that possible?" I whispered in reply. "You just saw me a couple of days ago."

"A couple of days? Has it been that long?"

A smile cracked my face into a wide grin and even though I wanted to pull away so I could see if he was beaming right back at me, the movement was unnecessary. The love swelled and built between us, and I didn't need to see how Nate was reacting to our reunion—I could feel it.

We held each other for a long time, simply standing there near the bridge, not saying another word, not even chirping at each other as the mockingbirds had done. It was enough to just be with him, to hold him close, to feel the way his pulse thrummed in his neck, and to know that this moment, if we wanted it to, didn't have to end.

But then, as if allowing myself to have such flippy, flighty romantic thoughts was the catalyst that brought reality rushing back in, I remembered all the questions that had ushered us to this point. I wanted to continue holding Nathan, but I also, pragmatically, needed to keep him at arm's length, at least until I knew the truth.

"What is it?" He asked when I pulled out of the embrace. "What's wrong?"

"I need to know…everything," I answered.

Nate pivoted, then nodded at the nearest stone bench. It was settled just a foot or so away from the path and was nestled underneath the maple tree the birds were sharing.

Seems an appropriate place for us to have this conversation.

He took my hand and led me to the bench, but when we slid onto our seats, I let go of his fingertips. Intentionally, I laced my own fingers together, locking them there, then laid them gently in my lap. "So..." I prompted, remembering what Steve had told me about approaching this whole thing like a hard-nosed reporter, "what's your story?"

Nathan inhaled slowly and I watched the way his lips twisted down at the corners. I knew from just that one simple gesture that he didn't relish getting into all this with me, so I silently vowed to stay quiet and let him tell the tale in his own time at his own pace.

"Thirteen years ago, I stood on this bridge for hours...waiting for you, Missy." I inhaled sharply and he nodded. "We've already gone over this, I guess, but I think it bears repeating because what happened here, or rather, didn't happen, impacted what was about to come next."

I fussed with my fingers, gripping them tighter, then nodded for him to proceed.

"That afternoon, I waited much longer than I should've. We both knew I needed to get on the road and head back to Pittsburgh, but I stood here, making excuses. Maybe you got called into work or it could've been that you lost your way coming down the path." He sighed wearily. "But that was all semi-wishful thinking. When you didn't show up, as I'd hoped, I dragged myself back to my truck and got going. But I didn't get very far. I'd been in such a rush the day before to make it to your apartment complex on time that I hadn't stopped to refuel when I probably needed to. So..." He paused and waved his hand at an indeterminate spot in the distance. "I pulled over at the first gas station. And that was when my life changed."

I leaned forward, intrigued. "What happened?"

"While filling up the tank, I popped into the convenience store to pick up a bottle of water and that's when I saw her."

"Lana?" I breathed and he nodded.

"She looked the same way she did when she worked on campus. Long, red hair, freckles faintly dusting her pale cheeks." He lifted his hand and touched his own freckles. "The only difference was as she skipped down the aisle, picking up packages of sandwich cookies and grabbing for a bottle of sweet tea that she had a little man trailing along behind her…"

"Was that…was it…?"

"Jordan." Nathan said his son's name reverently. "When I first set eyes on that kid, it was like looking in a mirror." He chuckled mirthlessly. "I hadn't known of his existence, had no clue the one night we'd spent together had sparked a whole chain reaction of repercussions, but there this kid was, looking all the world like the kindergarten picture of me my mom has framed and still keeps near the side of her bed."

"I remember," I whispered, fondly thinking of the countless times I'd gone home with Nate when we were dating. His family lived a few hours from Charlotte, but they were closer to campus than mine were, so it had been a natural conclusion for the two of us to visit sometimes. For holidays or family celebrations, I'd been right by his side at the Hamilton household and on more than one occasion, his mom had gone back to her bedroom and proudly produced her favorite portrait of her son. Little Nathan had been such a beautiful boy. His brown hair had been silky smooth then and his eyes had sparkled mischievously. In the picture, the photographer had captured an impish grin, which was only rendered more adorable because he was missing one of his front teeth in the image.

"Yeah," Nate muttered, "it was a real shot in the arm. I'd gone into that gas station moping, even dragging my feet a little, thinking of what I might say to you when I finally got up the nerve to call, but then, I saw Jordan and Lana and…"

"Everything changed?" I finished for him.

He made a soft sound in the back of his throat, like maybe he was fighting back his emotions, keeping them in check, just so he could continue with his story. He deliberately sat up straighter on the stiff bench, then cleared his throat loudly before answering. "Maybe not as much as you'd think…at least initially."

"Why not?" I asked. "If you recognized your features when they were right in front of you…?"

"I had to be sure," Nate explained. "There were some tests that needed to be done and plenty of long conversations ensued, but eventually, once the paternity test confirmed it, Lana and I were forced to determine how best to move forward."

"What did you do?"

He shrugged. "I offered to move to Charlotte so I could be a part of Jordan's life, but Lana didn't want that. She'd had a rough couple of years, after leaving UNC and having the baby. She'd stopped working in admissions offices and taken a job waiting tables sporadically, whenever she could get help watching Jordan. I think… in a lot of ways, she'd been looking for a way out of town. And that day we ran into each other at the gas station…well, I think that little meeting was an answer to her prayers."

"Okay," I ventured, "so what happened next?"

Nathan sat as far back as he could get and tipped his head, so he was staring straight up at the sun. He squeezed his eyes shut, then all at once, the lids sprung open, and he continued with his narrative. "We got married."

"What?" Now, I was squawking, just like that pair of mockingbirds.

"I told myself it was the right and honorable thing to do," Nathan said quickly, hurriedly allowing the rest of his story to pour out. "She and Jordan moved to Pittsburgh. We found a little two-bedroom house in one of the suburbs, where there was a decent school and then we tied the knot. The trouble was…" He paused and chewed on the corner of his lip. "…Lana and I didn't have a lot in common. We'd only hooked up that one night in college and that wasn't much to build a relationship upon. We stayed married for a little less than five years, but that's when we decided that our shared love for Jordan wasn't enough to keep us together as a couple. We figured we could still be his parents, and love him completely, but we didn't need to spend the rest of our lives cohabiting just to make everything seem perfect."

"So…you and Lana…?" I allowed my words to disappear, hoping he'd understand what I meant to ask.

He nodded, fully comprehending what I wanted to know. "We've been divorced for almost seven years. While we were married, she was able to get back on her feet and secured a cushy job as the head of admissions at Duquesne University. Housing benefits were discussed and before I knew it, she and Jordan moved out. I was glad they landed at Duquesne because it wasn't far from the house I owned. I could still spend time with Jordan every day…which was exactly the way I wanted it." He fished his phone out of his pocket and instantly, without needing to unlock the screen, a photo of Nate and his son flashed to life. They had their arms swung around each other's shoulders and both wore identical grins. Immediately, I could see the resemblance. Jordan's eyes were the same bright blue as Nate's and even the expression on his face, one of delight and merriment, matched his father's.

"He's beautiful," I whispered.

"Yeah," Nate agreed, "he's really something. A good kid. A real pal." He snorted. "Other people give me grief for treating him like my buddy, but I can't help it. Just look at that grin. Who wouldn't want to be friends with a kid like that?"

He slid the phone back in his pocket, then sat on his hands, and I said, "So, that's it? Have we finally reached the point where you've told me everything?"

Nate cocked his head to the side and looked at me with soft, adoring eyes. "There's a little bit more."

"Okay." I prepared myself for what was to come next. While his tale so far had been slightly surprising, nothing had truly shocked me. I'd been mostly ready. But now…now I figured was the time when he told me the worst of it. I gulped. "Go on."

"Jordan and I came up with this plan a few months ago," he said slowly. "We were sorting through some college brochures, trying to decide which places to visit over the summer, when he got all excited looking at a UNC-Charlotte catalog. We talked about the campus and before I knew it, the two of us had come up with this genius plan." A small smile crept onto his face. "Jordan liked the idea of being a legacy and roaming around the same places where I used to, and I liked the idea of embarking on a new adventure together."

"Wait…what?" I felt like I was misunderstanding. "How do Jordan's college aspirations involve you?"

"Well," Nate replied, lengthening the word suspensefully, "I was thinking I might…"

"You…you're going to move back here?"

Chapter Thirty-Four

Do You Want Me to be Here?
Nathan

"I wanted to," I answered truthfully, not letting the moment simmer any longer than was necessary. "I was giving it some serious thought, but…"

"But what?" she demanded. I could detect Missy's building frustration. She'd been so patient throughout my entire story, not interrupting except to urge me onward, so I didn't delay my response now.

"But everything looks different now that I'm here. When I thought…when I dared to dream that I'd come back to town and reunite with you, the idea of moving here seemed pretty great. But now…I can't do it."

"Why not?"

I softened my tone and gazed at Missy; certain she already knew the answer to that question. "I can't be here without you."

She scoffed. "That's ridiculous. Charlotte's a big city. If you came here with your son and lived over by the university, we'd probably never even see each other."

I laughed loudly, which felt almost cathartic, seeing as how tense I'd been just a few moments ago. "You might never see me, but I'd definitely get an eyeful of you, Miss. You're on TV every day and I do believe I saw a photo of you and Steve gracing a billboard over on Sixth Street."

Missy sighed and hung her head dejectedly. "I don't want to upset your plans because there's been this rift between us. If you want to move here with your son…with Jordan…then, that's exactly what you ought to be able to do."

"But what about you?" I asked, scooting closer to her on the bench. There remained a few inches of space between us, but it felt right to move nearer to her. "Do you want me to be here? If I were here, in town, would you want to see me?"

"I always want to see you," she whispered. And then, when our eyes met, I saw just how honest her words really were. The spaces we'd created around ourselves, our hearts, and our secrets had been hampering not just me, but Missy too. With just those few softly spoken words, she'd finally revealed the truest part of herself, the part she was afraid to let anyone else see, the real, slightly vulnerable, Missy Lawrence.

I leaned nearer, ready to bridge this divide and thank her for her honest reaction by kissing her sweet lips, but as I drew closer, Missy scooted away. "What?" I asked, stymied by her movements.

"Thank you for telling me everything…allowing me to see your side of things. But as far as I'm concerned, nothing's changed. We can kiss and flirt and even go out on dates, but I'll never be able to give you the future you want."

My heart thumped madly in my chest, urging me to act. Daringly, I reached out and cupped Missy's chin with my hands, forcing her to look at me, to meet my gaze completely. "I need you to hear this. I'm pretty sure I said it before…just the other night, but it doesn't seem like you were listening." She opened her mouth to protest, but I leaned nearer and hushed her. "Or maybe you were listening, but I don't think you truly appreciated what I was saying." I paused and licked my lips. "The only future I ever wanted was one with you, Missy. I know I said I wanted to have a bunch of kids, but I was just a kid myself when I spouted that foolish nonsense. What did I know about life or about raising a pack of children?" I shook my head ruefully. "I have a son and he's great. But now…now I'm ready to experience everything else life has to offer. Love…being with my one true love…that's what I really want."

Missy swallowed heavily then whispered, "So, what are you saying?"

An idea came upon me, and I let go of Missy's face. Springing to my feet, I reached for her hands and pulled her up with me.

"What…what are we doing?" she asked. "Where are we going?"

I ignored those questions and spoke from the heart. "Over there," I said, tilting my head to the side and gesturing to the creek that was burbling noisily below. "Years ago, I asked you to marry me. I begged you to meet me here because I wanted, more than anything, to make you my wife. Today, Missy, today, *you* were the one who suggested this meeting place. That can't be a coincidence, can it?"

Chapter Thirty-Five

Keep the Gold or…?
Missy

I shook my head. "You know I didn't just choose this spot randomly, Nate. My message was so vague…so nondescript. You and I had to be on the same page for us to end up here together."

"But why?" he pressed. "We had a lot to discuss, and that conversation could've taken place anywhere. Why did you want to come here?"

I stared into his gorgeous aqua blue eyes and knew that the answer was so obvious, it hardly bore stating it plainly. But I indulged him and did just that. "I wanted to meet you at Blessed Creek because I finally made a decision. I know…I know it's been a long time coming, but I do love you and I want to marry you—if that's still something you want, too."

Nathan's arms were around me at once, pulling me into the most splendid, loving embrace.

"Oh," he moaned, "I can't think of anything better."

A funny quip rose to the tip of my tongue, and I couldn't stop myself from uttering it. I whispered, "It might've been better if I'd reached this conclusion thirteen years ago. If I had, I could've saved us both…"

"No." He wriggled back a little so that I was able to glance upward and see the sincere look on his face. "You couldn't have saved us any of the hassle or heartbreak that ensued, and I wouldn't have wanted you to do that. I needed to feel dejected that day. If I hadn't been so down in the dumps, I wouldn't have pulled into the gas station and gone inside to buy something to drink. And if I hadn't done that, I'd never have run into Lana and Jordan." He relaxed his hold on me slightly, then lifted both hands and ran them through my hair, pulling the long tendrils away from my face. His fingertips floated softly through my locks, flicking aside the tresses, almost in the same manner a gentle breeze might. "I got to spend so many wonderful years with my kid and I wouldn't give up those moments for anything." A soft small tugged at the corners of his lips. "And I'm sure, for your part, you've had your own share of adventures."

"I have," I whispered.

Nate's left hand crept forward, and he caressed my cheek, gently stroking his fingertips against my flushed skin. "If you've got the time," he said simply, "I'd like to hear all about what you've been doing."

"I've got some time." I turned my head infinitesimally and nuzzled my cheek against his palm. "For you—I'll always make the time."

"Good."

He beamed affectionately at me. The queasiness that had roiled through my stomach all week dissipated and the riot of questions that had been clamoring for attention in my head quieted themselves, too. Nate and I were together again, and our closeness made everything else seem inconsequential.

As we stood there gazing into each other's eyes, I slowly slid my hand down the length of my body, and plucked the small, careworn penny from my pocket.

"What's that?" Nate asked, then when I lifted my hand and showed him what I was holding, his hands fell to his sides, and he took a step back. "Is that…?" His voice was tinged with awe and the look of surprise on his face was so cute and comical that I just had to laugh.

"What'll we do now?" I said, holding the penny he'd given me all those years ago up in between us. "Do we keep the gold or stay together forever?"

"Like you even have to ask," Nate quipped. Then, he plucked the penny from my fingertips and tossed it over his shoulder. He hadn't even bothered to look at the creek, but I watched the coin arch over the bridge railing before falling out of sight and presumably disappearing in the rushing waters below.

With that, nothing else stood between us, blocking our path to happiness. Nate wrapped me in a tight hug and whispered, "I love you so much."

Then, luxuriating in those beautiful, blessed words, I kissed him.

Epilogue

You Never Really Gave Up on Us, Did You?
Nathan

The next six months flew by at a breakneck pace. There was so much to be done in such a short span of time that most nights, I fell into bed, utterly and completely exhausted.

Thanks to Adair and Wesley, I was able to secure a new position and start my job immediately after selling my house in Pittsburgh and making the move to Charlotte. I bunked down with Missy over at Fountain Park and while it took a minute for us to adjust to living together, we figured the growing pains were worth it. She met Jordan for the first time when the kid accompanied me and stayed in the apartment with us during his spring break from school. We took full advantage of the time together to shepherd him around the city and finally got around to taking that tour of the college campus.

A full half year elapsed while Missy and I ran around, getting ready for our wedding, and preparing to live the life we'd put on hold for so long. Sometimes, I had to stand back and take a deep breath, just so I could appreciate how good it felt to finally…finally…be putting the finishing touches on our story.

And I was having one of those rare moments of repose when my lovely bride came to my side, sliding her hand through the loop in my arm and hooking it around the crook of my elbow.

"What are you doing over here by yourself?" she asked. She looked lovelier than ever today. I know many men think that much about their wives on their wedding day, but in my case, I'm sure those words had never been truer or more accurate. Because Missy was such a loyal friend and nurtured her pals, keeping in touch with most of them over the years, we'd needed to opt for a grand wedding *fete*. And that also meant that nothing about our wedding or reception could be simply done.

Missy wore a champagne-colored dress with a sweetheart neckline and a drop waist. From there, the gown sprung out wide, almost as if a hoop were holding it in place, and it was covered in yards of glorious silk. Tiny crystals dotted the bodice of the gown, and they shimmered every time she turned or twisted.

Adair, who was serving as the matron of honor, had loaned Missy the tiara she'd worn on her wedding day—as her *something borrowed* token—and it glistened ostentatiously in the afternoon sunlight.

We'd elected to have our wedding and reception at Blessed Creek. It seemed fitting and after some wheedling and making a sizable donation to the local parks and recreation department, we'd been able to convince the park ranger to let us take over the place for the day. The ceremony had been simple and sweet, but now, standing next to my wife, gazing in her pretty eyes, and seeing the look of pure joy on her face, I realized that while things seemed great at present, my life was only going to get better, day-by-day.

Missy bubbled with excitement and pinched my arm playfully. "Don't you think you ought to be mingling with our guests?"

"You mingle," I joked. "I'm happy to just stand here and watch you do your thing."

"Come on," she cajoled, tugging on my arm gently, leading me toward the makeshift dance floor we'd had specially laid for the reception. "I know there are plenty of people you haven't said hello to yet and some of the girls are just dying to congratulate you."

"Of course they are," I snickered. "They know I've finally managed to marry the best girl in the world."

She giggled and continued to tow me across the grassy field. I nodded at Adair and Wes who were standing close to the disc jockey table, swaying from side to side, perfectly in time with the music. Right next to them were Tom and Steve. Missy declared early on that it was imperative for Steve to be part of the wedding party, so he was dressed in a tux that glistened with a silvery, sparkly sheen. I'd come to regard this whole foursome, Adair, Wes, Tom, and Steve, as some of my own dearest pals and gave them all a happy grin as we walked by the quartet.

Then, I smiled broadly at Jordan and Lana. Some women might've balked over inviting the mother of my child and ex-wife to our ceremony, but Missy wasn't one of them. She'd insisted that Lana be here mostly because she wanted to get to know her better. She was a big part of my life after all and I was sure, once all the wedding stuff died down, Missy would be ready to grill Lana and find out everything I might've forgotten to mention previously.

Jordan waved at us, giving me a cheesy grin, and I marveled at my kid. In a few weeks, he'd be starting classes…My little guy was all grown up and just weeks away from becoming a college freshman. In many ways it seemed odd to pick up and move, just so I could stay close to him, but none of those mattered to me. I was just glad I got to be a part of Jordan's life and grateful for the way he'd embraced Missy, readily and eagerly willing to see her as his stepmother.

We'd tried to keep the wedding party small, so that meant many of the girls had only just arrived in town for the ceremony and this was my first-time reconnecting with them.

"Well, well," Brooklyn said, fluffing the ends of her naturally curly hair when we sauntered up next to her. She narrowed her eyes and pierced me with a patented Brooklyn Smythe glower. She was still stunning after all these years and because I knew her so well, I understood that she wasn't really glaring at me, but rather sizing me up and making sure I was good enough for her best bud. "What do we have here?" she said and then a slow grin spread onto her face.

"It's good to see you, Brooks," I said, leaning in and giving her a hug.

She was wearing a cobalt blue dress as well as a pair of enormous dangly earrings and one of them whipped me in the face when we embraced.

Yeah...that seems about right.

"You look nice, Nate," she said, backing away and smoothing down the creases that had sprung up in the folds of her dress. "Happy, I think."

"I am," I replied, "which makes you just as intuitive as ever." It was then that I noticed the hulking beast of a man at her side. "And who is this?" I asked, tipping my head so I could look upward at this behemoth. He couldn't have been shorter than six foot five and his shoulders were as broad as a bull's backside. His hair was short, dark, and spiky, and he had a scruffy chin strap beard.

"This is Travis McGibbins," Brooklyn said as a smug smile drifted onto her face.

"Travis McGibbins...like the linebacker for the Minnesota Vikings?"

Travis nodded curtly at me by jutting his chin, then he offered me a firm handshake. His hand was massive, like a bear's paw, and I was slightly starstruck when I realized who he was.

"You...you led your team to the Super Bowl last year..." I stammered.

He gave a deep, self-deprecating laugh. "I wouldn't claim to be the team leader or anything."

"But you are," I argued. "Without you, the rest of the line would've fallen flat on their faces and…"

Travis nudged Brooklyn's shoulder. "You didn't tell me the groom was a football fan."

Brooklyn rolled her eyes. "Once a caveman…always a caveman."

I got excited just being in Travis' presence. I wanted to talk to him about every play that he'd taken part in over the last season. "Hey," I said, leaning closer, "do you remember that tackle you…"

"Come on," Missy said, tugging on my arm gently.

"What?" I asked. "You said I needed to mingle and I'm pretty sure I've found the group of guests I want to mingle with."

She and Brooklyn shared a gleeful smile, then laughed perkily. "You boys can talk more later," Missy assured me. "For now, we've got to at least drop in on everybody else."

"Fine," I huffed, then turned back to Travis. "But don't go anywhere, okay? I really want to pick your brain."

"All right." Travis shrugged his beefy shoulders. "It's your day, man. You can spend it how you like."

Missy towed me away from Travis and we spent the next half hour greeting our guests. Autumn was there, looking as flawless as ever. We found Renee, Benson, and their respective husbands chatting while keeping a close watch over their broods. Maria, Sophia, and Jules all came to the party. They were holding things down over by the bar area. Savanna and Eve were seated at table number two, and they were trying, unsuccessfully, to convince my parents to join them by playing a round of poker. Sean and his wife were at the same table, and he was doing his best to calm the ladies and remind them that nobody wanted to lose a bunch of money tonight.

Just as Missy and I backed away from that table, quietly chuckling over my parents collective dismay, we bumped into Jack and Missy squealed.

"Jack! What are you doing here?"

At some point over the last six months, Missy had more explicitly explained how years ago, Jack had changed her image. She'd gone to LA, dyed her hair, bought some new clothes, and adopted a fresh musical sound. She'd even taken to calling herself Jackie Rose. But now, the woman standing in front of me looked just like the girl I remembered.

Jack was grinning from ear to ear, wearing a dress that was bright white and covered in a sunflower pattern. Her hair was twisted into a messy knot at the nape of her neck, and she looked good, natural, and most of all…pleased with herself for having surprised us so greatly.

"I know I wasn't invited, so I guess you caught me crashing but…" Jack began, and Missy let go of my arm so she could wrap her pal in a big hug.

"No," she said loudly, refuting the claim immediately. "You're not crashing. You were invited…or…at least we would've invited you if we'd have known where to find you."

Wes and Adair shimmied in our direction then and Adair caught my eye, giving me a big, conspiratorial wink. I hadn't known that Adair planned this little reunion for Missy, but I was appreciative of her thoughtfulness. It had destroyed Missy to have to leave Jack's name off our guest list, but what could she do? She didn't know how to locate her and well…I guess that didn't matter now. Adair took care of tracking down their long-lost gal pal and Jack was here, hugging Missy fiercely.

When they finally broke away, Missy made Jack promise she wouldn't slip away quickly. "We have to greet all the other guests, but I want to talk to *you*." She placed special emphasis on that last word and Jack smiled sheepishly.

"I'm not goin' anywhere, Misdemeanor."

"Good," Missy laughed, "'cause if you tried to leave now, I'd make the wedding party track you down, Jack-o-Lantern."

It was tough tearing the two of them apart, now that they were back to using their affectionate nicknames for one another, but I managed to coax Missy away, reminding her that Jack wasn't likely to break her promise. She'd still be here later.

We circled around the space, stopping every few feet to talk to more well-wishers.

When we encountered a few of Missy's former coworkers, Ethan and Mel, an odd couple who'd been married for ten years, my attention slid elsewhere and I spied Missy's little sister, Hope.

Hopey had been part of the wedding party, so it wasn't my first time seeing her today, which I was glad for because when I caught sight of her, she was chasing S.J. around the dance floor, waddling a little from the strain of her bulging baby belly. I knew her fourth child would be born any day now and I prayed she wouldn't go into labor tonight...during our wedding reception. I didn't mind so much sharing the spotlight with my dear sister-in-law and her husband, Skeeter, but I wanted everything to be just right for Missy. She deserved to have this day be very special.

Just as that thought flitted through my mind, the DJ quieted the soft pop music he'd been playing and spoke clearly and loudly into the microphone. "We need Mr. and Mrs. Hamilton to report to the dance floor, please. Mr. and Mrs. Hamilton."

Missy turned to look at me and when her hand slid down my arm so we could interlace our fingers, I was filled with a rush of ebullience.

"That's us, ya know," I whispered.

"It sure is," she said, leaning forward and giving me a quick kiss on the lips.

The partygoers who were standing nearest to us made gentle cooing sounds, but then, before I could deepen the kiss, Missy stepped back and started towing me toward the center of the floor.

She nodded at the DJ. "Okay," she said. "We're ready."

For our first dance as man and wife, we'd chosen a song, *the song*, that I used to play when we were riding around campus together, basking in the sunshine. So, the tune was a little old, and Jordan had reminded us that it was slightly uncool, but that didn't matter to me. Holding Missy in my arms, knowing that we'd made it over the last hurdle and finally taken our vows, swearing to love, honor, and cherish each other for the rest of our lives...that was all I really cared about. Well...that and my wife's happiness being equal to my own.

As we swayed around the dance floor, some of our friends wished us well, others cheered, and S.J. shouted petulantly, "I wanna dance with Aunt Missy."

Even though we usually indulged Missy's nieces and nephews, his words only made me want to hold my wife closer and treasure this moment that was just between the two of us. When I tightened my grip on her, she stepped nearer and leaned her head against my chest, making it so I was able to whisper directly in her ear. "Is this wedding everything you ever hoped it would be?"

"It's better," she said, emitting a soft sigh along with her response. "I'd given up hope of getting married and starting a family with you a long time ago, but now, I know I was underselling what I already had." She straightened up and looked deeply into my eyes. "I've always had a loving, supportive family surrounding me. My sister,

Adair, Steve, Brooklyn, Autumn, Benson...ahh...the list goes on and on. But you, Nate...now that I have you here, I have everything."

The music slowly faded then and was replaced by an upbeat dance number. I didn't know the lyrics to this song, but the bass line was kind of catchy, so I bopped back and forth, moving right along with Missy, just trying to keep up.

She tipped her head back and laughed jubilantly, then shouted a little so I could hear her over the music, "Is this wedding all you were hoping for?"

I tugged on her hands, pulling her as close to me as she could get, then I lifted my hands and lovingly placed them around the back of her neck. "Seeing you smile...knowing that I'm making you happy...that's the best thing about being here." I kissed Missy sweetly, relishing the exhilarated feelings that came over me when our lips collided.

Knowing that Missy and I had the power to make each other happy, understanding that we'd been brought back together for a reason...for this reason...was a truth I wholeheartedly acknowledged. And I made a silent vow, right then and there, while kissing my gorgeous bride and swaying with her in my arms around the dance floor, that this privilege was one I would never, ever take for granted.

Extended Epilogue

Can We be Done with the Questions Now, Please?
Missy

"In here," Jordan whispered, motioning Nate and me forward.

"Do we need to whisper, too?" Nathan asked, nervously smooshing the bundle of flowers and mylar balloons he was carrying against his chest so he could try to do the gentlemanly thing and hold open the door for me.

"No," Jordan chuckled. "I'm not sure why I'm doing that. Both Donna and the baby are wide awake, and I know the little one is excited to meet her grandparents."

I snickered. "She was just born, Jordan. So, she doesn't even know we're here."

"Sure, she does," Jordan replied in that light, airy way of his. "She's been listening to your voices the whole time she was in the womb. So, she might not comprehend everything that's going on around her, but trust me, my little one is fully alert and ready to greet her visitors."

He led the way into the labor and delivery room where his wife, Donna, had just given birth to their first child, a little girl, who, according to the chart on the wall already weighed six pounds, twelve ounces and was twenty-four inches long.

Tears of joy welled in my eyes when we rounded the pale pink, peach, and white privacy curtain and I saw the proud new mama, snuggling her newborn close to her chest. Donna's fair skin was mottled and blotchy. Her black, springy curls had been tugged back into a loose ponytail and tiny tendrils had escaped during the delivery, fluttering around her face, giving her almost an ethereal glow. The babe she held in her arms had Donna's same hair or at least it seemed that way because the child's locks were black as coal, but they were matted to her head. Just as I was making this observation, a nurse scurried forward and offered to put a blue, white, and pink striped hat on the baby's head, and I nodded approvingly at Donna. "Go on," I urged. "Teach your girl an appreciation for hats right from the start."

Donna tittered and then her pretty face split into a broad grin. I loved that girl. She and Jordan had met toward the end of his freshman year at UNC, and even though they'd had their fair share of disagreements over the years, they rarely parted ways. For the last eight years, Donna had been a permanent fixture in mine and Nathan's household, accompanying Jordan to family gatherings and even joining us occasionally on Sunday evenings when we hosted game night. When she and Jordan tied the knot eighteen months ago, Nate and I were sure, if it was in their power, that a baby would be joining our little family before long. And now, here we were, beaming at the precious child and her radiant mother.

Nathan and I followed Jordan around the foot of the bed and while Nate placed the gifts we'd brought on an end table near the window, I sidled right up to Donna and the baby so I could get a better look at the two of them. "How are you feeling?" I asked, lifting my hand, and brushing back a few of Donna's errant locks.

"I've been better," she said managing a weak smile.

"Was it rough?" I questioned.

"Doctor Gilbert said I did beautifully."

"She was a real champ," Jordan added, coming to my side. "The doc said she and our little lady were the easiest delivery she's done in a long time."

"It didn't seem easy," Donna whispered as her eyes left the face of her child and roved toward mine.

"You'll forget how difficult it was soon enough," I assured her. "My sister, Hope, says that's the way of it. In the moment and directly afterward, you feel like you've just finished running a race. But once you go home and get to spend time with your little one, the whole process doesn't seem so bad."

"She's beautiful, isn't she?" Nate said, touching my elbow gently and squeezing between Jordan and me so he could get a look at the baby. "I think she even has my eyes."

Jordan laughed. "The doc said most babies have blue or black eyes when they're first born. But she prepped us so we'd know that could change at any time."

"She'll have blue eyes," I said, grabbing ahold of Nate's hand and giving it a reassuring squeeze. "Both Donna and Jordan have blue eyes, so…it's just genetics."

"You're right." Nate lifted his free hand and tapped the side of his head where the gray that had started to show itself in his sideburns years ago had multiplied and given the locks nearest his ears a thicker smattering of silvery gray. "I should've thought of that."

"That's why I'm here, darling," I said, returning my gaze to the baby. "What you forget, I remember and vice versa."

We stood there for a few moments, talking quietly, and cooing over the baby, but then, just as I'd hoped, Donna's eyes drifted toward mine and she offered, "Would you like to hold her, Grandma?"

My heart melted. I'd known, of course, that I was going to be a grandparent once the baby was born, but I hadn't considered how it would feel to have Donna call me a grandma for the very first time.

"Please," I said, "give me just a minute." After being by Hope's side throughout all her pregnancies, I knew the drill. I crossed the room and washed my hands with warm water and soap, then used a paper towel to make sure they were dry and clean. Then, I walked slowly back to the bed and held out my arms, ready to receive.

With Jordan and Donna's daughter cradled gently in my arms, I felt a sense of belonging, one like I'd never known. My love for Nate was never-ending and I adored my great group of friends. But this baby, this gorgeous, sweet child was just here, needing and wanting to absorb all the love I could give her.

"What do you think you'll name the baby?" I asked after cuddling with her for a few minutes. The last two months of Donna's pregnancy, she'd carried a baby name book with her almost everywhere. Nate and I even bought her a few because we wanted her to really consider all the great options out there.

When I lifted my head to look at her, I saw that Donna's cheeks had become a shade pinker than they'd been before. "What?" I questioned. "Did I say something wrong? Did you want to keep the name a secret for a little while longer?"

"No, no," Jordan said hastily, reaching out and touching my elbow, careful not to jostle my arms or the baby I was holding. "We know what we wanna name her, but we sort of need to ask your permission first."

"My permission?" My eyes flicked toward Nate and his grin broadened. I got the feeling that he understood what his son was saying perfectly, but I was still at a loss.

"We'd like to name our daughter Melissa," Jordan said softly, smiling at me gently.

"My…my name?"

"Yeah," he replied. "If it's all right with you, that is."

"Me…me?" I didn't normally stammer this way. Years of television training usually helped me articulate exactly what I was thinking. But I was so shocked…so honored by this gesture, that I couldn't get the words out properly.

"Jordan is always talking about how you're the greatest stepmother in the world," Donna inserted. "And you know my backstory. My mom passed away when I was just five. But you, Missy, you welcomed me into your home the very first time we met, and I've always sort of felt like you were my chosen mom, the one who's been there for me, no matter what."

"*Aww*…Donna…Jordan…" My heart was beating rapidly. I'd considered myself blessed just a moment ago, but now, this…I still didn't know what to say to show my appreciation.

"We're thinking of putting the name Melissa on her birth certificate," Jordan continued with his explanation, "and we'd like to call her Liza."

"Liza," I echoed, loving the way it sounded. "Little Lady Liza…it's lovely."

Donna giggled. "That's what we think."

I nodded my head approvingly, fighting to hold back the tears that were threatening to leak out of my eyes. "Thank you," I whispered. "This is such a nice gesture. I'm so proud that you thought of me."

Nate stepped nearer and wrapped his arm around my shoulder, giving it a gentle squeeze. We stood, gazing down at baby Liza, and after basking in the happy silence for a minute, he said, "I love you."

I smiled and replied, "I couldn't love you more if I tried."

THE END

About the Author

Mindy Killgrove

Mindy Killgrove is the author of the KATE KELLNER TRILOGY, the MISSY LAWRENCE TRILOGY, the novel ROYALLY ENGAGED, and is the creator of the RILEY ROUNDTREE SOCIAL STORY LEARNING ADVENTURE SERIES. Most notably, Killgrove is a professional ghostwriter. She has penned one play, forty-one short stories, and thirty-six novels all while working as a freelance author.

She has a bachelor's degree from Heidelberg University and a master's degree from Bowling Green State University. She lives in Orlando, Florida with her adoring husband and three rambunctious, but beautiful children. When she's not writing or reading, she's exploring local theme parks, lounging on the beach, or aiming to bake the very best chocolate chip cookies in the world.

Explore more at www.mindykillgrove.com

The *Mindy Killgrove* Collection

Don't miss one of Mindy Killgrove's stories.

THE MISSY LAWRENCE TRILOGY
Meet Me at the Pond
Meet Me at Fountain Park
Meet Me at Blessed Creek

THE KATE KELLNER TRILOGY
Kate Kellner Throws a Wicked Changeup
Kate Kellner Throws a Filthy Drop Curve
Kate Kellner Throws a Perfect Game

KANEDY PRODUCTIONS PRESENTS TRILOGY
Royally Engaged
Majestically Married
The Princely Prize

EDUCATIONAL MATERIALS
If Teachers Could Talk…

CHILDREN'S BOOKS
The Riley Roundtree Social Story Learning Adventure Series

Did you enjoy reading the conclusion to Missy and Nate's story? If so, give the Kanedy Productions Trilogy a try. Attached here, you'll find the first chapter of *Royally Engaged*, starring Finnegan Kane and Samantha Mulligan.

Prologue

Twenty Years Ago
Nashville, Tennessee

"*Shh*! It's his turn," Samantha hushed her older brother, Will, who was laughing raucously following one of the quips made by the host of the television program.

"Ease up, Sam-Sam. They're just introducing him now," Will shot back. She resisted the urge to stick her tongue out at her sibling because that would mean taking her eyes off the screen. And that Samantha just couldn't do.

Finnegan Kane was about to step into the center spotlight, and she didn't want to miss a second of his performance. Since this new singing competition featuring young children and teenagers from all over the nation began three weeks before, Samantha had been glued to the screen, patiently waiting every week to see Finnegan Kane take the stage. And while he was obviously one of the best singers she'd ever heard, she was drawn to him for so many other reasons.

She couldn't quite pinpoint if it was his curly hair, with the tips bleached an outrageous shade of blonde, or his intense steel blue eyes that just seemed to beckon to her. But she knew, even though she was only eight years old, and he was just a few years her senior, that Finnegan Kane was destined to be a featured star in her life story.

As the house band began playing the opening bars of the song and Finnegan Kane started to sing, Samantha joined him. "Sam," Will snickered, "you don't even know the words to the song."

She shrugged. "I'm supporting Finnegan Kane, no matter what."

Will groaned. "He can't hear you. The only people who can wish you'd stop." At that, Samantha cast a look at her parents. Her mother sat in a recliner near the television. Her dainty feet were tucked beneath her, and she had a novel open on her lap. She clearly wasn't watching or even paying attention. Her father, likewise, was fiddling with his watch, looking at the face plate and scrunching his lips as if to indicate time was moving more slowly than he would've liked.

Sam lowered her voice but continued to sing quietly along with Finnegan Kane.

He's so amazing. He'll probably win this round of the competition.

As Finnegan held his hands up in the air and stretched out the last note of the song, Samantha spontaneously rose to her feet and applauded.

Will made hissing noises as he booed obnoxiously. Samantha tossed a red and white throw pillow at his head, but then focused back on the television screen. The host of the show was playfully toying with pieces of his hair that were styled as if he'd stuck his finger in an electrical socket. He smiled charismatically, then rushed across the stage so he could briefly interview Finnegan Kane post-performance. Samantha was mesmerized.

"Finnegan Kane!" The host, with his gleaming white teeth and dashing smile said. "That was one for the record-books. Do you have anyone out there you want to shout a hello to this evening? A Wife or girlfriend, perhaps?" The audience erupted into peals of laughter and Finnegan smiled shyly.

"At my age, I'm not even thinking about a wife, but ask me again in a few years. Someday…maybe," Finnegan replied, smirking at the host as if they were in on some private joke together.

"Someday," Samantha repeated. "I'm going to marry that boy."

"*Pft*…" Will blew a raspberry and guffawed stridently. "Try again, Sam-Sam. A guy like Finnegan Kane is gonna grow up in the spotlight. Where would you even meet a guy like that? And if you did, what would he want with someone like you?"

Samantha's face fell. She'd never thought of the world this way. She saw Finnegan Kane on TV every week and knew that if they ever met, he'd be able to sense their connection, too. It was undeniable.

"Will," their father scolded. "Give your sister a break." He looked up from his watch. "If she wants to marry that young man on TV, then I'm sure she will."

Samantha smiled happily at her father, pleased that he had taken her side and restored the way she chose to look at the world, as if anything was possible. This only made Will laugh louder.

"Not a chance," he mimicked in a sing-song voice as he got up off the couch and exited the room.

But Samantha refused to let his bad attitude bring her down. She was in love with Finnegan Kane and someday—she was going to marry him.

Chapter One

Present Day
Nashville, Tennessee

"Hey, hey! Shut it off! I need to hear this."

Samantha Mulligan was standing in the kitchen of the apartment that she shared with a rather new roommate, Brie Thornberg. Hoping to wash a few of her cares away, Samantha hit the pulverize button on the blender and watched as the strawberries, bananas, and milk spun into life. She marveled at the riot of colors that washed around the glass and hoped the smoothie would taste as good as it looked. In her experience, nothing was ever quite what it appeared to be though.

"Samantha!" Brie shouted, "I'm serious."

She was a little startled but obliged quickly. Brie had been on her computer all morning and it was rather odd behavior to start squawking about something now. Brie knew Samantha was going to make smoothies. That meant she had to use the blender. Curious, Samantha peeked her head around the corner.

"Everything okay?" she asked.

"Yeah," Brie answered abruptly and then added, "Wait! You'll want to hear this, too."

Before Samantha had time to ask or Brie had an opportunity to explain, a loud, ringing voice, floating in a disembodied way out of the laptop exclaimed, "Finnegan Kane! Finnegan Kane! He's back, baby!"

"What's this?" Samantha asked slowly as she moved from the kitchen area into the connected living room. She felt a shiver run up her spine when her cold feet touched the hardwood floors. Hugging herself a little to fight off the chill, she went to peer over Brie's shoulder. Her roommate had coal black hair that she wore in a series of braids which were twisted and tangled into a high topknot. Her hand covered her mouth, and her sienna brown eyes were as wide as the gold hoop earrings she wore dangling from her ears. For a split second, Samantha feared something dreadful had happened to Finn.

Brie didn't bother to answer Samantha's question. She just kept staring at the computer screen. Samantha leaned over a little, so she could get a closer look. Simultaneously, Brie hit the volume up tab on the keyboard and it felt like the living room of the apartment was awash in sound.

The entertainment reporter could barely contain his glee. He was gazing into the camera and flashing his most hypnotic smile. Samantha felt a little bit of relief as she recognized that the newscaster would not be smiling in this manner if something bad had happened to Finn.

The newscaster repeated, "Finnegan Kane! Finnegan Kane! He's back, baby." And then he continued, "Ladies, hunting season is open, and your prize game is Finnegan Kane. He's officially back on the market, and this time he's looking for a wife." Samantha's shoulders slumped in dismay. Since they had broken up six weeks ago, she'd heard similar headlines many times. It was no surprise to anyone that Finn wanted to get married, and now that he was available, it was crystal clear that he'd be looking to date someone new. Samantha was just about to turn away from the screen and return to her smoothie making experiment when the newscaster proceeded.

"Just announced this morning, Finnegan Kane is going to headline a new program for Kanedy Productions. The reality television program will feature women, living in Nashville, Tennessee, as they vie for the heart of the wealthy heir to the Kane Empire." The newsfeed cut to a live shot of Magnus Kane, Finn's father. He was dressed in his signature navy-blue suit and standing in front of the Kanedy Production building which was conveniently located just a few blocks away from the apartment Finn and Samantha had once shared.

Magnus spoke quietly, as if he knew the audience would be on the edge of their seat, waiting to devour his every word. "This dating show will be unlike any other. First and foremost, Kanedy Productions wants to make this program as realistic as possible."

Samantha snorted. "As if a reality dating show could ever be realistic." Brie waved her hand in an agitated manner, trying to shush Samantha. They both leaned back towards the computer and kept listening.

"With that realism in mind, the women who appear on this program will come from a pool of eligible candidates right here in Nashville, Tennessee. They must prove they live in the area because there is no 'big house'. They've gotta be the kind of women who would naturally meet Finnegan, rather than ones who're just seeking a handsome husband. It's very important to Finnegan that the woman he elects to marry not have to change her life for him. He wants them both to be happy just as they are."

Samantha's face blanched and the ache in her heart that had been there the last six weeks, throbbing in a dull, ever-present way, intensified. She'd said something just like that to Finn when they broke up for good.

I don't want to have to change my life. And I don't want you changing who you are just to be with me, either.

Samantha's senses overloaded as her whole world tipped the wrong way on its axis. She took a deep breath and listened as Magnus continued to explain the program.

"Unlike other dating programs, Finn won't be asking the ladies out because he's feeling obligated, and the young ladies aren't required to stay if they don't wish. Everyone is free to come and go as they please. We're looking to mimic a true dating environment as much as possible." Magnus was giving the camera a very satisfied smile and Samantha was reminded a little of a shark. While she had only ever looked at sharks when visiting the aquarium, she was sure that Magnus's deep black eyes and sharp-tooth grin mimicked the predators exactly.

The scene cut away from Magnus and the fresh-faced newscaster, with a brilliant smile, was back on the screen.

"That's right, ladies. If you live in or around the Nashville area, it could be your lucky day. Casting for *Royally Engaged* will begin this afternoon, with the filming starting tomorrow evening. No specific number of spaces have been allotted for contestants, as women won't be living together, and dates will not be mandatory. The first episode of *Royally Engaged* is set to air on Friday evening.

"From what has been reported, it appears that Finnegan Kane has signed an agreement requiring him to be filmed continuously for twenty-four hours a day for the next six weeks. At the end of the six weeks, Finnegan Kane will select his bride from the pool of eligible women who're still a part of the show."

"Six weeks?" Samantha echoed as her heart leapt up into her throat. Mechanically, her feet led her away from the computer and the report. She couldn't listen anymore.

I can't believe Finn would do something like this. This is even worse than I feared.

She had always known that Finn was going to get back into acting, and maybe even do a reality television series. He'd been so successful in that arena previously, both when he'd been a contestant on *America's Superstar Singers* as a pre-teen and then again six years later when he was the youngest judge to ever sit on the panel for the same program. From such a young age, Finn had been in the spotlight. He had a knack for it, and that terrified Samantha. She didn't want to spend the rest of her life with the public scrutinizing her every move. That was part of what kept her from working for the Kane Empire. She didn't want people to know her middle name or the fact that she liked to eat tacos every Friday night. She hadn't wanted that for Finn either and was sure that if one or both kept working for his father, they'd be sucked into that type of life. Magnus would force them into the limelight, just as he was doing to Finn now.

It had taken right around six weeks post-break up for Finn to do exactly as Samantha had dreaded and now, on top of all that, he was going to dive in over his head and marry someone else in another six weeks' time. Samantha felt this whole notion was preposterous.

"Finn *can't* marry someone else," she whispered to the deserted kitchen and the smoothie ingredients sitting partially annihilated in the blender. She knew they'd broken up, but after eight years of being together,

Samantha hadn't quite given up hope that Finn would come back to her. He would decide that being with her was more important than being a celebrity, and he'd return. But now, that possibility seemed impossible. He was going to date someone else. He was going to *marry* someone else. And she was going to be forced to watch it all. The tears trickled out of her eyes. She couldn't stop them.

How could he do this? Why would he marry someone else? How is he ready to move on so quickly?

She pondered all those notions as she reached for the blender. Hitting the pulverize button once more was cathartic and this time she relished the sight of the tearing and spinning of the fruit within.

Samantha wasn't paying attention because she was so focused on her own misery. So, when the door opened unexpectedly, she didn't even hear the turning of the door handle or the creak of the hinges.

She also missed when a voice timidly called out, "Hello." Samantha stared at the strawberries and thought of how Finn's latest adventure with Kanedy Productions was wringing her heart exactly like the fruit in the blender.

"Hello," Finn said softly one more time as he poked his head into the kitchen. Without thinking what she was doing, Samantha smiled. The blender was still running, drowning out the sound of his voice, but that didn't matter because her reaction was instinctive. She was so relieved to see him standing in her doorway that she simply grinned in response.

He's here!

He could tell her everything she'd just heard and seen was a lie. He wasn't going to date someone else. He wasn't going to marry someone else. That entire nightmare had just been made up for the Kanedy Production team to get some publicity for a different show they were considering airing.

Samantha clicked the button on the blender, silencing it. She turned towards Finn and felt underdressed. She just had on an old pair of sweatpants and a tank top she'd worn a million times. Tugging at the hem of the tank top, she wished she'd already changed out of her sleep attire. Remembering the tears streaking her face, she rubbed her fingertips over her cheeks, trying her best to smooth away the signs of sadness. Looking down for a moment to collect herself, Samantha took a deep breath, then slowly raised her chin. She peered up at Finn, hoping he hadn't noticed the tears.

"So," he said, shifting from foot to foot, "you've heard."

"Royally engaged?" Samantha returned, conjuring up a bit of a laugh. "Who picked that name?" She was holding it together remarkably well if she did say so herself. Moments ago, she'd been near the edge of hysteria, but seeing Finn, standing there in his standard Sunday morning attire—faded blue jeans and a robin's egg blue t-shirt—made her feel calm almost instantly.

His mouth quirked up into a smile at the corners. "My dad," he replied with a roll of his stunning blue eyes.

"And that's what you think, is it? Some girl gets to marry you and that automatically makes her American royalty?" Samantha was still attempting to be playful, but her tone was changing without her permission. She couldn't decide whether she wanted to keep this interaction light-hearted, or if she wanted to sling mud at his beautiful face.

Finn knew her so well and obviously caught the shift in tone, so he humbly looked down at his sneakers again. He crossed one leg over the other and tried to adjust his position leaning against the wall. "Samantha, I wanted to be the one who told you."

He started to explain, but his words cut Samantha to her core, so she muttered sarcastically, "What do you mean? You didn't want me to hear about your search for a wife elsewhere?"

"Samantha," Finn said, and his voice was pleading with her. It was evident that he wanted to have a conversation, but for the first time since she'd met him, he seemed stymied and incapable of finding the right words.

"Yes," she said, belatedly answering his query. "I heard." She turned away from Finn and started up the blender. Even though the fruit within had been demolished and the smoothie was most likely inedible at this point, she felt good punching the button, watching the contents spin, and blocking out the sound of his voice. Finn took a step towards her. He placed his hand on top of hers.

She hit the pause button and turned her body so only her head was facing him. A curtain of her long brown hair partially blocked her face and Finn deftly pushed the locks aside, brushing her temples gently as he did so.

"Samantha," he said softly, and her hands started shaking uncontrollably. She was going to cry again. He reached out to envelope her in a hug, but when her cheek drifted near his neck, her lips began kissing the familiar spot she knew so well. Now she felt the electricity pulse through her own body and into his and she remembered. She recollected what it meant to be in love with Finnegan Kane. It was thrilling.

He didn't let her kiss his neck long before he shifted his head slightly and pressed his own mouth against hers. She moved her lips in time with his and it felt wonderful. Samantha's heart began to soar. Her hands raced across his back and up through his hair. Urged onward by the swirl of emotions that were tumbling tumultuously inside of her, she tugged on one of the errant tendrils of his thick hair and ran her fingers along the ends to help smooth it back into place. Meanwhile, he moved his hands from her waist up her back. He was slowly tracing lines up and down her spine and it felt so good. Samantha lifted the tail of Finn's shirt and allowed her fingers to prance up and down his bare skin.

He moaned, "Samantha," and she pressed her body into his. He moved his hands down to the waistband of her loose-fitting sweatpants and ran his finger along the seam.

"Finn," she whispered his name in his ear and let her tongue tickle his earlobe. He pulled away just slightly and smiled at her briefly.

"Samantha, I'm so glad you understand. This is how it's supposed to be. It's just me and you and . . ." She didn't let him finish. She was pressing her lips against his again, silencing whatever he was about to say. She held him in her arms and felt that the world was about to be right again. They were about to get back together for good and this entire nightmare could end.

"We need to talk," he breathed as he moved his mouth away from her kiss. Gently, he started placing slow, loving smooches on her neck. She arched her back a little to give him further access.

"Do we?" she replied.

"We can be together now." He paused to kiss along her collar bone. "If you just come to the audition today . . ." There was nothing else Finn could have said that would've made Samantha snap out of his embrace faster.

"What now?" she asked, her words laced with hostility as she pushed away from him. Finn looked a little disheveled, and if she hadn't been steaming mad, she would've felt sorry for him. But, right now, she couldn't get there. She was angrier than she'd ever been in her entire life.

He looked at her and started to stammer a response. But she wasn't going to let him. "*Where* do you want me to go?"

Finn tucked his shirt into his jeans. He was stalling for time and in those precious moments, Samantha thought she understood.

"You want me to be on the show?" she asked, tremors of outrage coursing through her voice.

"Well, yeah," Finn replied meekly, ducking his head a little and giving her a sheepish smile. "I thought you understood that." He motioned to the divide between them, as if to indicate the fact that she'd kissed him just now proved the point.

"I don't." Samantha groaned and leaned back against the kitchen counter. Suddenly she wanted to put as much space between herself and Finn as possible. "I don't understand at all. And I certainly do *not* agree. What would make you think that I wanted to have my personal life publicized?" Finn started to interject, but she was having none of that. "I've told you hundreds of times that I never wanted this to happen."

"*This?*" Finn began and his incredulous reaction only flared Samantha's temper further.

"Not *this*," she snapped, with emphasis, motioning to herself first, then to Finn. "I never expected you to put your entire dating life out there for everyone to watch and . . ."

"Sam-Sam, it's not as bad as you think," Finn responded.

"You…" She stepped toward him swiftly and stuck her finger in his face. "You do *not* get to call me by my pet name."

"Okay," he nodded. "I shouldn't have done that. I'm sorry."

"You're sorry. You're *sorry*?" Samantha was beside herself. "I don't even know where to begin with that . . ."

Finn moved as close to the kitchen door frame as possible and put his hands in his pockets. "Samantha, I'm sorry for so many things. I'm sorry that the news this morning surprised you. I'm sorry that it wasn't something you wanted to hear. I'm sorry that. . ."

She cut him off, "But you're going to marry someone else!"

And then, out of nowhere, Finn lost *his* temper. Even though she'd quite literally backed him into the corner of the room, his eyes flared and sparked as he shouted, "But I wanted to marry *you*! I asked and you turned me down, remember?"

A small squeak escaped Brie's lips and she slid from her seat in front of the laptop. She ducked her head and raced as fast as her fuzzy slipper covered feet would carry her back to her bedroom. She didn't slam the door behind her but closed it as quietly as she possibly could. Samantha had entirely forgotten that her roommate had been in the adjoining room. And she didn't have time to feel ashamed about the way she'd been kissing Finn because her mind was consumed by what he'd just said, and she felt awful.

"I know," she mumbled.

"So, you don't get to be angry with me for trying to find someone else," Finn muttered thickly while his lower lip pooched out in a despondent way. "I told you I wanted to get married. I told you years ago that having a wife was important to me. I wanted it to be you. I'm thirty years old, Samantha. How long did you expect me to be happy just being your boyfriend? I couldn't do that forever. I needed to grow up and I wanted . . ."

"But what about what I wanted?" She argued. "I wanted to be your wife, but I won't be a cog in the Kane Empire. I will not allow your father to make a mockery of me and to put you on display like some prized hog."

"We can't be having this argument again," Finn grumbled and shook his head.

"And yet, we are!" Samantha shouted with indignation. "Finn, we only broke up six weeks ago. Six weeks, Finn! I'm still hanging around in my ratty sweatpants, but you? You and your father have come up with a way for you to be married two months from now!"

He gave her a shocked look. His eyebrows were furrowed, and the corners of his mouth were turned decidedly downward. Maybe she should've stopped there and let him process what she was saying, but Samantha knew what was on her mind and she wanted to speak.

Who knows when I'll have the chance again?

"Okay, Finn. I get it. This is not about me. It's about you. *You* want to be married, and that's fine. If you think this is the right way to go about finding your bride, I won't stop you. But I won't be a part of it, either. Because here's the dirty secret that I'm sure your father has concealed." She paused and sucked in a deep inhalation, then whispered, "What happens next?" Samantha swept her hand wide, gesturing around the entire space of the kitchen.

Finn just stared at her, so she continued. "What happens next, I ask you. Do you get to find your wife and then go off and live together happily ever after? Hardly," she scoffed. "When this is done, you'll be forced to let the world watch your wedding. *Majestically Married*, I'm sure. Then, you and your new wife are part of some show about being newlyweds. A few years later, the world holds their breath while your wife gives birth to your first child. All of it has been filmed and delivered to an audience of millions of people. And then what? What happens when the world is tired of Finnegan Kane? Then, what happens?" Samantha dreaded saying the next part, but she needed to illuminate this possibility for him. "Then, it's time for Jase and Joss to get engaged."

"No," Finn interjected. "Jase and Joss have nothing to do with this."

"No?" Samantha challenged, her eyebrow arching significantly. "I beg to differ. While Jase and Joss aren't as comfortable being filmed the way you are, they're both beautiful and charismatic." Samantha pictured Finn's younger twin brother and sister, Jasen and Jossalyn, and her heart smashed into a thousand pieces. "If you think this exploitation of your family ends with you, you're wrong."

"That's not how it's going to work," Finn protested. "Jase and Joss have no part in this. They don't want any part of it. They're like you."

Samantha rolled her eyes. "Good for them."

"You don't understand," Finn returned pleadingly. "I volunteered for this project. But, as the auditions got closer, I began to doubt that I could do it without you. Samantha, I need you to be there."

"You want me to help pick out your next girlfriend?" Samantha wrinkled her nose in disgust. "I won't."

"Of course not," Finn said, shaking his head emphatically. "I want you to be on the show. I want you to be there with me. I could go on dates with you. I could even pick you to marry me... if you wanted." Finn looked so hopeful when he said those words that Samantha nearly cried on his behalf. Now, she knew what he was asking, but it was impossible. She couldn't be a contestant on this show any more than she could help select the next person he'd marry. She reached out and grabbed his hand.

"You know I can't do that," she said and gave his icy cool fingertips a small squeeze. He pulled his hand out of her grip.

"It's not that you *can't* do it. It's that you don't want to," Finn answered in an injured tone. Samantha eyed him sorrowfully. They were never going to see eye-to-eye on this topic. She was never going to agree to have her personal life splashed across all the media outlets for public consumption and he was never going to see why that was not the life she wanted.

"I love you, Finn, but I can't, *and* I won't." Samantha shook her head dejectedly.

"I love *you*, Samantha. That has to be enough." He tried to reach out and touch her again.

"But it's not." Samantha turned away from him. "I think you should go now." She wasn't looking at Finn, and she wouldn't be able to look at him when he walked out the door. When he left the first time, Samantha hoped he'd come back, but she knew in her heart of hearts that when he left this time, that was the end. He would never come back here. He'd find a new girlfriend and soon, sooner than she cared to imagine, that woman would become his wife. She might never see Finn again, except on television.

"We can't," Finn begged. "We can't end it this way. Please think about it. Think about coming on the show."

Samantha said nothing. Finn rushed forward with a slurry of information. "I'm going to Johnny's show tonight. We're gonna introduce the program properly. Watch it. Learn what this is all about. Think about it. Really think about it, Samantha," he said, then sighed dramatically. He wanted to reach out and touch her. Samantha could feel that. He wanted to hold her in his arms, but she wasn't going to allow that again.

As tears threatened to spill onto her cheeks once more, all she could do was nod.

Finn moved out of the corner of the room and headed toward the door. He stopped and placed his key on the countertop, turning it over so she could see it.

"Thank you," Samantha said nodding at the thoughtfulness of the final gesture. As she did, the tears began to flow. She didn't reach up to block them. It wouldn't help. Finn stood, framed in the doorway. She didn't know how long he lingered there as she finally succumbed to her grief and walked out of the room.

"Goodbye, Finn," she said quietly as she shut the door to her bedroom and threw herself, face down, onto her bedspread. "Goodbye."

Made in the USA
Middletown, DE
01 April 2024

52260986R00116